D0053271

The Wicked Flea

The Wicked Flea

A DOG LOVER'S MYSTERY

Susan Conant

BERKLEY PRIME CRIME, NEW YORK

THE WICKED FLEA

A Berkley Prime Crime Book
Published by The Berkley Publishing Group,
a division of Penguin Putnam Inc.,
375 Hudson Street, New York, New York 10014.

Visit our website at
www.penguinputnam.com

First edition: March 2002

Library of Congress Cataloging-in-Publication Data

Conant, Susan, 1946–
    The wicked flea : a dog lover's mystery / Susan Conant.— 1st ed.
        p.   cm
    ISBN 0-425-18334-3 (alk. paper)
    1. Winter, Holly (Fictitious character)—Fiction. 2. Cambridge
(Mass.)—Fiction. 3. Women journalists—Fiction. 4. Women dog
owners—Fiction. 5. Alaskan Malamute—Fiction. 6. Dogs—Fiction.
I. Title.

PS3553.O4857 W43 2002
813'.54—dc21

                                                        2001052580

PRINTED IN THE UNITED STATES OF AMERICA

10   9   8   7   6   5   4   3

ACKNOWLEDGMENTS

For the appearance of Alaskan malamutes CH Jazz-land's Embraceable You and CH Jazzland's How High the Moon, I am grateful to Cindy Neely as well as to Emma and Howie. Many thanks to the members of Malamute-L who responded to my eccentric author queries; to Martha Kalina of the Perry Greene Kennel, for letting me use the perfect domain name; to Charlene LaBelle, for allowing me to share her liver recipe; to my feline malamutes, Chartreux cats G. R. P. Janvier Pandora Spocks of Ajolie and Ajolie's Shadow Dancer; and to my beloved Alaskan malamute, Frost-field Perfect Crime, C.D., C.G.C., W.P.D., Th.D., who is called Rowdy. For help with the manuscript, my profuse thanks to Jean Berman, Wren Dugal, Roseann Mandell, Judy Margolis, Cindy Neely, Geoff Stern, Anya Wittenborg, Corinne Zipps, and to my astute editor, Natalee Rosenstein.

In loving memory of my beautiful boy,
Frostfield Firestar's Kobuk

Through many dangers, toils, and snares
I have already come.
'Tis grace hath brought me safe thus far
And grace will lead me home.

—JOHN NEWTON 1779

The wicked flee when no man pursueth.

—PROVERBS 28:1

CHAPTER 1

My father's new wife, Gabrielle, was determined to enlist my help in disposing of her first husband.

Naturally, I protested. "I'm hardly the most suitable person," I argued in our final phone conversation on the subject. "Besides, we don't want to end up in jail, do we?"

Gabrielle was adamant. "It's important, Holly, to liberate oneself from the remains of the past. Even *fond* remains," she added before continuing in that extraordinary voice of hers, which is low, throaty, and infinitely persuasive. How persuasive? Well, my father married her, didn't he? And Buck is not an easy person to persuade to do anything. Believe me, I've tried. Not that I'd wanted to talk him out of marrying Gabrielle. On the contrary, I like Gabrielle tremendously, and I'm convinced that falling in love with her is one of the sanest things my father has ever done. Given Buck's eccentricities, that's not saying much, I guess, but I'm always surprised and relieved when he does something even remotely normal, and when it comes to choosing wives, Buck is a model of mental hygiene, perhaps because he's had only two. But maybe I'm being unfair to Buck. In any case, like Gabrielle, my late mother was a wonderful, warm, and sensible, if somewhat controlling, person.

"It just doesn't feel right," Gabrielle went on, "to have a second husband when the first is still around."

"It's illegal," I countered.

"Marginally," Gabrielle admitted, "but if we were caught, which we aren't going to be, the fine would be, uh, let's see, not less than one hundred nor more than five hundred dollars, and I can afford that." She paused. "Or imprisonment," she conceded, "but technically, it would only be for six months or so, and no one is actually going to throw us in the hoosegow for scattering Walter in Harvard Yard."

"*Hoosegow?*"

"Spanish origin," she said smugly. "Isn't it charming?"

"The reality wouldn't be," I said, "and in Massachusetts you can't go around blithely sprinkling people's ashes wherever you feel like, Gabrielle. Among other things, you'd need a permit from the board of health, and you'd have to get Harvard's permission. What's wrong with Mount Auburn Cemetery?"

"It's terribly expensive," she whispered, sounding hurt, as if I'd been cruelly referring to her recent financial losses. "And we don't want a public event, do we? I just want to say a quiet good-bye. That doesn't seem too much to ask, Holly. And we'd do the same for your father, wouldn't we?"

Since Harvard Yard is useless for hunting, fishing, or showing purebred dogs, it's one of the last places on earth that my own father, Buck, would choose as a final, or even transitory, resting place. Still, I refrained from making the obvious reply, which was, What's this *we*? Gabrielle has a likable habit of thinking of everyone as *we*. If I'd asked her to join me in dispersing the cremated remains of some homicidal fiend who'd been a stranger to both of us, she'd have hurled herself into the project with great enthusiasm. It was easy to imagine her reading a carefully selected verse over the monster's ashes and shedding genuine tears at the thought of how much *we* would miss him.

When Gabrielle arrived at my house a few days later, I presented her with printed copies of a great many web pages on two topics: Massachusetts law concerning dead bodies and what are fancifully known as "creative scattering options." My house, I might mention, is the barn-red one on the corner of Appleton and Concord in Cambridge, Massachusetts, about a twenty-minute walk from Harvard Yard. I live on the first floor with Rowdy and Kimi, the two most stunning and brilliant Alaskan malamutes in the world—that's an objective description—and Tracker. Having offered an objective description of the dogs, I should probably do the same for Tracker, but I can't stand people who disparage their animals, no matter how hideous, pitiful, or mean-tempered—in Tracker's case, all three—so let's just call her a cat. My second-floor tenant, Rita, is my best friend, as well as a clinical psychologist and the owner of a Scottie, Willie. My third-floor tenants, a circuit court judge and her husband, have two handsome Persian cats. I may be the only landlord in Cambridge, or possibly the only landlord anywhere, who won't rent to you *unless* you have at least one pet. Anyway, my proximity to Harvard and my, shall we say, positive attitude toward dogs were central to Gabrielle's dispersal plans for the late Professor Beamon. She had decided that we were going to avoid arrest under Chapter 114 of the General Laws of Massachusetts, Cemeteries and Burials, Miscellaneous Provisions, Section 43 M, Permanent Disposition of Dead Bodies or Remains, by disguising ourselves as dog walkers.

"Disguising ourselves?" Gabrielle was offended. She sat at my kitchen table drinking a cup of strong coffee with tons of cream and sugar. In her lap was her bichon, Molly, who is spoiled rotten. Bichon is short for bichon frise, French for curly-haired lapdog, all-white, jaunty, cute, member of the American Kennel Club's *Non-sporting* Group, an unfortunate term for certain nonhunting breeds that misleadingly connotes poor sportsmanship and a sort of joyless attitude never observed in the bichon frise. "We *are* dog walkers!" Gabrielle exclaimed. "We'll just happen to walk our dogs into the Yard. What we do with Walter when we're there is none of Harvard's business. I won't be bossed around by a lot of silly paperwork."

You can see why Buck fell in love with Gabrielle. For one thing, they met at a show, a dog show—when it comes to my father, *ça va sans dire,* as he would never say—and for another, she has that low, seductive voice. The American Medical Association would probably describe Gabrielle as too heavy, and her skin makes it obvious that she has never bothered to use sunblock. Her hair is a mixture of blond and white, possibly natural—she's in her late fifties—and cut in a feathery style that flatters a face that needs no flattery. She has incredible bone structure and blue eyes that most people would compare with such prosaic objects as oceans, skies, and cornflowers. From Buck's viewpoint, his bride's eyes are Siberian husky blue.

In declaring that she wouldn't be bossed around by paperwork, Gabrielle was not just speaking figuratively. Spread out on my kitchen table were the printed web pages. "These have nothing to do with us," she said dismissively. "*Body after dissection!* I ask you! I did not donate Walter's body to science. And these people can't even make up their minds what to call these laws. Annotated? General? But the point is, Holly, that they're meant for grave robbers and shady morticians and sneaky murderers. They aren't meant to apply to people like us. And these so-called creative scattering options are ridiculous. Turning Walter into a living coral reef? Or throwing him off a boat? Or rocketing him into outer space?"

"If we avoided archeological sites and Native American burial sites and that kind of thing, we'd be allowed to use a state park in California," I pointed out, tapping a finger on one of the pages.

"Three thousand miles from home? Harvard Yard is right down the street." Gabrielle picked at the sleeves of her long, loose white blouse, a cross between a smock and what I think is called a poet's shirt. Molly's eyes followed Gabrielle's sun-spotted hands. Sighing, Gabrielle rose and put the little dog on the floor. With an involuntary, reflexive jerk, I looked around to make sure that Rowdy and Kimi hadn't escaped from my bedroom. The AKC may classify the bichon as Non-sporting, but the Alaskan malamute disagrees: small furry things belong to the Fair Game Group. Although neither Rowdy nor Kimi has ever hurt or even threat-ened Molly, they still need careful watching when she's around. As I always tell Rowdy and Kimi, the only reason I don't trust them is that they're not trust-worthy. Molly wasn't the only reason I'd incarcerated them. The other was a premonition that I'd capitulate to Gabrielle's demands. On principle, malamutes don't back down, and they don't think highly of anyone who does. To the dogs, I'm supposed to be Holly Winter, She Who Must Be Obeyed, not Holly Winter, She Who Caves in to Her Stepmother.

I said softly, "Okay, Gabrielle, I give up. We'll scat-ter the ashes anywhere you want."

"Are you sure you're well enough?" she asked.

"There is nothing physically wrong with me," I as-sured her for at least the hundredth time. "A few little neurological blips. I'm supposed to avoid another head injury." Honest to doG, that was the medical advice I'd been given, as if I'd have intentionally gone around searching for new and yet more skull-shattering ways to concuss myself.

The crack on the head was one of the twin traumas I'd suffered about two months earlier. While hiking with the dogs at Acadia National Park, I'd plummeted down a rocky little mountainside only to collide with a boulder. The damage suggests that I landed head first. When I regained consciousness, the fragmentary remains of my memory left me unable to retrieve an alarming number of ordinary words that would've come in handy. *Amnesia,* for instance, and *Holly Winter.* Forgetting my own name wasn't necessarily all that big a deal, but as a real dog person, I'm still horrified at my initial failure to recognize Rowdy and Kimi as my own dogs. Their names were lost to me, too. But I did, of course, know that they were show-quality Alaskan malamutes.

The other trauma was a broken heart. My lover, also my vet, Steve Delaney had married someone else, and not just any old someone else, either, and not just a young, beautiful someone else, but a damned disbarred lawyer. Her name was Anita Fairley. I can't bring myself to say more about Steve or Anita right now, except that I needed a new vet and that I hated Anita as ferociously as she hated dogs.

"Even so, I think I can probably manage to make it from here to Harvard Yard," I told Gabrielle.

Consequently, on the following evening, a bleak and weirdly mild one for mid-November, Gabrielle and I

set out on foot for what's known as Tercentenary Theater, which, in Harvardian fashion (*"When I use a
word,"* Humpty Dumpty said, *in a rather scornful tone,
"it means just what I choose it to mean—neither more
nor less"*), isn't a *theater* by any normal definition of
the term, lacking as it does such theater-defining essentials as a stage and seats, for instance. In fact, it's
the flat, grassy area of Harvard Yard between Memorial Church and Widener Library, which are, respectively, a church and a library, perhaps by mistake. It's
called a theater, I suppose, because it's the venue for
Harvard's graduation ceremonies, which are known as
commencements, another term that baffles me. For
most alumni, going to Harvard is the apex, like reaching the summit of Everest, and leaving Harvard is the
commencement of the descent into the dreary, litter-
strewn base camp below.

Theater or no theater, the area between Memorial
Church and Widener is, indeed, a spot fair to the eye,
a quadrangle bounded on the other two sides by Sever
and University halls and planted with numerous species
of deciduous trees, all of which were indistinguishable
from one another when Gabrielle and I arrived, because
they had lost their leaves, and the lights shone on the
paved walks and the entrances to the buildings, not on
the treetops.

"Not that I can tell one tree from another," I told
Gabrielle. "Maybe you can. Did Walter have a favorite
species? Kimi, not there!" I used to think that the leg-
lifting frequently observed in female malamutes was a
sign of dominance, but someone who works with

8

wolves told me it had nothing to do with dominant or submissive rank within a pack and everything to do with self-confidence. Kimi would have made a great suffragist. Any male who'd tried to deny her the vote would've found himself pounced on, knocked to the ground, and pinned there until he not only conceded her right to cast a ballot, but promised to help elect her. Anyway, Kimi marks her turf all the time, but the prospect of having her drench a funeral marker struck me as unseemly. I'd left Rowdy at home. If you want to be dismissed as just one more dog walker, an Alaskan malamute is already a poor choice of breed to walk. And in a populous area like Harvard Yard, Rowdy is a shameless, hopeless, uncontrollable attention-grabber. Both dogs are wolf-gray, with plumy white tails, stand-off coats, and lovely little ears. But Rowdy is bigger than Kimi—about eighty-eight pounds to her seventy-five—and he's a better show dog than she is, not because judges necessarily prefer his white face to her black facial markings, but because Rowdy radiates an animal magnetism that dares people to look elsewhere when he's around. Also, Kimi can sometimes be persuaded to mind her own business, whereas Rowdy will not be stopped from singing loud peals of *woo-woo-woo*. We didn't have the Yard to ourselves. Students passed by, alone, in couples, and in groups.

"Walter was partial to pines," Gabrielle said, "but there aren't any here." For once, Molly was on the ground instead of in Gabrielle's arms. Gabrielle held the little white dog's leash in one hand. Her other hand supported one of those green and white L. L. Bean tote bags touted in the catalog as useful for everything, including, presumably, the transportation of human remains. "Not that it matters," she added. "What I had in mind was Widener. There's something religious about it, don't you think? More than Mem. Church, really."

Widener Library is a temple to academe, with tremendously long stone steps all across the front that lead up to the main entrance. The steps are reminiscent of those you see in pictures of pre-Columbian ruins, not that ascending them is any sort of prelude to human sacrifice, even in the case of undergraduates with failing grades, but Gabrielle was nonetheless right about Widener's religious quality. "Yes," I agreed, "there's something wonderfully eternal about it. But there are people sitting on the steps."

"There's no wind," Gabrielle observed, "so it's not as if . . ." She broke off. "Did you know," she asked, "that Harvard is the second-wealthiest nonprofit organization in the world? Second only to the Roman Catholic Church."

"No, I didn't know that," I said.

"Well, it is," Gabrielle said, as if Harvard's endowment somehow entitled her to deposit her first husband's remains on university property. "Even so," she said, "the earth is probably better. Mother of us all, and so forth. Right over there would do nicely, I think."

She pointed to a clump of young trees with Molly's leash and then strode toward the chosen spot. Kimi and

I followed. Reaching her destination, Gabrielle stopped, put the tote bag down, and bent over to remove its contents, which consisted of a flashlight, a sheet of paper, a pair of eyeglasses, and a square cardboard box. Before I could stop her, she turned on the flashlight.

"Gabrielle, that's not a good idea," I warned. "And we really don't need any extra light."

"We do," she said. "Or I do, because I have a little something I want to read. You didn't think we were just going to dump him on the ground and run off, did you?"

"People are going to wonder what's up."

"Let them!" she exclaimed. At the same time, however, having apparently thought the matter over, she turned off the light. "Oh, well, I know it by heart, I think." Replacing the flashlight and eyeglasses in the tote bag, she opened the cardboard box. "Molly, sit!"

Copying Gabrielle, I said, "Kimi, sit!" Onlookers, I hoped, might imagine that we were training our dogs.

"The plastic bag is already open," Gabrielle informed me. "I haven't come totally unprepared. Well, I suppose we're ready."

All on its own, my body adopted a prayerful posture; I could feel my shoulders straighten, my head bow, and my eyes close. Like Molly and Kimi, I waited silently.

Gabrielle lightly cleared her throat and, in that resonant voice of hers, said with great solemnity, "Goodbye, Walter. 'Strength without insolence, courage without ferocity, and all the virtues of man without his vices.' Good-bye, good-bye."

11

The quoted words were familiar. No, more than merely familiar. I, too, knew them by heart. Had I chosen to do so, I could have continued where Gabrielle had left off:

> *This Praise, which would be unmeaning flattery*
> *If inscribed over Human Ashes,*
> *Is but a just tribute to the Memory of*
> *Boatswain, a Dog*

Boatswain had belonged to Lord Byron, who had written the inscription for the Newfoundland's monument.

Gabrielle still maintains that it was my inexplicable coughing fit that alerted the Harvard University Police to our presence. In my defense, let me say that the fit was uncontrollable. But something certainly drew the attention of the young man in the Harvard University Police uniform, who came striding up to us and said in a what's-this-all-about tone of voice, "Lovely evening, isn't it?"

"Bracing," Gabrielle replied.

"Something I can help you with here?" he asked.

Under the circumstances, there was one right answer to that question: *no.* Even polite elaboration would have done nicely: *Thank you so much for asking, but we're just out for a stroll with our dogs.*

Gabrielle, however, always assumes that the entire world is on her side and that every stranger is about to become her best friend. She blabbed the entire story.

The late Walter Beamon returned home with us.

CHAPTER 2

Subj: My Support—and a brag!
From: Gabrielle@beamonres.org
To: HollyWinter@amrone.org

Dearest Holly!

I am fully supportive of your decision to see a psychiatrist. How lucky you are to have Rita as a
trusted friend who can recommend the best possible person! Knowing your father as you do, you will
understand that the wisest and most tactful course
will be to say nothing to Buck about the psychiatrist, whom I have described to him as a neurologist. The departure from the precise truth is very
slight. After all, both examine heads.

Buck intends to E-mail you about the neurologist.
I do wish that he could be persuaded not to write

E-mail in ALL CAPS. He has repeatedly been informed that the usage makes his communications look as if he is SHOUTING. Buck's invariable reply to me when I draw his attention to the matter is that he IS shouting. Thank heaven, he is just kidding as usual. :0 (Is that right? It's supposed to be a smile, but it looks peculiar, like that painting, "The Scream," by Munch, isn't it?)

Molly went R.W.B.* on Saturday. I was moderately pleased with the Reserve. Buck was not. Your father felt that the Winners Bitch was inferior to Molly and said that the judge, Lester Offenbach, chose the incorrect bichon over Molly because the other one had a pretty handler. It's certainly true that our own dear Horace Livermore is not pretty! But even Buck admits that Horace is an excellent handler. And Molly went W.B. on Sunday! Only one point, but who cares? Well, your father does, but I don't! I must confess that I am still not entirely comfortable in spelling out the B. in W.B., so to speak. Buck correctly points out that if "bitch" (There! I've done it!) were other than a proper term for female, the American Kennel Club would ban its use, as is certainly not the case since you-know-what is every other word spoken at AKC shows.

---

*Reserve Winners Bitch. My stepmother is talking about a dog show. Naturally she is. She's married to my father. She means that in the competition among female bichons who weren't yet champions, Molly just missed the championship points, which went to another female, the Winners Bitch. W.B. Winners Bitch. R.W.B.: close but no cigar.—H. W.

We really must have another go at Harvard Yard. It's a shame that we were foiled in our previous attempt. I won't feel quite right until the deed is done.

Your loving stepmother—Doesn't that make me sound like a witch!

Gabrielle

CHAPTER 3

Subj: BORDER COLLIE
From: BUCKWINTER@MAINELY-DOGS.COM
To: HOLLYWINTER@AMRONE.ORG

GABRIELLE SAYS THAT RITA HAS PACKED YOU OFF
TO A NEUROLOGIST. REAL DOCTORS ARE OK, BUT
DON'T LET ANY OF THOSE CAMBRIDGE TOFU GUM-
MERS TALK YOU INTO THINKING YOU NEED YOUR
HEAD EXAMINED. THE ONLY THING THOSE JOKERS
ARE AFTER IS YOUR MONEY. THERE'S NOT A DAMNED
THING WRONG WITH YOU THAT DOGS AND HARD
WORK WON'T CURE.

GIVE SERIOUS THOUGHT TO THE BORDER COLLIE.

CHAPTER 4

Vee Foote. I ask you! What kind of stupid first name is *Vee*? It isn't even a name; it's an initial. And *Foote*? *Dr.* Foote? For a *psychiatrist*? It sounded to me as if her idea of treatment would be a swift kick. On reflection, however, I decided that a swift kick might be precisely what I needed. Besides a new vet, of course. As I've mentioned, my last vet, Steve Delaney, married . . .

Well, enough about Anita Fairley-Delaney. For now.

For whatever reason, I found myself in the Proverbial situation of the wicked, who, as the Bible says— Proverbs 28:1—"flee when no man pursueth." Steve, having plighted his troth to Anita, was no longer pursuing me. My next-door neighbor and thoroughly admirable longtime admirer, Lt. Kevin Dennehy of the Cambridge police, finally had a girlfriend, a cop named Jennie, as opposed, for example, to a dog writer named Holly. I'd seen almost nothing of Kevin lately. He hadn't even introduced me to Jennie, whom I imagined as thin, blond, and gorgeous, in other words, remarkably like Anita Fairley. Dog clubs and dog shows are lousy places to meet men. They're disproportionately packed with women, and the men tend to be married or gay. Indeed, the world of dogs is a microcosm of the world at large, or so it often seems to me.

"Hunting attracts men," I told Dr. Foote, "but malamutes are useless for hunting, and besides, the last thing I want to do is kill animals. AA is supposed to be great, but I'm not alcoholic, and it seems a little risky to make myself eligible. AA or no AA, I might not dry out."

"Tell me more about Steve," said Dr. Foote, whose home office was in a big single-family Victorian house that must have been undergoing renovation. Or were the workers possibly putting up a kennel run? In any case, the curb was lined with contractors' trucks and vans. Hammers banged. There weren't any tricycles in the front yard or anything like that, and Dr. Foote was a little old to be the mother of toddlers. She looked forty-five or fiftyish, my senior by a decade or more, and had long, dark, gray-streaked hair that fell loose around her shoulders, Cambridge style, even though she lived in Newton, the suburb of suburbs, which according to an article in one of the Boston papers had recently won an award for being the safest city in America. The rankings were based on crime statistics, not on psychotherapy ratings, but Newton had also made the news lately for having the highest number of psychiatrists per capita of any city in the U.S. A connection there?

Anyhow, especially because I'd never consulted a therapist before, it felt comforting to know that I was seeking help in not just any old safe place, but in *the* safest city in the entire country. Dr. Foote's office had apparently been furnished to convey that same impression. The walls were lined with books, the carpet was a tweedy tan, and the chairs were upholstered in a velvety brown. There was nothing threatening-looking about Dr. Foote, either. She wore a loosely draped dress in gray jersey with a red-patterned scarf and chunky gold earrings. Her footwear consisted of black flats, not boots.

"Steve," I repeated. "No matter how we'd split up, I'd miss him. Even before he fell into Anita's clutches, I was lonely for him. In so many ways, we liked the same things. Hiking with our dogs. Eating out. I don't really cook. For people. I cook for dogs. But that was okay because Steve likes restaurants. And no one could ask for a more attentive—" I stopped. As maybe you've noticed, I don't hold back a lot, but I didn't feel like talking to Dr. Foote about sex. "Except that asking for someone else was basically what I did. I was unappreciative and ungrateful. And stupid. I miss Steve a lot. And India and Lady. With India around, I used to be able to let Rowdy and Kimi off leash once in a while, in the woods, where there were no cars anywhere nearby, because India would watch out for them. She's a shepherd. German shepherd dog," I explained. "Very responsible. Incredibly obedient. The perfect dog. I've thought about getting one myself."

Dr. Foote raised her eyebrows. For some weird reason, her mouth twitched.

"A shepherd. Or a Border collie. But I can't, really, not where I live. If I got a male, there'd be trouble with Rowdy, and Kimi wouldn't accept another female, and I don't have room for kennels. The timing's bad, too. I'm not back to normal yet. I'm a lot better, a million times better. My memory is fine, except that once in a while, I have trouble—I'll read an article, and when I get to the end, I'll have trouble remembering the beginning. And I don't exactly have insomnia. I just wake up too early. Like four A.M."

"That is early," Dr. Foote agreed.

"And then I can't go back to sleep."

"What do you do then?"

"Get up. Feed the dogs. Work. Not that I exactly enjoy writing at five o'clock in the morning, but I get a lot done. I'm doing an article on fatal dog attacks, which is a fairly depressing subject, obviously, but it's particularly depressing before dawn. Or sometimes I take the dogs to Fresh Pond, which is the kind of thing I always tell other people to do instead of going to singles bars or taking adult ed courses."

Dr. Foote looked puzzled.

"World's best dating service," I explained. "A flashy dog. Two of them. The theory is perfectly sound, and I don't *want* to take up swing dancing, and I don't believe in personal ads—I think they're dangerous—but I walk the dogs all the time, so I already know all the other dog walkers at Fresh Pond and in the rest of my neighborhood, and I'm not interested in them."

"Have you let people know that you're interested in meeting men?" Dr. Foote asked.

I thought the question over. It struck me as sensible. Had I let people know? "More or less," I replied.

She smiled. "More *or* less?"

I smiled back. "Less."

"They may assume that you're not ready. Or not interested. You do have an air of self-sufficiency, you know."

"Me?"

"You."

"Well, in a way it's true. I mean, Rowdy and Kimi and I are . . . How do I say this? There's a way in which we're complete. Not exactly complete. A unit. One. We're the *we* in my life, if that makes any sense." The first thing I'd done on arriving at Foote's house had been to scrutinize the premises for any sign of a dog. I'd found none, unless you count the possibility of a kennel run in progress.

"Does it make sense to you?" she asked.

"Yes."

"And is there room for another person there? In that *we?*"

"Not just anyone. But yes, there is. The right one."

"I'd suggest that you let people know that."

Close to the end of the fifty-minute hour, we made another appointment. The "session," as Rita, my therapist friend and second-floor tenant, calls such meetings, had been different from what I'd expected. Unlike movie psychiatrists, Dr. Foote didn't have a foreign accent and didn't ask weird or corny questions about my father and mother. Rita does have a foreign accent—New York—and she's obsessed with parents. Mine, I might add, were not the reason Rita had talked me into seeing Dr. Foote. Rather, Rita had argued that the combination of my head injury and the loss of my relationship with Steve were too much for me to bear by myself. I'd countered with a lot of claims about dogs, friends, and relatives, but Rita, who understands me, had pointed out that if Rowdy or Kimi had suffered a concussion and a traumatic loss, and had sporadic memory problems and early-morning insomnia, I wouldn't hesitate to seek professional help. According to Rita, I should be as good an owner of myself as I was of my animals.

As I was passing through Dr. Foote's waiting room on my way out, the door to the outside opened, and two thoughts leaped to my consciousness. The first was that since the bland-looking fortyish man who entered the waiting room was evidently Dr. Foote's next patient, he must be totally out of his mind. The second was Rita's assurance that seeing a therapist was invariably proof of sanity, not madness. The man's appearance and demeanor supported Rita's view. He was about five ten and had light brown hair, blue eyes, and a fading tan. Not that the mad are necessarily tall or short, pale or dark, but if they look and act like some of the obviously deranged people who hang out in Harvard Square, they seem anything but ordinary. Dr. Foote's patient wasn't wearing jingle bells, hadn't embroidered bizarre words on his clothing, and didn't

shout or whisper to imaginary listeners. On the contrary, he was well groomed and wore a dark business
suit, and he dealt with the awkwardness of confronting
a possibly insane person, namely, me, by nodding his
head almost imperceptibly and giving a slight, formal
smile. With equal courtesy, I returned the acknowledgment. What are manners for, after all? Disguising embarrassment, among other things. You'd have thought
we were in the waiting room of a V.D. clinic.

CHAPTER 5

Subj: Your referral
From: DrVeeFoote@post.harvard.edu
To: Ritatheshrink@psychesrus.net

Hi Rita,

I tried to call to thank you for the referral, but your line was busy. In any case, thanks for referring Holly Winter. I really appreciate this gesture of confidence. As we discussed, I have a strong interest in neurology, as well as in loss, grief, and attachment, and always welcome referrals where these and other issues are paramount.

The plans for the new kitchen and baths are taking shape. David and I are very excited about the proj-

ect. You'll have to come and have a drink with us
when all the work is done.

Once again, many thanks for the interesting referral. I still have a few hours open I'd like to fill, so
bear me in mind!

Best,
  Vee

CHAPTER 6

Male dogs strut around and even roll onto their backs in public without visibly blushing at the prospect of embarrassing remarks about whatever surgery they may or may not have had. The canine inability to wish for medical privacy is not limited to males. If Kimi, for example, felt the need to consult a mental-health professional, and if her dog-psychiatric records eventually fell into her paws—or were dropped there by Rita—she wouldn't object to my publishing them in *Dog's Life* magazine or otherwise letting everyone on dog's green earth read them. I, however, belong to a lesser species and am thus tempted to suppress documents I acquired months after they were written. Alternatively, I could annotate them at length. As it is, I'll limit myself to a single comment: Had I but known!

Winter, Holly
P. referred for emotional aspects of recent head
trauma w/ amnesia lasting ca. 1 week. Now neur.
ok except for reported early A.M. awakening, minor
difficulty in concentrating, and reported problems
in sequencing. Denies headaches. Injury concomitant with marriage of p's former lover (Steve) to
"consummate bitch." Claims new wife indicted for
embezzlement! Also concomitant w/ marriage of
widowed father. Denies rivalry, resentment of new
wife. Note marked idealization of late mother. De-
scribes occupation as "dog writer"! Can this be??
Reports owns two, idealized—See late mother note.
Perseveration on topic of dogs, deflects own con-
flicts to the animals, consequent to trauma?

COUNTERTRANSFERENCE!!!

CHAPTER 7

Instead of going home after my session with Dr. Foote, I set out to pay a purely social call on a pair of elderly sisters, Althea Battlefield and Ceci Love, who were friends of mine and lived in Newton. Rowdy and I had met Althea on our therapy dog visits to a nursing home, and after she'd moved out of the facility and in with Ceci, I'd stayed in touch with both sisters. After my head trauma, they'd insisted on my staying with them for a few days. Incredibly, Ceci had welcomed my big, hairy, demanding dogs as well. She knew the medicine I needed most. Both sisters were now my adopted aunts. Althea looked about a thousand years old, but was only in her nineties. Ceci, the baby of the family, would object to a bald statement of her true age. Althea was tremendously tall and bony, with big hands, big feet, and a large brain capacity that she had put to use throughout her long life by devoting herself to the study of Sherlock Holmes. Although Ceci

took advantage of Althea's immenseness and scholar-
liness as foils for her own petite frivolity, she had been
trained in investment strategies by her late husband, a
stockbroker, and was far less featherbrained than she
took pains to appear.

My appointment with Dr. Foote had been at 2:10. It
was after three when I pulled up at Ceci's house, a
beautifully tended white colonial in a charming gas-
lighted neighborhood of big houses with big yards.
Real gaslights. But the yard was what I envied, a half
acre or so that ran downhill behind the house and was
fully enclosed by a high, sturdy fence, originally
erected for the Newfoundlands Ceci had owned. When
I'd met her, she'd been mourning the death of the last
of her beloved giants, Simon, whose oil portrait occupied the place of honor above the fireplace in Ceci's
living room.

Soon after I rang the bell, Ceci opened the door and
launched into one of her usual nonstop and over-
whelmingly hospitable greetings. "Holly, I'm so glad
to see you, and Althea will be terribly sorry to have
missed you, and I should have told you when you
called, but I forgot, Hugh and Robert have whisked her
off, so you'll have to settle for me, if that's all right,
and Quest, of course, I'm dying for you to meet him!"

Ceci liked to present herself as a vision in cham-
pagne. Her soft, pretty hair was tinted that shade, her
face was always carefully made up in pinkish beige,
and she favored flowing jersey garments in pale, pink-
toned tans. Today she wore a light beige knit dress
with a swath of black hairs across the skirt. The acci-

dental ornamentation constituted my introduction to
Quest, a Newfoundland she had just adopted from a
breed rescue group. "Quest is shedding," Ceci said,
"not that I mind, I'm perfectly used to dog hair. Home
isn't home without it, is it? Althea begs to disagree,
and she was determined to change his name to something from Sherlock Holmes—can you imagine a Newfoundland named Mycroft? And he is not fat!—but I
said that being abandoned by his owners because he
was supposedly *defective* was terrible enough, and it's
hard on any dog to adjust to new people, and I was
not going to make things more difficult for him by
changing his name, and there's nothing wrong with
Quest, is there? Especially when you consider that he's
been *rehomed.*" Her smug expression suggested pride
in the term, which was the new and fashionable way
to refer to the rescue and placement of unwanted or
abandoned animals. Ceci hated to feel outmoded. "In
other words," she explained, "he *was* on a quest, but
his search ended right here."

As I trailed after Ceci, I tried to ask polite questions
about Hugh and Robert, who are dear friends and ad-
mirers of Althea's, but Ceci was obsessed with her new
dog, who turned out to occupy a gigantic cedar-filled
dog bed at the far end of the living room in a sort of
mini conservatory with a tile floor, potted palms, and
wicker furniture. The black bear of a dog looked at
least as old as Althea. He was fast asleep.

"Quest, wake up!" Ceci demanded. To me, she said,
"As I may have mentioned, Quest has hip dysplasia,
only mild to moderate, thank goodness, but no one else

wanted to adopt him, and his age didn't help, either, although we're not quite sure what it is, maybe eleven, maybe more, but possibly less, so he wasn't exactly the dog of most people's dreams, but with Althea the way she is, we couldn't have a young dog bounding around and bumping into her, but I had my heart set on a Newfoundland, and Quest is really very sweet and gentle, and he's the perfect dog for us. Quest, wake up! We have company!" Turning to me again, she confided in an unnecessary whisper, "We think he may be a little hard of hearing."

As if awakened by the whispering, Quest raised his mighty head. His eyes had the opacity of old age. Like other giant breeds, the Newfoundland has a short life span. I've known Newfies to live to thirteen, but the average is more like nine years. Considering Quest's elderly appearance and the hip dysplasia, he rose to his feet rather easily. The condition, a malformation of the ball and socket at the hip, is eventually accompanied by osteoarthritis, which is, in effect, the body's effort to stabilize the unstable joint. Make your left hand into a tight fist. That's the top of the dog's thigh bone. Wrap your right hand snugly around it. That's the part of the pelvis known as the acetabulum. The ensemble, a good femoral head set snugly in a correctly formed acetabulum, is a good hip joint. Loosen your right hand. Or make your left fist into a strange shape. Or pull your fist all the way out of the surrounding hand. As Tolstoy intimates in *Anna Karenina,* all happy hip joints are alike, but unhappy hip joints are unhappy in lots of different ways. And there you have dysplasia.

Tolstoy, great family vet. I needed a new one, just as I needed a new man in my life. Steve Delaney had been both. Too bad Tolstoy was before my time.

After offering a hand for Quest to sniff, I said, "Hi there, big dog. It's a pleasure to meet you."

"You can pat him," Ceci assured me. "He's a glutton for affection. For a Newf, he's not really very protective. But you're used to that." Malamutes are *not* guard dogs or watch dogs. That's what she meant. As I stroked the giant dog, Ceci went on to say that she was convinced that he came from show lines. "Doesn't he have a lovely broad head? Good ears. His gait is less than ideal, but he can't help that, can you, Quest? And he does very, very well, considering. And his anti-inflammatories help a lot, don't they?" On all subjects and in all circumstances, Ceci was a garrulous person. But when it comes to dogs, especially their own dogs, even laconic dog people turn voluble. Ceci continued for the next half hour, by which time we were having tea and cookies in the living room. Although Quest appeared to see and hear very little and to fall asleep at every opportunity, he followed Ceci in an endearing way and was now dozing at her feet. "He needs exercise," Ceci rambled, "not that he can be expected to go running, which would be beyond me, if it comes to that, and he has the run of the yard, so to speak, but when he's out there, he doesn't actually run—dogs don't, do they, unless you have more than one?—so I've been taking him to Clear Creek Park, where there's a very nice dog group. Have I mentioned that Quest just loves other dogs?"

"That's wonderful," I said before seizing the chance to follow Dr. Foote's advice. "Speaking of the need for companionship, Ceci, I thought I might just mention that, um—"

Before I could finish, she broke in, her face alight with glee. "You need to meet *men.* Of course you do. I understand completely. My marriage to Ellis was a very happy one, you know." She glanced fondly at the tiny framed photo of her late husband that sat on a side table, then up at the mammoth portrait of the New-foundland, Simon, that hung over the fireplace.

"I thought I should say something," I told her, "and not expect people to guess. Or think I wanted to be alone. Especially with Rowdy and Kimi, I think maybe, uh, the three of us can seem sort of self-sufficient."

"I have the perfect man for you," Ceci announced. "He's part of the dog group." In asking an elderly woman about relatively young men, I'd had in mind the brokers at her late husband's firm, maybe, or men who'd grown up in her lovely neighborhood. "His name is Douglas, and he is a lovely person. He has such a funny dog, a hound mix, heaven knows what, everything, adopted from a shelter, a sweet dog, big, smaller than Quest, of course, but a big dog, Ulysses, and the dog group could use your help. As a matter of fact, I was going to ask for your advice even before this came up, because, you see, it's really rather awkward, but one of the nicest people there, Sylvia, has a dog that, if the truth be told, does *not* belong off leash. And I know that look on your face, Holly! No dog belongs off leash, but the dogs at the park stay together in a little group, and they have such fun, and it's wonderful exercise for them. The only problem, really, is Zsa Zsa, Sylvia's dog, who has a *less* than ideal temperament and is making things difficult for all of us."

Temperament is a dog-talk euphemism. A "bad temperament" usually means that the dog bites. Weak versions of the phrase—an "iffy temperament"—usually mean that the dog hasn't bitten anyone yet.

Just to be sure, I asked, "Has Zsa Zsa bitten anyone?"

"Oh, no, no, no, not so far, not exactly, and she's much worse with other dogs than she is with people, although I must admit that I don't feel entirely comfortable with her, and she has a really unfortunate way of bothering people who don't even like dogs, which is most unwelcome because not everyone at the park is happy to have the dogs play there, and the rest of us knock ourselves out, really, to be responsible and not to make matters worse by giving dogs a bad name."

"Zsa Zsa jumps on people?" I guessed.

"And chases after them, especially runners. And people on bicycles. But the worst part is that she picks fights with other dogs, and we don't know what to do about it without offending Sylvia."

"Maybe you can't. Have you tried talking to Sylvia?"

Ceci made girlish faces. "Sylvia doesn't seem to appreciate the extent of the problem, because you won't believe it, but Zsa Zsa is a golden retriever! Of all breeds! They're usually angels, but you know that, don't you? You used to have them." Did I ever! My native breed. "And Sylvia's son-in-law," Ceci continued, "Wilson Goodenough—such a striking name— has tried to talk to her, I'm sure, because Wilson is a perfect paragon of responsible ownership, and Zsa Zsa embarrasses him, and I'm sure that if he could do anything about her, he would. Wilson did persuade Sylvia to stop breeding Zsa Zsa, but that's as far as he got. But what I'm driving at, Holly, is that we could use your help, and so we'll go to the park with Quest in a completely natural way." Ceci smiled impishly. "We won't say that you're there to meet Douglas, you see," Ceci declared. "We'll say that you're there about Zsa Zsa. You and Douglas can just bump into each other."

"Oh?" I said.

"That way," Ceci concluded, "Douglas won't be scared off."

CHAPTER 8

I awoke the next morning at the undogly hour of four and couldn't get back to sleep. At quarter of five, after a shower, breakfast, coffee, and a hit of E-mail, I should have done some work, but as I'd told Dr. Foote, fatal dog attacks are not a sunrise topic. I had a second project, but Rita and my third-floor tenants had made me promise to conduct the research for it only when they were out of the house. They'd also made me swear to ventilate the building after each experiment. I'd have done that anyway. You can grind chicken livers and mix them with cornmeal, or douse calves' liver in garlic powder and sherry, or just nuke a slab of lamb's liver in the microwave, but no matter what kind of liver you use and how you cook it, it stinks. Dogs disagree. Yes, indeed, as you've probably guessed, my new project was a cookbook. The original working title had been *A Hundred and One Ways to Cook Liver*. It soon became apparent that I'd underestimated the scope of my subject. *Two Hundred and One...? Five Hundred and One...?* Or even (gasp!), *A Thousand and One Irresistibly Tempting Ways to Cook Liver, Liver, and More LIVER?*

Times best-seller list, here I come!

Anyway, in Ceci's case, the observation about elderly people waking early was true, and she'd mentioned that her dog group began to gather in the park at dawn, so I felt free to call her and accept the invitation to accompany her. I offered to drive and consequently needed room for Quest, whose monumental size would mean that I'd have space in the back of the Bronco for Rowdy or Kimi but not both. I hate to bad-mouth my own dogs, but strictly between us, it's often hard to estimate which one will act worse in a particular situation, especially when the situation involves anything remotely akin to sharing a prized possession, such as food, water, space in our car, or, for that matter, the God-given dominion of the Alaskan malamute over every other creature in the solar system. When it comes to dog aggression, a rule of thumb—rule of dew claw?—is that same-sex dogs are more likely to fight than are dogs of opposite sexes. But Kimi makes her own rules, which stipulate, in essence, that she's the one who does. Rule. The universe.

In brief, my intuition advised that Rowdy would behave slightly better than Kimi. To protect Rowdy from the hideous sight of a male Newfoundland occupying space is *his* car, I removed the metal travel crates from the Bronco and incarcerated Rowdy in a blessedly opaque Vari-Kennel. Furthermore, Ceci and I wisely abided by a second rule of dew claw, the one that says to introduce dogs on neutral turf. Rowdy and Quest met a few houses down the street from Ceci's rather than in Rowdy's precious, if ancient and dented, Bronco.

The moment Rowdy saw the monumental black Newfie, he obviously came to an important decision, which was that Quest did not exist. After a single initial glance, Rowdy stared right through the big dog. Inside his Vari-Kennel on the drive to the park, Rowdy didn't growl, rumble, or fuss at Quest's proximity. Why protest the presence of a dog who wasn't there? Even a dog whose weight had practically broken my arms and back when I'd half lifted him into the car? When we arrived at the park and took both dogs out of the Bronco, Rowdy surveyed the scene with his usual curiosity. Clear Creek Park, I should mention, was not some stingy patch of vegetation, but a generous area of perhaps thirty or forty acres that included open fields and dense woodland. Now, Rowdy scanned the blacktop parking lot, the tennis courts, a playground, a large wooded area in the distance, the cloudless sky, and a vast playing field, its grass still green, where four people in bright parkas huddled together near a group of frolicking dogs. He took in absolutely everything except Quest. Etiquette provides a term for this extreme form of snubbing. As I recall, it's known as *the cut direct.*

"Oh, I do think that our boys are going to be dear friends," Ceci gushed. As always, she was carefully made up and becomingly dressed. Her champagne-

colored jacket had a hood trimmed with what she had
assured me at stupefying length was artificial fur. Although I'd heard all about her devotion to Newfoundlands, I suddenly realized that one source of her
attraction to the breed was the startling contrast between her pale daintiness and the breed's dark monu-
mentality. "Rowdy has been very good with Quest,
hasn't he? Good boy, Rowdy! You can always tell
when dogs form friendships, can't you! You can see it
in their eyes. Rowdy, you've taken a real liking to
Quest, haven't you? What a good dog! Oh, there's
Noah. He's the round little man, and those four brown
shepherd mixes are his, all from shelters, he's such a
noble soul, Matthew, Mark, Luke, and Jonna, isn't that
cute?"

It seemed to me that the hour, seven-thirty A.M., was
too damned early for cute, especially canine cute, but
I was delighted to hear the enthusiasm in Ceci's voice.
Althea had spoken to me in private about her worry
that Ceci felt obliged to spend most of her time at
home. Althea actually liked to have her sister go out,
not only because Althea didn't want to be a burden,
but because Ceci's unending chitchat grated on Althea's nerves. Now, making her way eagerly toward
the group of dogs and people, Ceci picked up her pace
and tried to cajole Quest to do the same. "Sweetheart!
Let's go play with our friends! Let's go!" she enjoined
loudly. Quest raised his tremendous head a bit and may
have picked up his lumbering pace a trifle, but Ceci
was satisfied. "He just loves coming here, don't you,
sweetie? Who is Mommy's best boy? Is Quest? Is

Quest Mommy's good boy who loves to play with the other doggies?"

In public! With someone *listening*! I cringed at the prospect of Ceci's introducing me in a similar fashion to Douglas, the man she had in mind for me: *Now Dougie, this is Holly-Wolly, and she is Mommy's best girl, isn't she? She's a good girl who just loves to play with the men, aren't you, Holly?* But Douglas wasn't there; Noah, owner of the four Gospels, was the only man in the group. The three women with him were presented to me only as the mommies of Chomsky, Princess, and Henry David Thoreau. Chomsky was a soft-coated wheaten terrier, a male in desperate need of grooming. That's the hitch about wheatens. They're cheerful, perky, friendly, cooperative, charming, medium-size dogs, perfects pets, except that they absolutely, positively need regular brushing, bathing, and trimming, and when I say *need*, I'm speaking (as usual) from the dog's point of view. If that soft coat gets filthy and matted the way Chomsky's was, the dog's skin becomes irritated and sore. Why do people who hate grooming insist on getting these high-maintenance breeds?

As is perhaps all too apparent by now, the attitude of dog-show types toward pet people is the attitude that concert pianists take toward enthusiastic amateurs who struggle to pick out "Go Tell Aunt Rhody" on the glockenspiel. Our justification for the insufferable condescension is that they know nothing, we know everything, they're always wrong, we're always right, and what's more, when we try to educate them, are they grateful? No! Gee, I can't imagine why. For once, I refrained from lecturing. Fortunately, the remaining two dogs were black Labs and thus had short, smooth, easy-care coats. Princess was young, lean, and fit, but poor Henry David Thoreau was grotesquely fat, like a whale with legs, as I did not say aloud.

As Ceci had said in pointing him out, Noah was a round little man. He had the fuzzy brown hair and the warm, safe appeal of a teddy bear, an image he probably sensed and hated. Even so, his red parka, which matched the red collars on his shepherd-mix dogs, would've been suitable for the L. L. Bean toy known as L. L. Bear. Together with the mommies, clad, respectively, in purple, blue, and yellow, Noah extended an enthusiastic greeting to Rowdy and expressed a gratifying interest in him.

"We used to have a husky here," said the woman in purple, "but he got run over."

The woman in blue corrected her. "This is a malamute. Isn't he?"

"Yes," I said.

"You might want to think about getting him neutered."

"He's a show dog." I could've elaborated by sharing the news that a highly esteemed breeder of malamutes who lived in the state of Washington had just E-mailed me, inquiring about the possibility of using Rowdy at stud. The breeder, Cindy Neely, also happened to be a friend of mine and a fellow soldier in the trenches of malamute rescue. That is, Cindy and I devoted the spare time we didn't have to finding homes for home-

less malamutes. In that case, why breed more malamutes? Where else were healthy, correct dogs like hers
and mine supposed to come from? But I digress.

"You can let Rowdy loose," the woman informed
me. "There's a leash law, sort of, but the dogs always
play here, and people turn a blind eye, more or less.
Lately, it's been less, but no one minds this early.
Rowdy is beautiful. I'm sure he wins all the time."

Pet people! There isn't a show dog on earth who
wins *all* the time. Still, I intended to thank her and to
say something nice about the dogs romping in the field,
but before I had a chance, Ceci said, "Holly has two
malamutes, a male and a female, the girl is Kimi, and
we'll have to get Holly to bring her here sometime,
too, she's a sweetheart, but the point is that Holly
knows everything about dogs, and she's going to solve
all our problems with Zsa Zsa."

I do know some things about dogs. For example, I
understood that Rowdy was at that moment allowing
Quest to sniff his big rear paws only because Quest
was an imaginary dog and thus wasn't there. "What I
know is far from everything," I protested. "But Ceci
was telling me about the problem, and she thought it
might help to have a fresh perspective."

"We were just talking about Zsa Zsa," Noah said.

The woman in yellow laughed. "She's all we ever
talk about !"

"That's not true," objected the woman in purple.
"We talk about how well all the other dogs get along.
Chomsky—he's the wheaten—is the most self-
directed. He pretty much does his own thing *around*

the other dogs, on the periphery, and he likes them, but after he runs with them for a few minutes, he loses interest. And then he sniffs things."

"I've deprived Chomsky of the benefit of siblings," explained the woman in yellow. "He's an only child, so he's had to learn to entertain himself. Aren't you going to let Rowdy play?"

"He isn't necessarily good with other dogs," I said apologetically, meaning that the handsome boy was my life's blood, and I didn't want his flowing in the street after he'd been hit by a car.

"Unsocialized," the woman said matter-of-factly.

OBEDIENCE-TITLED-CANINE-GOOD-CITIZEN-BREED-CHAMPION-BREEDING-QUALITY-CERTIFIED-THERAPY-DOG! I wanted to reply just like that! Hyphenated, all one word, all capital letters, one long, loud, dog-proud brag. But like Rowdy and Kimi, I am socialized. Also, her wheaten, Chomsky, was peacefully wandering around off leash without getting into dog fights or any other trouble, and in that limited sphere of behavior, he probably was superior to Rowdy. Not that there's so much as a competitive metatarsal in my body, but as a dog show type, I find myself oddly reluctant to enter a My Dog's Better Than Your Dog contest that my dog is bound to lose.

"There you have it." Noah spoke with the cadence of a radio preacher. "Dogs that come to the park and socialize all learn to get along together." He didn't actually finish with *amen,* but the word hung in the air all the same. Could he really be a minister? The Gospel

dog names—Matthew, Mark, Luke, and Jonna—
sounded a bit blasphemous even to me, but maybe the
intention had been devout. In any case, the loose dogs
seemed to support his contention about the benefits of
off-leash play. Chomsky remained happily on the
fringes of the group, as Noah's mixed breeds and the
Labs tore around. With a guilt-ridden glance in my
direction, Ceci removed Quest's leash. The excitement
of meeting Rowdy and riding in the car, however,
seemed to have exhausted the old dog's energy. He
sank to the grass in a bearlike heap.

"That hardly applies to Zsa Zsa," one of the women
pointed out. "I mean, Zsa Zsa isn't exactly a walking
ad for playing with other dogs, and Sylvia's yard is
next to the park. It's five minutes from here. Zsa Zsa's
been coming here for ages, and you couldn't exactly
call her socialized. Really, she's just getting worse and
worse."

"I hate to say it," another woman remarked, "but I'm
afraid the truth is that Zsa Zsa just is not a very nice
dog. Naturally, you can't expect Sylvia to see it that
way."

"Has anyone tried talking to Sylvia?" I asked.

"Sylvia knows damn well that Zsa Zsa's ruining the
park for the rest of us," Noah said. "Hey, who keeps
the park safe? We do! Dog walkers. The rest of us
knock ourselves out to fight the antidog sentiment. We
go around with our pockets full of plastic bags. We
clean up after our dogs. Our dogs don't go around
chasing the joggers and jumping on people and scaring

little old ladies." Suddenly aware of Ceci's presence, Noah reddened and had the sense not to elaborate.

"It's true," said the woman in purple. "Technically, there's a leash law, but no one used to care all that much, except for a few cranks who complained if they stepped in dog doo, but really our dogs just play together." She swept an arm toward the nearby pack. "They're not bothering anyone."

"Does Sylvia—?" I started to ask.

Noah interrupted me. "Sylvia knows. Her son complains to her all the time."

The woman in purple corrected him. "Son-in-law. He's married to Sylvia's daughter. I forget his name."

"Leo's daddy," someone said. Or that's what it sounded like.

Ceci spelled out the name. "L-l-i-o. Llio is a Pembroke Welsh corgi, just like the Queen's dogs, although I must say that despite the Welsh and all that, tradition, respect for the breed's origins, and so forth, it still strikes me as a foolish name for a girl, because after all, we're not in Wales, are we?" She had a momentary look of genuine puzzlement. As if announcing a comforting discovery, she cried, Columbus-like, "We're in America!" Ceci's daffiness, I might mention, drove her sister wild. Or as wild as the logical Althea ever got. "It's not mental deterioration," Althea had informed me. "That sort of lunacy used to be fashionable in young women."

"Be that as it may," Ceci continued, "Llio is perfectly charming, not to mention quite, quite beautiful, and her daddy is a model of responsible ownership. So we feel certain that he has talked sternly to Sylvia."

"I wonder," I suggested, "whether all of you might try putting the problem to Sylvia directly. Sometimes people don't pay all that much attention to members of their own families."

"You don't know Sylvia!" one of the women exclaimed. The other people laughed.

"That's true," I agreed.

"Sylvia makes a joke out of everything," Ceci explained, "including poor Wilson, her son-in-law, who is really a very nice young man." She broke off. "Speaking of him, there he is now."

Rapidly approaching from the direction of the woods was a tall, dark-haired man carrying a retractable lead, at the end of which was a really beautiful Pembroke bitch, which is to say a show-quality Pembroke Welsh corgi female. Corgis are tough, sturdy herding dogs, with substantial bodies and short legs. Handy mnemonic: long tail, long sleeves, Cardigan. As in sweater. Cardigan Welsh corgis have long tails. The ones with the short tails are Pembrokes. Llio, whose name had come up earlier, stood about ten inches at the withers, the withers being above the forelegs, more or less where a dog's back stops and the neck begins. She must've weighed about twenty-five pounds. Her head was what the standard—the official description of the ideal Pembroke—calls "foxy," meaning what it says, reminiscent of the head of a fox. Ears are terribly important in Pembrokes. In fact, the language of Pembrokes abounds in derogatory terms for bad ears; the breed is not supposed to have bat ears, hooded ears, catlike ears, button ears, rose ears, or drop ears. Llio's were lovely: medium sized, erect, and neither too pointed nor too round at the tips. Color and markings are also important in the Pembroke ring. In fact, the standard is exceptionally detailed, so almost every feature is vital. Llio was black and tan with white on her legs and chest, where it's allowed. She had an intelligent expression and a smooth gait. Suddenly, the sun was shining a bit more brightly than it had been only moments earlier. Ever noticed that phenomenon? It happens whenever a beautiful dog appears.

Human and canine members alike, the dog group had an endearing habit of greeting each new arrival with warmth and enthusiasm. The people welcomed Llio by name and called out to their own dogs: "Llio's here! Come say hi to Llio!"

"Llio stays on leash, too," the woman in purple informed me. "Don't you, poor girl?"

"She's beautiful," I said to her owner, the tall, dark-haired man. From a distance, he'd looked moderately attractive, but viewed from up close, he was unappealing. Although he'd shaved, his hair was greasy, and his teeth needed the attention of a skilled hygienist. He was munching on a jelly doughnut. Grains of sugar clung to his thin lips. Someone should have told him to close his mouth when he chewed. Still, his bitch was beautiful. "Do you show her?"

After replying that he did, he complimented Rowdy and asked whether I showed him, as I did and do, and then naturally I recounted a few high points of

Rowdy's career in the breed and obedience rings, and
Llio's owner reported that she needed only one major
to finish, meaning, as almost no one else there understood, that Llio needed only one major win (a win
worth three or more points) to finish her championship.
My own bitch, I said, hadn't finished yet. My cousin
was handling her for me, but I always used a professional handler for Rowdy. Did my new acquaintance
handle his bitch himself? No, he didn't. By now, Noah,
Ceci, and the other mommies had tuned us out and
were saying hello to a variety of people and dogs join-
ing the group.

Having discovered that we were both show people,
Llio's owner and I ignored the proletarian hordes surrounding us and continued to converse about bitches,
majors, professional handlers, recent shows, upcoming
shows, and various other topics of exclusive interest to
the dog elite. Eventually, I said that my name was
Holly, and he said that his was Wilson, and then we
were off again. Long before that, it had become apparent to me that Wilson's dog–social standing was not
quite . . . what's a nonsnobbish way to say this? In the,
a-hem, highly structured social world of the dog fancy,
my own standing borders on the illustrious, not so
much because of my own accomplishments as because
of my late mother's. She was not only a famous
breeder of golden retrievers and a successful obedience
competitor, but the sort of personable personage who
joins everything and knows everyone who's anyone in
dogs, including, for example, Mrs. Nigel Waggenhoffer, whose name Wilson dropped. And when I say

dropped, I mean let fall with a bang. Mrs. Waggenhoffer is big in goldens and is the president of the
prestigious Micmac Kennel Club, to which I belong
and Wilson didn't.

"I was the co-breeder on some of my mother's litters," I explained modestly. "I'm sort of a legacy ad-
mission. I'm not active in the club at all." *So don't
even think about asking me to sponsor you,* I wanted
to add.

Changing the subject, Wilson said, "You hardly ever
see any show people at the park."

"We don't let our dogs off leash," I said. "That's
one reason."

In low tones, Wilson confided, "These pet people
don't know anything. Take the wheaten. Chomsky. Jesus, the poor dog, he's all matted. She lets him get like
that, worse than that, and then she takes him to the
groomer and has him shaved. It's awful. And Thoreau,
that's that fat Lab over there, is a blimp. She's killing
him."

"The dogs really do seem well socialized," I pointed
out.

Wilson rolled his eyes. "What's it going to matter if
they're dead?"

CHAPTER 9

As Wilson and I were chatting, yet more new people and dogs arrived. By now, there must've been a couple of dozen dogs of all sizes, shapes, and colors, including two standard poodles, one black and one white, a pair of yellow Labs, three West Highland white terriers, and some of those fascinating mixes whose ancestry inspires guessing games with no known right answers. The big spotted dog gently herding the Westies could well have been a Border collie-Newfoundland cross. A medium-size, short-coated tan dog looked like a million other All-American dogs, except for the peculiar and distinctively Chinese crested patches of long white hair on his head and tail. What had been a unified play group now consisted of three or four subgroups with a few lone dogs hanging out on the periphery and few happy pairs playing together. Ceci's great big Quest had risen to his immense feet and was gently looming over an adorable Shih

Tzu, who was barking directly into his face while executing the front-down, rear-up play bows that dogs use to invite one another to romp. Was I tempted to let Rowdy join the free play? Oh, yes I was. Did I remove his leash? I did not.

Although it was still early morning, the temperature was rising, and the mommies I'd identified by color had removed their parkas, as had Noah. Ceci was by far the oldest person there. A young Asian woman and a hefty, dark-skinned man added a little variety. As is usually the case, by comparison with the dogs, however, the human beings were annoyingly homogeneous. Some were taller or shorter, heavier or leaner than others, but no difference in human appearance began to rival the marvelous contrast between the giant Quest and the little Shih Tzu. Naked, we'd've looked even more uniform than we did with our clothes on. As I was reflecting on the aesthetic superiority of Rowdy's species to my own, a male Dalmatian who'd been flying around in circles with a couple of buddies suddenly split off and sprinted toward the woods.

"Lydia," someone called out. "Lydia!" Weird name for a male, right? These pet people! But Lydia turned out to be the owner, a red-haired woman in jeans and an "I Love My Dal" sweatshirt, who shouted, "Buster! Buster, you come right back here! Buster, bad dog! Damn it all!" Still hollering, she marched off in the direction the Dalmatian had taken before he'd disappeared into the woods.

Almost immediately, another woman appeared. This one was also looking for a dog. Slim and neat, she had shoulder-length brown hair streaked with gray. She wore a pale green coat over a matching suit. On her feet were cream-colored pumps, what I think of as real shoes, meaning that they made walking difficult and running impossible. Reaching the dog group, she exclaimed cheerfully, "The tart!" Then she bellowed, "Zsa Zsa, here! Damn it! Zsa Zsa!"

"Probably thinks that Damn It is her name," Wilson murmured to me. "It's all Sylvia ever calls her."

Turning toward him, I noticed something to which he seemed oblivious, namely, that Llio, his corgi, was not just squatting close to him, but was soaking his left shoe and the cuff of his left trouser with urine. Averting my gaze, I noticed people glancing at Wilson and Llio, and exchanging low-key smirks and silent snickers.

"Wilson," the new arrival said loudly, "that dog is pissing on your foot again. Your pants are soaked."

Poor Wilson looked down at Llio and his left foot. Not everyone felt as sorry for him as I did. Giggles were audible.

"Thanks, Sylvia," Wilson said with an edge in his voice. "Llio, bad dog!"

"Too late now," someone told him gently.

"Zsa Zsa!" Sylvia bellowed. "There she is! Zsa Zsa! Get over here before I strangle you!" Sylvia's tone, however, was affectionate.

Heading toward the group from the direction of the woods was a morbidly obese golden retriever.

"Sylvia, you've got to get that dog on a diet," someone said.

"I tried diet food," Sylvia replied, "but she didn't like it. All she wants to do is pig out on burgers and fries."

It seemed to me that if Wilson had had any pride, he'd have gone home to change his pants and shoes. But he was still hanging around. Watching his face, I could almost read his mind. His thoughts seemed identical to mine. Then, to my astonishment, he spoke them aloud.

"Then don't give them to her," he said. "If she doesn't like low-calorie food, she won't eat it, and she'll lose weight."

"The dog expert speaks!" Sylvia crowed. "At least Zsa Zsa's housebroken. Llio's ruined every rug in my house."

Meanwhile, Zsa Zsa plodded toward us. To anyone who cared about dogs, she was pitiful. To someone who knew a bit about canine gait (yes, guess who the someone was), it was hard to know where to begin enumerating what was wrong with hers. As she drew close, I could see not only that she was grotesquely overweight, but that the excess pounds were badly distributed. Her shoulders were overdeveloped, and her whole front was monstrously heavy, but her hips and rear legs were scrawny. Her forelegs bowed and her back sagged as if she were carrying a cruelly heavy pack. With her hind legs, she took the mincing little steps of a woman in stiletto heels. In other words, because of weakness in the rear, her front end was doing all the work of dragging her around. When she ran, her rear legs moved under her in unison like a rabbit's; the gait is known as "bunny hopping." It's hard to evaluate structure and movement in a fat dog. Still, Zsa Zsa was the picture of severe hip dysplasia. As Ceci had said, Quest was dysplastic. By comparison with this poor golden, he moved like a dream. And he wasn't in pain. I'd have bet anything that Zsa Zsa was.

Empathy blinded me, as did anger. My own hip joints ached. And damn it! That pain was preventable. Where did dysplastic dogs come from? From dysplastic lines, that was where, and if every breeder would X-ray the hips of all breeding stock, the incidence of the disorder would plummet. Why breed Rowdy? So there'd be malamutes with his effortless gait. From the looks of Zsa Zsa, she'd come from a pet shop or a backyard breeder. If buyers would shop as carefully for puppies as they did for cars, then . . . cars? Hell, if they'd shop as carefully for puppies as they did for beer! Well, then—

When Zsa Zsa struck, Rowdy was ready. He's a good dog, but he's not big on empathy for other animals. Also, he cares nothing about the ethics of dog breeding; if the choice were his, he'd be the sire of thousands. Instead of wasting his time on thinking, Rowdy had watched Zsa Zsa and risen to his feet. He doesn't believe in taking anything lying down, especially when the thing in question is an attack by another dog.

Zsa Zsa caught me completely unaware. The silence, suddenness, and power of her attack astounded me. In seconds, Rowdy and Zsa Zsa were one violent mass of writhing bodies and flashing teeth. Then Rowdy locked those massive malamute jaws in a vice grip on the skin of Zsa Zsa's neck. The air itself reeked of a fight. The crowd of people around us parted to make room for the brawl. Sylvia was shouting at Zsa Zsa, and Ceci was shrieking a high-pitched, "No, no! Stop! Stop it!"

I had no excuse. In the eyes of other dogs, the stand-up ears, stand-off coat, and high tail carriage of the Alaskan malamute look aggressive. Even peaceful malamutes get attacked. And Rowdy wasn't exactly Gandhi. Bad enough to have a fight. But a fight between two big dogs when all those other dogs were running around loose and might join the fray? Or start battles of their own? Rowdy was my responsibility. I should have been vigilant. After all, Ceci had warned me about Zsa Zsa. The second the notorious golden appeared, I should have done what I did now. With one hand gripping Rowdy's leash, I stuck the other into one of the big pockets of my jacket and pulled out a small aerosol can with one visibly unusual feature. In place of a nozzle, it had a red plastic cone-shaped device. Brandishing the spray can, I reached outward and downward to position it as near as possible to one of Zsa Zsa's ears. Then I pressed the button. The resulting clamor was almost unbelievable: WWAAAMMAAA! Imagine the wailing of a police cruiser combined with the greatly amplified mooing of an enraged cow. MMAAWWWWAAA!

The dogs sprang apart. To the relief of everyone within a mile, I suspect, I released the button, thus silencing the aerosol horn. Clasping Rowdy's leash tightly, I called to him and bolted. If he hadn't followed, I'd have dragged him, but he now had eyes only for me. I'd bought the aerosol alarm at a marine supply shop on the coast of Maine and carried it in case the need for it ever arose. Rowdy had never heard it before. Not that he'd previously underestimated my prowess as a mighty hunter and master of the universe! For years, he'd seen me leave on courageously lone pursuits of wild game and, in no time at all, return bearing slaughtered beasts all ground up and packed into forty-pound bags. Impenetrable obstacles gave way when I poked them with bits of metal. But never, ever had Rowdy even dreamed me capable of this monstrous roar!

Still clutching the horn in one hand, I used the other to check Rowdy for injuries, especially puncture wounds. No blood was visible, and my fingertips found no damage. As I went over him, I congratulated myself on having decided to bring Rowdy instead of Kimi. Rowdy had defended himself. He'd been ready to have the fight end. If Zsa Zsa had gone after Kimi, Kimi might have ignored the horn in favor of pursuing the famous best defense. The expression *bitch fight* sounds pornographic, but it's the common term in the dog world for a fight between females. It connotes menace and fear, because at least one of the combatants often tries to go for the kill. Sexism? No, realism. Anyway, surveying the scene, I saw that Zsa Zsa had retreated to the periphery of the woods and that Sylvia had followed her there. Every other dog, however, and every other person was staring at me in amazement. Slowly and cautiously, I led Rowdy back to the group. "I'm sorry," I said, "but I didn't know what else to do."

Far from blaming me, everyone deluged me with questions about the means I'd used to perform the miracle. What *was* it? People were fascinated. By comparison, the Greek armies at Troy gave only a cursory glance at Achilles' sword and shield. What's more, so far as I could remember, Achilles' comrades hadn't flooded him with inquiries about where he'd bought his weapons and where they could get the same kind for themselves.

"It's no magic bullet," I kept warning. "It won't break up every fight. It won't even scare off some dogs." I went on to suggest spray bottles or squirt guns filled with vinegar and water, even though I avoided them myself because they were a nuisance to carry in my hand and a worse nuisance in my pockets, where they always leaked. I'd never tried pepper spray and didn't suggest it.

"What about those, uh, what do you call them?" someone asked. "Personal alarms?"

"Personal alarm devices," someone supplied. "They're smaller. Those things are really small. And they're even louder."

Ceci reveled in my effectiveness. "You see, Holly? I knew you'd know what to do, but you're so modest, you just won't give yourself credit, and didn't I say she knew everything about dogs, well she does! I have to get one of those things immediately, because poor Quest, he's really a bit beyond being able to defend himself properly, not that he'd ever start trouble, but who knows?"

"What we need to do," said Noah, the group's un-official leader, "is to make sure that everyone, including Sylvia, carries one of these horns from now on. Or a personal alarm. *Especially* Sylvia. The problem is that she has no control over Zsa Zsa. With one of these horns, she could stop Zsa Zsa before things got started."

I'd been trying to make myself heard. Giving up on getting the group's attention, I spoke to Ceci. "This is totally out of hand! It's hardly going to improve things at the park if all the dog walkers suddenly start blasting horns and alarms. People who already object to the dogs are going to have two things to complain about instead of just one. And isn't there some kind of or-dinance against loud noise?" I stopped. I'd assumed that Sylvia would catch Zsa Zsa and take her home. In fact, Sylvia was heading back toward the group with Zsa Zsa trailing after her.

"You see what we're up against?" Ceci commented. "I think maybe it's time to go home."

But Wilson started toward his mother-in-law. He pulled a spare leash from his pocket. When he reached Sylvia, he handed it to her. He must have said some-thing, but he was too far away for me to hear. Perhaps because Zsa Zsa's head was still reeling from the blast in her ear, she proved easy for Sylvia to catch. Wilson didn't help Sylvia. Rather, he and his lovely corgi headed toward the woods. With Zsa Zsa on leash, Syl-via, however, returned to the group. I expected her to reenter by apologizing to me for the unprovoked attack on my dog. Instead, she repeated all the questions the others had asked about the aerosol horn.

Once again, I pointed out that arming the dog group with horns and alarms, far from solving public relations problems with other users of the park, would exacerbate the situation. Instead of complaining about dogs, the public would call the police about the noise, and when the police started showing up, all the dogs would have to be leashed. Eventually, feeling that I'd sounded enough loud and sour notes, I said lightly, "I've had one recent encounter with the police. I don't really need another."

"Oh, people won't make *noise*," Ceci assured me, "unless they really *need* to, the way you did. You're just not giving yourself proper credit for a wonderful idea, but I knew you'd know exactly what to do! And so you did! It's just too bad that you-know-who wasn't here this morning to see what a miracle worker you are." Somehow managing to whisper at a volume only slightly lower than the boat horn's, she added, in case my recent concussion was impairing my reason, "Douglas! That's who I mean, but we won't say a word to anyone, will we?" Returning abruptly to my reference to the police, she asked, "Were you arrested? Of course you weren't. What could you of all people possibly have done, I mean, Holly, you are perfectly law abiding, you probably got a parking ticket, or maybe you were walking your dogs and forgot to carry a plastic cleanup bag and—"

Sylvia interrupted her. "*Were* you arrested? How interesting!"

To avoid a second fight between Zsa Zsa and Rowdy, I'd been back-stepping a bit. Consequently, I had to raise my voice to respond and thus ended up telling everyone the story of my new stepmother's abortive attempt to scatter her late husband's ashes in Harvard Yard.

Sylvia was tickled by the idea. "Marvelous! Maybe that's what I should do with Ian! He's been sitting in an urn at home gathering dust. Dust unto dust, as they say, but—"

Someone asked dryly, "Wedding bells in your future, Sylvia?"

"You never know," she replied, "although marriage isn't exactly what I've been thinking about." Smiling, she hummed a tune that everyone must have recognized: "There'll Be Some Changes Made."

It always irks me to hear someone hint at some drastic change without going on to specify what it's going to be. So what if Sylvia sounded hostile? What could she do that would have any effect on me? Nothing! If she dyed her hair chartreuse, moved to Brazil, and married *two* men, her green-coiffed South American bigamy would have no impact on me, except that I'd be able to accompany Ceci and Quest to the park without the risk of having Zsa Zsa attack Rowdy. Preoccupied with this senseless resentment, and still monitoring Zsa Zsa, I didn't notice the pretty, petite young woman in black spandex until she'd practically hurled herself at Sylvia.

"Dear God, Pia, what's the matter now?" Sylvia said. "Pia panics at everything. She always has."

The runner looked genuinely distressed. Her hair contributed to her startling and startled appearance. It was short and dark, and stood up in locks and tufts, almost as if it were standing on end. She probably just hadn't brushed it before going for a morning run. Exercise could have reddened her face. But her expression was anxious and aggrieved. "Mother, really! A lot of help you are! Where's Wilson?"

A couple of people started to tell the young woman that Wilson had left a while ago. Ceci, however, responded to her obvious disquiet. "Something happened to you," she said. "What is it? It wasn't that foolish man again, was it?"

"Yes, it was! Miracle of miracles, someone finally noticed. Thank you! Yes, it was the same one."

"In the ski mask?" someone asked.

"Yes. And the trench coat. Corny, huh? But let me tell you, when it happens to you, it's not very funny."

"No one said it was," Noah told her.

"My mother did."

"She didn't mean that," Noah assured Pia. "Did you, Sylvia?"

"Pia, grow up!" Sylvia ordered. "These things happen. There are a lot of sick people in the world. This exhibitionist is one of them."

"If you'd had a dog with you—" Noah began.

"It'd still have happened," a woman finished. "It happened to me three weeks ago, and Pasquale was with me"—she pointed to yet another black Lab—"and he didn't deter this guy one bit."

"Did you report it to the police?" someone asked her.

"Yes, and all they did was put it in the Crime Beat column in the paper. Big help that was. At least they didn't print my name."

"It's nothing to be ashamed of," Ceci said, "since after all, you were the victim of this deviant person, and it isn't as if you had done anything except just take Pasquale for a walk, speaking of which, my sister will wonder where on earth Quest and I have gone to, we're usually not this late. Holly?"

As I drove Ceci and Quest home, she lamented Douglas's absence, but said how glad she was that I'd solved all the problems with Zsa Zsa and had a chance to meet all of Quest's friends at the park. "And their mommies and daddies, too, of course," she added.

When Rowdy and I were finally alone in the car driving home, I said to him, "Rowdy, I'm your best friend, and I'm Kimi's, too. I'm your owner, your hired help, your trainer, your handler, your groomer, nutritionist, nursemaid, and partner. I am all things to you. Except one. I am *not* your goddamned mommy."

CHAPTER 10

Subj: Re: Your Rowdy
From: Jazzland@pnwmals.org
To: HollyWinter@amrone.org

HollyWinter@amrone.org writes:

<<What are you looking for? I'm wondering why you're not using one of your own males.>>

My males are too young or too old or too closely related to Emma. She is CH Jazzland's Embraceable You. Emma's claim to fame is that she went R.W.B. at the National.* I'll send you her pedigree. She is

---

*Reserve Winners Bitch at the Alaskan Malamute National Speciality, the annual nationwide all-malamute show. In contrast to going R.W.B. at a little local show, going Reserve at the National is a

the product of an outcross. Sire is AM/CAN CH Brae-mal's Alyeska Tuaq, and dam is Jazzland's Fly Me to the Moon.** I want to go back into the dogs on the mother's side of the pedigree, and those are the dogs that are in Rowdy's pedigree. Any chance you could send a video of him?

I want a standard size stud, no bigger than 26", good coat, good bone, dark, obliquely set eyes, lit-tle ears, a PERFECT tail set, and EFFORTLESS move-ment. Emma and Howie (her brother, CH Jazzland's How High the Moon) regularly run through the woods on our property. They cruise at top speed over fallen trees, rocks, and shrubs, and their top-lines barely move. They look like they are flat out on a ROAD. They absolutely float. I love to watch them.

Cindy
Jazzland Alaskan Malamutes
WAMAL—WA Alaskan Malamute Adoption League—
President
AMAL—Alaskan Malamute Assistance League—WA

---

great honor, like getting a silver medal at the Olympics or having your novel short-listed for the Booker Prize, only more so.—H. W. **Sires are fathers, and dams are mothers. An AM/CAN CH is an American and Canadian champion. When Cindy writes that Emma is the product of an outcross, she means that Emma's father and mother were unrelated.—H. W.

CHAPTER 11

Rowdy and I next accompanied Ceci to the park about two weeks later. It was early on a Thursday morning. Very early. Too early. So far, Dr. Foote had provided no cure for my predawn insomnia, and since dogs don't suffer from the symptom, I had no idea how to rid myself of it. The only remotely applicable home remedy I could think of was the ridiculous notion that babies who sleep all day and stay awake all night can be made to reverse the cycle by being held by their heels and whirled around in the air. Absurd! But spun around by my heels was more or less the way I felt when Ceci and I were in the middle of the field with her dog group and she finally had the opportunity to introduce me to the much-talked-about eligible gentleman, Douglas.

I'll begin my own introduction of Douglas by saying that his dog, Ulysses, was a large, silly-looking mix of what were probably a dozen breeds, most of them scent hounds, including bloodhound, basset, and black-and-tan. Ulysses was long and tall, with floppy ears and an improbable coat consisting of blotches, tufts, and bristles. His predominant color was grayish brown, but a brown splotched with large white splashes and dotted, spotted, and ticked with shades of black. He looked like a long-haired dog who'd been shaved to the skin some months earlier and had then had the misfortune to stand next to someone who spilled a gallon jug of bleach on him. Ulysses' soulful basset eyes were his best feature. His nose never wandered far from the ground.

Ulysses' owner, or in park parlance, his daddy, was a pleasant-looking fortyish man, about five ten, with blue eyes and a fading tan. Sound familiar? If not, it will. When I'd seen him before, he'd worn a suit. Now, he'd apparently been running. He had on gray sweatpants, a gray sweatshirt, and expensive running shoes, white with turquoise flame-shaped decorations, probably intended to connote speed. I studied his shoes for a few seconds. It was easier than meeting his gaze. When I raised my eyes, we exchanged knowing smiles. Douglas and I had something in common. We were both in therapy with Dr. Foote.

"I'm so glad that you two have finally had a chance to meet," Ceci gushed. "I knew that Holly would just love—"

I held my breath.

"—Ulysses," she finished, to my great relief.

"Ulysses is wonderful," I said to Douglas. "He's"—I sought the right word—"unique."

Douglas's eyes twinkled. "He's that. Your dog is beautiful."

Rowdy was again enjoying the privilege of accompanying me. I hate to play favorites. Most of the time, I take both dogs everywhere. But if Zsa Zsa tackled Kimi? There wasn't going to be an *if*, not with Kimi at home. "Thank you," I said. "He's a good boy." Standing at my side, his eyes fixed on me, Rowdy wagged his perfect tail.

Douglas was beginning to reply, but a horrendous noise drowned him out. If every horrendous noise I'd heard at the park that morning had been a drop of water, we'd all have drowned. There was no actual rain. On the contrary, the sky was a wintery blue. Despite the chilly weather, the park was a popular place this morning. In the distance, graceful figures danced across the basketball courts and tennis courts. Runners ran, and congenial-looking groups of people, mostly women, walked briskly, as if determined to shake the blubber off their thighs. A few dozen delightfully assorted dogs fraternized in the field, while their self-proclaimed parents exchanged the human equivalents of sniffs and play bows.

If it hadn't been for the intervention of a certain supposed dog expert, the whole sunlit scene would've been a sort of impressionist study in the mundane beauty of middle-class recreation. The appearance of harmony was illusory. When I'd picked Ceci up that morning, she'd shown me two letters to the editor she'd clipped from the *Newton Pulse*.

Ban Dogs!
Bad enough that Clear Creek Park is already
polluted by dog feces without the latest, which
is noise pollution from loud noisemakers blown
at all times of the day and night to supposedly
stop dogs from fighting with each other and at-
tacking innocent persons like myself who seek
exercise and peaceful solace in the publicly
owned woods. Enough is enough! It's high time
to clean up Newton's parks by banning dogs
totally and outright.

—Doug Hare
Newton Centre

People Will Be Next!
Regarding grumbling throughout the City about
"noise" in Newton parks, Newtonians are harboring under a false assumption. Concerned
dog-owning citizens in the futile (!) hope of
placating anti-dog factions at Clear Creek Park,
in fact, sought the advice of a professional dog
training expert who recommended the applica-
tion of loud auditory stimuli as a scientifically
proven method of modifying the behavior of
dogs which were offending non-dog users of the
park. Now those same complainers are whining
about the efforts to modify the very same behavior which was the cause of the original com-
plaints! Some people are never satisfied. Watch

out! If dogs are banned from parks, people will
be next!

—LIONEL BROWN
NEWTON HIGHLANDS

As it was, the jolting blasts of air horns and personal
alarm devices kept interrupting the harmony of man,
woman, and dog. No sooner did the joggers resume
jogging, the walkers walking, the dogs frolicking, and
the mommies and daddies chatting, than someone just
had to go and try out one of the damned noisemakers.
The most active experimenters with the gadgets were
the adult human males, who seemed determined to support the stereotype that men are no more than large
preadolescent boys. Two outwardly mature men kept
miming a quick-draw contest with their air horns. Or,
maybe they were reenacting the gunfight at the OK
Corral. Miming was at least silent. The shrieks of the
personal alarms were, if anything, worse than the sick-
cow blasts of the horns.

"It's a good thing for Quest that he's a little hard of
hearing," Ceci said. "But the other dogs! Their poor
ears! Men! They're nothing but little boys."

"Where did all these things come from?" I asked.
Boston is, of course, on the Atlantic Ocean, and the
Charles River, which empties into Boston Harbor, has
lots of small-boat traffic. Even so, the marinas and
marine-supply shops are mainly in the seacoast towns
north and south of Boston, not in the western suburbs.
As it turned out, someone had bought a whole case of

air horns for almost nothing at a gigantic discount store and handed them out to all the dog walkers. The personal alarms had come from electronics shops, both local and online.

Wilson's corgi, Llio, had her ears flattened. She looked miserable. "This is misguided," Wilson said reasonably. "Among other things, if the dogs get used to the noise, it won't stop fights. And Pia had to go and get a personal alarm after what happened with the, uh, sick individual in the ski mask. But what good's it going to do now?"

"Crying wolf," his wife agreed. She again wore a running outfit—cream-colored tights and layers of sweatshirts. "Although I must say that I'm not sure these personal alarms do any good, anyway, in terms of personal safety. What if no one hears them? Or hears them and doesn't do anything? A dog might be afraid of the sound, but a flasher?"

"Low curs, aren't they?" Douglas joked.

Oddly, Pia didn't seem to object to his making light of her unhappy encounter. On the contrary, she smiled flirtatiously at Douglas. "You and your puns, Douglas," she said.

"It isn't a laughing matter," Wilson protested.

"I've recovered," his wife told him. "The police said these sickos usually just do what they do. They get off on exposing themselves. They aren't rapists. If they were, they'd—"

"Pia, enough," Wilson ordered. "We know what they'd do. It's obvious. Enough."

Pia flushed. "Would you not talk to me like I'm a dog?"

Wilson apologized and went on say, "I didn't mean it to sound like that."

"Well, that's what you always say to Llio. *Enough!* Not that she listens."

"Llio listens better than Zsa Zsa does," her husband countered. "Not that that's saying a lot. Oh, God! Here she comes."

A glance showed Sylvia emerging from the woods. Zsa Zsa was waddling beside her.

"Rowdy and I are going to disappear," I said, "and Ceci, I think you should get Quest away from here, too."

"Don't you have your—?"

"We were lucky last time. It might not work, especially . . . let's just go."

Ceci being the upbeat, if somewhat unrealistic, person she was, said, "Well, yes, it probably is time for us to head home. You have work to do, I'm sure, Holly dear, and we've all had our *exercise* for the day, haven't we, Quest?"

Although our exercise had consisted of traversing the short distance from the car to the middle of the field, I didn't argue. Ceci believed so fervently in the benefits of fresh air that she considered outdoor breathing to be a vigorous aerobic activity. I intended to have a talk with her about the importance of maintaining muscle tone in dysplastic dogs and to prod her to walk Quest on the paths in the park. But not now.

I cut her good-byes short. As she, Rowdy, Quest,

and I made our way toward my Bronco, I checked on Zsa Zsa's whereabouts. Sylvia and the golden had covered about half the distance from the woods to the dog group, which is to say, about half the length of a football field. I relaxed. Even if Zsa Zsa decided to tackle Rowdy again or to go after Quest, we'd reach the Bronco before she could get to us. In passing, I noticed a runner whose route would intersect Sylvia and Zsa Zsa's. Someone had mentioned that Zsa Zsa pestered runners. I couldn't remember whether she chased them, jumped on them, nipped at their heels, or irked them in some other way. This runner, a dark-haired woman, moved with speed and energy; she looked more than capable of outdistancing a dysplastic dog. Besides, even from afar, she somehow radiated an air of taking no grief from anyone, human or canine. She wore black, a bulky black top and, in defiance of the cold weather, black stretch shorts.

Ceci spoke. "I can't decide whether to tell Althea, because, you see, in some ways, Althea is quite worldly, if you know what I mean, and in others, she is really very sheltered, living as she does in a world of books with all that Sherlock Holmes make-believe and so forth, not to mention that I am her junior by more than a few years, and once a little sister, always a little sister no matter how many years pass and how much water runs under the bridge, don't you think?"

The language-processing centers of Ceci's brain must be larger and more complex than mine. Even before my concussion, my mind would digest the first half of one of her sentences and then choke on the final half. "Tell Althea about what?"

"The man!"

"Douglas?"

"No, no, the one in the ski mask. And trench coat." Ceci lowered her voice. "That silly man who, uh, shows himself. To women."

Before I report what happened next, I want to make it clear that the moment Ceci raised the topic of telling or not telling Althea about the exhibitionist, I turned my eyes from the field to Ceci, and thus was not watching Sylvia, Zsa Zsa, and the runner in black. Ceci wasn't looking at them, either; she was looking at me. In other words, I didn't see what happened and have never said otherwise. Ceci didn't see what happened, either; she couldn't have. Neither of us looked in that direction until we heard shouting and barking. When we did, we stopped, turned around, and saw the source of the hullabaloo. The first thing I noticed was that Sylvia was, for once, holding Zsa Zsa's collar. Specifically, Sylvia was bent over a little and grasping the collar in her left hand. With her right, she was jabbing a fist at the runner in black, who stood a foot or two away from her. I had the impression that Sylvia was gesturing. It's possible that Sylvia's fist made contact with the runner's body. I was too far away to judge accurately. Zsa Zsa was certainly barking, and the women were undoubtedly shouting at each other. I made out only two words: *you* and *dog*.

Sylvia, Zsa Zsa, and the runner were closer to the big group of dog walkers and dogs than they were to

Ceci, Quest, Rowdy, and me. By the time I turned to watch the dispute, some members of the dog group were rounding up their animals and putting them on leash. A few people, however, were heading toward the scene of the altercation. Pia must have gotten there first. She was followed closely by Wilson, who had had Llio on leash to begin with. Noah was another speedy arrival. His dogs, Matthew, Mark, Luke, and Jonna, got along well with the other dogs and showed no desire to wander from the group, so he probably felt comfortable in taking his eyes off them.

"There goes Noah!" Ceci exclaimed. "He's our mayor, you know. That's what we call him. The mayor of the dog group. He'll get things straightened out, but doesn't Sylvia look furious! And that other woman, whoever she is, is really quite, quite angry, and what do you suppose happened? I'll bet Zsa Zsa chased after her, and then she said something not very nice to Sylvia, and . . ." By this time, Ceci was eagerly heading toward the quarreling women, her progress impeded by Quest, who shared none of his owner's inquisitiveness about the drama. "Quest, do stop being a mule!" Ceci commanded.

In contrast to Quest, Rowdy was almost uncontrollably eager to get to the scene of the conflict. Human discord would've been of passing interest to him, but in his ears, Zsa Zsa's insistent barks demanded his intervention. Malamutes are convinced that the world is run, if you can even call it that, by a bunch of spineless incompetents with no sense of order and no ability to enforce rules. Border collies share the conviction, but are committed to rising above the chaos or herding it neatly into enclosures. Malamutes use brute force. Cheerful creatures that they are, they *like* using brute force. Furthermore, they avoid the periphery in favor of the center. In this instance, Rowdy was just positively itching to pounce on Zsa Zsa and teach her a lesson, thereby restoring order and, of course, making himself the star of the show.

I didn't permit Rowdy to play policeman. But I could have stopped him from dragging me across the field. I didn't. I'm human, therefore I'm curious. Also, I knew that Ceci was unstoppable. Consequently, Quest and I got hauled to the small group of people who now surrounded Sylvia, Zsa Zsa, and the angry runner. Ceci's and Rowdy's timing was actually good, because the four of us arrived at a key moment. From up close, where we now were, I could see that the runner must have taken a fall. One of her bare legs was covered with mud and grass, she had a smear of earth on her face, and she was brushing dirt off her hands. Her cheeks were bright red. At the time, I assumed that ire had made the blood rush to her face. I now know that she just had good coloring. For that matter, she had good everything: a pretty face, large eyes, great legs, and an enviably voluptuous build. Now, her dark eyes crackled, and as she shifted her weight from the ball of one foot to the ball of another, she reminded me of a Scottie sparring in the show ring in a display of the true terrier character that judges love.

Sylvia was screaming, "What the hell was I supposed to do? *You* lunged at *my* dog!"

"I did not lunge at him!" the terrier shouted.

"Her! Zsa Zsa! You made a vicious grab for her!" Sylvia screamed. "And you shoved *me*! You did it deliberately!"

Her opponent was suddenly and ominously motionless. Staring at Sylvia, she said, "I want your name and address."

"My name and address are none of your goddamned business," Sylvia told her.

"Oh, yes they are," replied the runner, reaching under her bulky black sweatshirt and pulling out, of all things, a pair of handcuffs. After once again fishing under her sweatshirt, she produced a black leather case that she opened and held out for Sylvia to see. "Police officer," she announced. "You're under arrest. Assault on a police officer. Resisting arrest."

With that, she quickly stepped behind Sylvia and, pulling Sylvia's hand from Zsa Zsa's collar, cuffed her hands behind her back.

"You moron!" Sylvia sputtered. "How could I have resisted arrest *before* you tried to arrest me? You just told me this second you were a cop! Am I resisting arrest? I'm not resisting! How was I supposed to . . . and I haven't done anything! You're the one who pushed me, you bitch! And for Christ's sake, would someone get Zsa Zsa! Pia, would you for once make yourself useful!"

Released from Sylvia's grip, Zsa Zsa had fallen silent. She continued to stand near Sylvia, but made no effort to protect her. The golden's expression was oddly sleepy or dazed, and she showed no inclination to go after any of the other dogs. I often carry a spare leash and was now glad that I had one with me. Pulling it from my pocket, I handed it to someone and asked to have it passed to Pia, who, in contrast to Zsa Zsa, was aggressively defending Sylvia. "My mother did not push you! You lunged at Zsa Zsa, and then you slipped and fell. Everyone saw you. If anyone assaulted anyone, it was you! When you put those stupid handcuffs on her, you wrenched her wrist, and I saw you! This is ridiculous! You can't arrest my *mother*!"

The officer paid no attention, mainly because she was busy talking into a mobile phone.

"Pia, shut up!" Sylvia ordered.

"I can't believe she's a cop," Pia went on. The leash had finally been passed to her. As she snapped it on Zsa Zsa's collar, she asked rhetorically, "Does she look like a cop? No! How was anyone supposed to know? She never said she was a cop. Did she?"

"Certainly not," declared Ceci, who, of course, hadn't witnessed the beginning of the episode. "She just went running up to Sylvia and made a *very* threatening move toward Zsa Zsa, and then she lost her balance and fell. No one assaulted anyone."

Stepping forward, Noah tried to take charge and restore peace. "Officer, there seems to have been a misunderstanding. Let's try to get this straightened—"

The cop cut him off. "There's no misunderstanding. What there is, is assault on a police officer."

Sidling up to me, Wilson whispered, "What a fiasco! Sylvia *did* push her. For heaven's sake, don't mention this to Mrs. Waggenhoffer! I suppose I'd better go call a lawyer. Except there's probably one here. Do you think I should ask?"

The notion struck me as ridiculous. *Is there a lawyer in the park?* "Ceci, I think we should leave," I said.

"Walk out on Sylvia? *Abandon* her?" Ceci was aghast. "Holly, I'm surprised at you! Are you feeling all right? We can't just run off. After all, we're witnesses!"

Although it seemed only seconds ago that the officer had summoned help, a siren wailed, and a cruiser sped into the park and came to a halt near my Bronco. The owners whose dogs were still loose got busy retrieving and leashing their animals. A few people joined the circle around Sylvia and the cop. The sensible ones strolled casually off. I envied them. Meanwhile, two uniformed men leaped out of the cruiser, which they left with its lights flashing and front doors open, and made a dash to assist their fellow officer. Like everything else about the incident, the response seemed disproportionate to the trivial nature of Sylvia's crime, if she'd even committed one. The only law I'd seen her break was the leash law. Was it illegal to call a cop a moron and a bitch? I didn't think so. It was possible that Sylvia had pushed or maybe tripped the runner without knowing that the woman was a cop, but she hadn't socked her in the jaw, pulled a gun, or otherwise committed an act of violence. Yet here she was, in handcuffs! Under arrest! Here in this pretty park in the Safest City in America. Weirdly enough, instead of normalizing the events, the presence of the uniformed cops only added to the sense of unreality. For one thing, the guys in uniform were incredibly handsome, with movie star looks too good to be real. Both were young and tall, with broad shoulders. One had short blond hair and fair skin, and the other, as if chosen by a casting director as the perfect foil, had short black hair and espresso-dark skin.

"One of the nice things about Newton," Ceci commented smugly, "is that it's always such a pleasure to call the police, not in *this* instance, really, but our police are so handsome that it can't be an accident, can it? The world is full of ordinary-looking people, so you'd think the police in Newton would be ordinary-looking people, too, but they're not, obviously, and it's nice to see that affirmative action hasn't changed things, has it!"

As Ceci babbled, the uniformed men, however handsome, led a protesting Sylvia to the cruiser. The reality of her predicament was now apparent to her and to everyone else. The anger had left her face, which was pale and tearful. Still, she had the presence of mind to shout instructions to Wilson and Pia about calling a lawyer and meeting her at the police station.

"We'll be there, too!" Ceci impulsively promised at full volume. "Holly, we need to go there right away so poor Sylvia doesn't have to face this trauma all alone. Headquarters is in West Newton, which you could reach by going back to my house, but that's the long way around, really, so we'll take the . . . what do you call it? Hypotenuse, just the way we learned in geometry, about squaring sides." She paused. As if the matter were of pressing importance, she asked, "Who *was* that man with the hypotenuse? Pythagoras! That's who it was. We'll do just what Pythagoras said."

I refused.

CHAPTER 12

On the following Tuesday morning, five days after Sylvia's altercation at the park and her subsequent arrest, I had a call from Ceci's sister, Althea. I should mention that Althea Battlefield, BSI, almost never asked favors of anyone. The letters after Althea's name signified her membership in the Baker Street Irregulars, an elite society of devotees of Sherlock Holmes. Revered by her fellow Holmesians as a sort of Irene Adler—*the* woman—she was universally acknowledged in Sherlockian circles to possess an intelligence that combined Sherlock's rationality with the limitless brain power of his brother, Mycroft. Like Mycroft, Althea seldom ventured far from her lodgings. In her case, the reason was not a sedentary disposition, but the physical infirmity of great age. As Ceci always took pains to emphasize, Althea was the elder sister. As I've probably made clear by now, Ceci was the silly one. Anyway, Althea never made frivolous requests. Consequently, when she phoned to ask for my help, I had to say yes.

"Two Adventuresses are calling on me this afternoon," Althea explained. The capital *A* rang in her voice. Althea's eyesight was poor, but her hearing remained acute, and she didn't shout. The capital pealed and chimed to distinguish the exalted New York visitors from run-of-the-mill, lowercase female adventurers who might pop in to advance some nefarious scheme by questionable or ruthless means. Indeed, Althea was herself an Adventuress, which is to say, a member of the ultra elite Adventuresses of Sherlock Holmes.

"The game is afoot!" I dutifully replied.

A lower-case, lower-class adventuress would have gone on to offer a trumped-up excuse for begging me to get Ceci out of the house or might even have spat out the truth. Capitalized Adventuresses, however, are extremely genteel. Althea didn't feign concern that Ceci would be bored by the Holmesian visit, and she didn't say outright that even in the presence of three Adventuresses, the game would never really get afoot with Ceci underfoot. Rather, she took the refined course of trusting me to use my common sense. "Could I prevail on you, Holly, to take Ceci and Quest to the park?" she asked. "My visitors are due here at two o'clock, and they don't have time for a long visit. I expect they'll be gone by four-thirty."

I agreed. About a minute after I hung up, the phone rang again. This time, it was was Ceci, who said, "I have a tremendous favor to ask you, not for myself, really, for Althea, who really does enjoy life, you know, despite the toll the years have taken on her. She's considerably older than I am, although we avoid mentioning it, but there it is, and facts are facts, and the fact is that she has friends stopping in this afternoon, two of them, Sherlock Holmes lunatics just like my sister and my late husband, of course, Ellis. These two are Adventuresses of Sherlock Holmes, which Althea is, too, ridiculous name, it makes them sound like women of ill repute, and the three of them are going to gab nonstop about the Canon and the Master and copper beeches and speckled bands and dancing men, which I can follow, more or less, but half of what they say about teapots and lions is completely lost on me, and the truth is that it's very boring to sit and listen to people go on and on in some foreign language you don't speak and don't care to learn, besides which if I'm here, despite all good intentions, I'll spoil the fun." She stopped to catch her breath. "I don't want to be rude and go running out of the house on my own as if I want to avoid the Adventuresses, so could you possibly *insist* that I have to go somewhere with you? Anywhere at all!"

"I'd be delighted," I said.

"The park would be lovely," Ceci said, "and the Adventuresses are arriving at two, so we can get there when it's still nice and sunny out and before too many other people get there, but if we stay long enough, Douglas could turn up, has he called you yet?"

Rowdy and I picked up Ceci and Quest at quarter of two. Rowdy, as usual, refused to admit that a monumental black male dog was occupying space in the Bronco that properly belonged to Kimi or to no one. As we drove to the park, I half-envied Rowdy his ability to pretend that Quest didn't exist. If I'd known the secret of Rowdy's mental knack, I'd have applied it to blotting out Ceci.

"Things at the park have really not been the same since that policewoman arrested poor Sylvia," Ceci rambled, "although I have been going there just the same because I feel that it's important for Quest to have the physical and mental stimulation, and I must admit that in terms of Zsa Zsa, things are better because miracle of miracles Sylvia has been keeping her on leash lately, not that Zsa Zsa is the nicest dog in the world even on leash, but it does help, has Douglas called you? Or have I asked you that already?"

She had. Repeatedly. I was almost sorry to have to admit that Douglas hadn't called, not because I had any romantic interest in him but because I'd have liked the chance to discuss Dr. Foote with another one of her patients. Specifically, I had the unaccountable sensation that something about me made Dr. Foote nervous, and I wondered whether Douglas sensed that he had that same effect on her.

When Ceci and I finally arrived at Clear Creek Park, only a few other cars were there, and the big field was empty. The unseasonably warm weather was persisting. The temperature must've been sixty, and the still air gave the sun a summery warmth. Although the trees had dropped most of their leaves, the grass remained green.

"What a perfect day for a walk!" I told Ceci, without adding that standing around in a field was not my idea of fun and that it wasn't Rowdy's, either.

Ceci voiced an objection. "That *man* skulks in the woods. The pervert, I mean."

The dogs were out of the car now. Anticipating a walk on the trails, I'd put Rowdy on a long retractable lead. He was bouncing around, his tail flying like a banner over his back. Quest was a bit beyond the bounce and wag stage of life, but at least he hadn't sunk to the blacktop and fallen asleep. Gesturing to Rowdy and Quest, I said, "Ceci, with these two big dogs around, no one is going to bother us. Their combined weight must be over two hundred pounds, and they love us. I don't think we need to worry. The exercise will be good for everyone."

Her expression remained hesitant. Hoping to lighten her attitude, I added foolishly, "If the exhibitionist tries anything, the four of us will chase after him, and the dogs will catch him, and then you and I will perform a citizen's arrest!"

Tickled by the notion, Ceci agreed to a walk and even led the way to a trail that began at a small footbridge spanning a dark, oily-looking stream and then entered the woods. Quest, for once, required no cajoling. Lumbering along, he reminded me of the grizzlies I'd seen on a TV show about hibernation. Ceci, in her pink-beige quilted jacket, personified traditional, civilized femininity. Taking advantage of Quest's burst of energy, she was stepping briskly along at a pace that matched Rowdy's and mine when all of a sudden that damned Zsa Zsa flew out of the underbrush only a few yards ahead of us and, as if determined to ruin our walk, flattened her ears, lowered her tail, put her hackles up, and came to a menacing halt. Her narrowed eyes were fixed on Rowdy. If Ceci hadn't been there, I'd have sworn loudly. As it was, to my astonishment, Ceci spat, "Damn it! What is wrong with Sylvia! She knows better than this! Zsa Zsa, bad dog! Go home!"

My temper snapped. Rowdy had emerged unscathed from his first encounter with the nasty golden. I had no doubt that he'd win a second fight. If Zsa Zsa tore one of his perfect ears or scarred his face, he wouldn't care. But I would! No one had the right to hurt any dog of mine. And absolutely no one was going to ruin the looks of one of the best show dogs I'd ever owned! All at the same time, I reeled in Rowdy's lead, called to him, and pulled the boat horn and my car keys out of my pocket. Zsa Zsa had probably been blasted with horns and alarms so many times by now that one more roar wouldn't bother her, but the aerosol can of noise was the only weapon I had. Pushing Rowdy behind me, I gave my keys to Ceci and ordered her to take Quest and head for the car. Frightened, she obeyed me and did it silently, too. Then I directed the inadequate weapon at Zsa Zsa and pushed its button. Over the sick-sounding clamor, I shouted at her, "NO! Go away! Go home!" Confident of not being overheard, I spoke bluntly. "You stinking, rotten, miserable bitch, make one more move, and I'll strangle you with my bare hands! Disappear!" In desperation, I scanned the ground, spotted a rock the size of a baseball, picked it up, and gripped it in my right hand. Zsa Zsa hadn't departed, but she'd stopped moving toward us and no longer seemed to be on the verge of attack. Keeping one eye on her, I began to take small, calm steps back down the trail toward the car. "Watch me," I whispered to Rowdy. "Let's not start trouble with her. Good boy!"

In almost no time, we reached the little footbridge. To my relief, Zsa Zsa wasn't following us. I picked up the pace, and Rowdy and I soon reached the Bronco. Only then did I remember that Ceci couldn't get Quest up into the car by herself. I apologized to her, put Rowdy in his crate, and boosted Quest into the back.

Ceci was furious at Sylvia. "This is not right!" She stomped a dainty foot on the blacktop. "Wouldn't you think Sylvia would've learned a lesson? But no! And to think that I have been taking her side. All along, Noah has been perfectly right about Sylvia. Zsa Zsa *is* ruining the park for everyone, and it's all Sylvia's fault."

"Ceci," I said forcefully, "Zsa Zsa is *not* ruining the park for *us* because I'm not going to let her. Sylvia lives right near here, doesn't she? Do you know which house? And how to get there?"

"It's a brick Tudor, or what's called Tudor, although I doubt that . . . well, it's a suburban Tudor, let's say, with cream stucco and a brown door and trim, and a slate roof. It's no distance at all, in fact, you can see the chimney and a bit of the roof from here. Wilson showed me one day." With that, she pointed out a brick chimney and a slate roof easily visible beyond a stretch of leafless trees. "That's Sylvia's house. If you go down the trail where we just were, you cut through the woods a little, and there you are."

After settling Ceci in the passenger seat, I armed myself with a leash, a training collar, and fresh supply of dog treats (liver, what else?), and set off to capture the wild beast, Zsa Zsa. I did not, of course, intend to carry out my threat of strangling her; I just meant to catch her and walk her home. If I sound confident or even arrogant about the prospect of dealing with an aggressive dog, it's because Zsa Zsa was a golden retriever, a horrible, atypical one in almost every way, but a golden nonetheless. The goldens I'd grown up with and the ones I'd owned myself had been sound of body and mind, strong, healthy, biddable, and angelically gentle, just as goldens should be and Zsa Zsa wasn't. Still, I felt a sense of control over any golden.

Soon after recrossing the footbridge, I began to call and whistle for Zsa Zsa. She didn't appear. I kept walking and, within a few minutes, ran into one of the women I'd met on my first day at the park, the owner of Princess, the lean black Lab, who was happily trotting along on a retractable leash. The woman and I exchanged nods and smiles, and I asked whether she'd seen Zsa Zsa.

Instead of answering, the woman said, "Is she loose again? I thought Sylvia had shaped up, but Zsa Zsa was running around yesterday. And Sylvia was nowhere in sight."

The woman hadn't seen Sylvia today, either. I continued my search for another minute or two and then caught sight of my quarry a few hundred feet ahead on the trail. Zsa Zsa proved surprisingly easy to lure. I held out a handful of liver treats and called sweetly. But when she got within a yard of me, she stopped. I'm an old fox with dogs. Instead of moving toward her, I inched backward. Happy sounds and liver did the rest. In no time, I had her on leash and was taking her home. A narrow footpath off the main trail seemed likely to lead to the house Ceci had pointed out and, in fact, did. Sylvia's irresponsibility about her dog and the scrappy nature of her family had somehow made me expect a house with vines running wild and architectural elements at war with one another. The little path ended at the rear of a neatly lawn-serviced yard with short grass, tons of mulch, and the inevitable suburban rhododendrons. The conventional brick Tudor matched Ceci's description. The only object in sight that showed any sign of neglect was a large, treelike wrought iron structure with a variety of empty bird feeders and empty suet baskets hanging like weird pieces of fruit from its numerous branches. But the house was Sylvia's. When I rang the bell at the back door, the young man who answered took one look at Zsa Zsa and, addressing me, asked, "Did my mother get arrested again?"

"Not that I know of," I said.

Although it was midafternoon, he'd apparently just awakened. His eyelids were puffy, and the inner corners were thick with the crud that is euphemistically known as "sleep." He wore two diamond-chip studs in one ear. On one side of his scalp, his hair was in rather rumpled spikes, but his pillow had flattened the hair on the other side.

"I'm Holly Winter," I said. "I'm returning Zsa Zsa. She really shouldn't be loose."

"Eric Metzner." He yawned. "Uh, sorry about the dog. I'll keep her in. Where's my mother?"

"I have no idea."

"There's no food in the house," Eric complained. "There was nothing when I got in last night, and now there's nothing for breakfast. If you see her, could you tell her?" He yawned again. "Is her car here?"

"I don't even know what Sylvia drives."

"You haven't seen her?"

"No," I said impatiently, "I haven't seen her."

"Well, hey," Eric said, "uh, sorry about the dog. I'll keep her in. Thanks for bringing her back."

Taking long, rapid strides back toward the car, I savored the heroic sense of being the park's bold, capable savior. As Saint Patrick had rid Ireland of snakes, so I had rid Clear Creek Park of Zsa Zsa! The world, it seemed to me, should be run by dog trainers. Instead of passively letting Sylvia and Zsa Zsa get away with spoiling the park, I'd taken decisive, effective action! Sylvia was the English, the park was France, and I was Joan of Arc! When I reached the Bronco, Ceci immediately brought me back to reality, or at least to her version of it. She was standing by my car with Douglas and his dog, Ulysses, the multi-hound mix. "Holly," she announced as I approached, "Douglas has offered to walk with us. So we won't have to worry about being bothered by the foolish *man.*"

"Hi, Douglas," I said. "Hello, Ulysses! Good boy!" I reached a hand out.

"Not advised," Douglas said. "He's been rolling in dead things."

"Ulysses is a great one for carcasses." Ceci's tone suggested that the predilection was greatly to the dog's credit and, by extension, to Douglas's. Beaming at Douglas, she said, "I'm sure that Rowdy would go after dead things, too, given the opportunity. Wouldn't he, Holly?"

Douglas caught my eye, nodded, and with a conspiratorial smile said, "Something in common!"

Having dogs who rolled in dead things wasn't a romantically wonderful something to have in common, of course. Neither was sharing a therapist. Still, I wished I found Douglas attractive. He wasn't bad looking. Just . . . bland. Average height, brown hair, no outstanding features. Not that I was in search of someone eight feet tall with green hair and the nose of Cyrano de Bergerac! And not that Steve Delaney . . . had anything to do with anything. Douglas, I told myself, was really *not* bad looking. He had an interesting dog. He was perfectly pleasant. Physically fit. Nice to old ladies. Be still, my heart!

"Speaking of dogs," I said, "I caught Zsa Zsa and took her home. Sylvia's son was there. Eric. He promised to keep Zsa Zsa in the house."

As I got Rowdy and Quest out of the car again, Ceci kept asking questions about Sylvia. Had I seen her?

Had Eric said anything about her? Had Douglas seen her? Not today? Yesterday? Was there any *news*? Had *anyone* heard *anything*? Ceci had heard that Sylvia was going to sue the policewoman. Was it true?"

Douglas, I might point out, really was nice to Ceci. He didn't ridicule or ignore her, and as we walked along the path that began at the footbridge, he matched his pace to hers and Quest's. After passing an area of deciduous trees, we climbed a gentle slope into a grove of pines and then descended into a shallow, dank valley of thick, weedy-looking underbrush. This being a suburban rather than urban park, there were no beer cans, candy wrappers, or other debris, but this little section somehow looked trashy in the absence of trash. Soon after we'd crossed the bridge, Douglas removed Ulysses' leash. The big hound trailed after us. But by the time we reached the dank valley, Ulysses had disappeared.

"He does this," Douglas said. "Ulysses! Ulysses!" He cupped his hands around his mouth and emitted a loud whistle. "Ulysses, here!"

Our little group came to a halt. Douglas called a few more times.

"Probably after a squirrel," Ceci said.

"A dead squirrel," Douglas said with regret. "Ulysses!"

Rowdy, who delights in the misbehavior of other dogs, was dancing around at the end of his long lead. He was, I thought, responding to Douglas's whistling and calling. Nothing in Rowdy's behavior suggested that his keen ears and nose had picked up a sign of the big hound.

Douglas sighed. "I'd better go after him before he eats whatever he's found." Thoughtfully glancing at Ceci to see whether she was comfortable about being left without male protection, he said, "I'll be right back."

As Douglas headed back down the trail toward the parking lot, Ceci said, "Such a lovely man." She paused. "What did you think of *that* Eric?"

"I thought that *that* Eric had just got out of bed." Feeling guilty about indulging Ceci's love of gossip, I added, "Maybe he works nights."

"Hah! He doesn't work at all," Ceci said.

"He wanted to know if I'd seen Sylvia. He was complaining that there was no food in the house. I thought that was peculiar. He'd never seen me before. And he asked me to tell Sylvia. If I ran into her. It was quite odd."

"Such *chutzpah!*" Ceci exclaimed. "That's Yiddish for *a lot of nerve.* One of the things I like about Newton is learning all these words. And bagels. And, *what are we, chopped liver?* That would be a good title for your book, wouldn't it? Of course, now there are all these national chains, but we always had bagels here, and good bagels, too, although I like the plain ones myself, not onion, and . . ."

Douglas and Ulysses suddenly crashed through the underbrush onto the trail only a few yards behind us. The big hound was on leash. His mouth was empty; if he'd found a carcass, Douglas must have persuaded him to leave it. Douglas came to an abrupt halt. His face was pale and grim.

"Ulysses," Ceci chirped, "did you roll in something nasty again? What was it this time? Another dead thing?"

In an oddly stilted voice, Douglas repeated her phase. "Another dead thing." He said it again. "Another dead thing."

"Douglas, are you all right?" Ceci demanded.

"Sylvia," he replied. "Ulysses found her."

"You're not making any sense," Ceci scolded.

"The dead thing," Douglas said, "is Sylvia."

CHAPTER 13

"Nihil nisi bonum," declared Ceci, "but there was something in the paper a few years ago about salmonella at one of Sylvia's restaurants, hot dog stands, really, glorified, but that's what they are, although it's no excuse for food poisoning, is it?" Apparently interpreting my bewildered expression as evidence that I needed a translation of the Latin, she added, "Nothing but good about the dead! Not that salmonella can exactly be called *good*."

"Sylvia didn't die of food poisoning," Douglas said hastily.

"Are you sure she's dead?" I asked.

"She was shot." Douglas amended the statement. "Someone shot her. There's no gun there."

I said the obvious: "We need to call the police." Although the need was self-evident, I felt sharply aware of making a charged statement. The Sunday papers had picked up the story of Sylvia's dispute and arrest. The journalists had dutifully tried to present objective accounts. As far as I knew, the background information about Newton was accurate: Newton was called the Garden City; it had a diverse population of Protestants, Catholics, and Jews; it boasted an excellent record of harmony among religious and ethnic groups and among clergy of all faiths; it had been named the Safest City in America; and most of its streets actually were lined with mature trees. The scene of the dispute was indubitably Clear Creek Park.

If the journalists failed to give a clear picture of what had happened, who could blame them? I'd been there, and I still wasn't sure. They'd done their best to present diverse points of view. Diverse they were! One story quoted Sylvia at length. "I was heading toward a group of friends when all of a sudden, this woman I'd never seen before came up and started screaming about the leash law. So I took hold of Zsa Zsa's collar. Zsa Zsa loves people, and she was under voice control. But I did it anyway. It still wasn't enough to satisfy the woman. She flew at her and grabbed her collar and twisted it. Naturally, I tried to protect my dog, but the woman got a grip on my arm and squeezed it. You can still see the bruises. I had no idea she was a police officer. No one could've guessed. I assumed she was mentally ill. She was acting deranged. She was out of control. I still think she must suffer from some sort of rage syndrome. I've wondered if she had some kind of seizure that made her lose her balance and fall down. I certainly never pushed her. But nothing excuses what she did. She used fascist tactics. She violated my civil rights."

According to the papers, Sylvia's opponent, Officer Jennifer Pasquarelli, contended that the incident began when Sylvia's dog snarled at her. The officer said that she then asked to have the dog put on leash. When the owner refused, the officer identified herself as such and asked to see the dog's rabies tag. She also requested proof that the owner was complying with the pooper-scooper law by carrying a means of picking up the dog's feces. The owner responded by screaming at her and violently pushing her to the ground.

What transformed the incident into a political dispute was a column in one of the Boston papers that showed no sign of any effort at professional journalism. Here's how it began:

> On a warm, peaceful November afternoon in the Safest City in America, Sylvia Metzner took a few minutes from her busy schedule to walk her beloved golden retriever, Zsa Zsa. The widowed mother of three children, Metzner was crossing the playing field of Clear Creek Park and looking forward to a chat with fellow pooch-proud Newtonians when violence reared its hideous head.

The episode occurred on a cold morning. Zsa Zsa wasn't exactly beloved, and Sylvia hardly fit the image of a widowed mother of three. The columnist went on to write that a Newton police officer with an Italian name, Pasquarelli, had been ill advised to use totalitarian tactics on an innocent citizen with a Jewish name in a city with a substantial Jewish population as well as large number of residents who'd fled Iron Curtain countries for the land of freedom and justice. The attempt to recast the incident as an act of anti-Semitism was ridiculous. There had been nothing to identify Sylvia as Jewish. What's more, in addition to a substantial Jewish population, Newton had a substantial Italian population and its own Little Italy, albeit a very little one. A Newton police spokesperson reported that an Internal Affairs investigation of the incident was under way. Although both Officer Pasquarelli and Sylvia Metzner were women, a feminist group hurled itself into the fray on Sylvia's side by interpreting her arrest as a diversionary tactic that perpetuated violence against women at the park. According to the group's leader, "If a woman were lurking in the woods and exposing her genitalia to men, she'd have been caught long ago!"

Ceci's response to the news of Sylvia's death was thus no surprise. "Officer Pasquarelli!" she exclaimed. "Rage syndrome! That's what Sylvia said she had! We should have listened. This is terrible! Sylvia was such a jolly person, wasn't she! And for all that she let her children take advantage of her, it was done out of love for them, wasn't it! Douglas, you don't suppose she's still around, do you?"

The shock of finding Sylvia's body had eroded Douglas's patience with Ceci. "How could Sylvia still be around? I just told you! She's dead."

"Not Sylvia. That policewoman who shot her. No one else carries a gun here. If she hears us talking, she might—"

Douglas now looked queasy as well as pale. "Ceci, uh, Sylvia has been dead for, uh, some time. And there's no reason to think that Jennifer Pasquarelli . . . I have no idea who shot Sylvia."

"We need a phone," I said. Although Sylvia's house was nearby, the prospect of going back there on an errand radically and gruesomely different from the first felt grotesque. *Well, Eric, nice to see you again! This time, it's not the dog I'm returning, it's your dead mother!*

"I have a car phone," Douglas said. His manner irritated me. He was just standing there aimlessly shuffling his feet on the dirt path. His uselessness in a crisis might, I thought, be one reason he was seeing Dr. Foote.

"Go and use it!" I ordered him.

Douglas looked offended. "There's no hurry, really," he said. "This isn't something that just happened. That's what attracted Ulysses—"

"Ceci doesn't need to hear the details." I gave Douglas what I hoped was a meaningful stare. Ceci was owed the deference traditionally shown to elders. Besides, I didn't want to have to hear about decomposition and its stench, either. I was a dog writer; I could guess what had attracted the attention of a scent hound. "Douglas, if Ulysses found the body, someone else could, too. Children could. *Please* run and use your car phone. Call the police."

As if to second me, Rowdy began issuing impatient, insistent Arctic-dog noises that were halfway between abbreviated growls and prolonged whines. His opinion was clear to me. What's more, I shared it. For once, Rowdy and I both wanted an authority figure to appear and take control.

"Douglas," I said calmly, "where is the body?"

He pointed in the direction of the parking lot and the field. "Back that way. Down one of those little paths. To the left. Not far. In a clearing."

"Fine. We're going to walk with you to the beginning of the path. We're going to wait there so no one else goes in. Then you and Ulysses are going to run to your car and call the police."

We followed my plan. The path Douglas meant diverged from the main trail in a pretty section of pines. The path was barely that; it couldn't have been more than six inches wide and looked more like an animal track than like a walking trail. "Hurry!" I told him. "Run!"

He finally did. When he'd taken off, I turned my attention to Ceci, who had been uncharacteristically silent. Her lips looked blue. "Ceci, are you okay?"

"I'm cold," she said. The temperature had, in fact, dropped, and the pines blocked the sun. The chilling element, however, must have been the news of Sylvia's murder.

"Zip up your parka," I advised. "Do you want to put your hood up? I can give you my jacket, too."

"You are a dear girl," she said. "Offering me the shirt off your back!"

"The police'll be here in no time, and then I'll get you home."

"They won't send the same policewoman, will they? Officer Pasquarelli? What am I saying? Of course not. She's been suspended. I hate that expression! It sounds as if she's been hanged." Healthy color suddenly returned to Ceci's face. "You don't think Douglas could be dramatizing things, do you?" Her glance eagerly traced the narrow track that meandered under the pines and disappeared in a dense thicket. "Sylvia might just have fallen, you know. Or fainted. Douglas doesn't strike me as a terribly imaginative type, but you never know, do you? I think we'd better go see whether Sylvia needs help."

"Ceci, I don't . . ."

By the time I realized that she wasn't just free-associating, she'd dragged the imperturbable Quest to his feet and was hauling him swiftly down the track. Too late, I realized that my promise to get her home soon hadn't conveyed the comfort I'd intended; rather, she'd viewed it as a threat to remove her from the action. Rowdy, who never wants to be left out either, was trying to pull me after Quest and Ceci.

"Ceci!" I called out. "I don't think this is a good idea!" I have to confess that as I was hollering to Ceci, I was also mulling over what she'd said about Douglas. He didn't strike me as the imaginative type, either, certainly not as the type who imagines dead bodies where there are none. On the other hand, as Ceci didn't know, Douglas was consulting a psychiatrist, my own Dr. Foote, about something. He seemed far too bland, too ordinary, to possess so vivid and unusual a symptom as the tendency to hallucinate corpses. Still, as Ceci said, you never know, do you?

Ceci had moved beyond the pretty pines to thick woods, which consisted of tall, bare trees, barren saplings, and weedy shrubs. I ran, with Rowdy dashing ahead. Mainly because Quest was slowing Ceci's progress, we quickly caught up. She and the Newfie had, however, come to a stop at the edge of a small clearing that was little more than a widening of the track. In its center stood a waist-high boulder, the kind that the last glacier deposited in great numbers as it retreated from New England. Steeling myself for the macabre sight of Sylvia's body, I came to a halt next to Ceci, maybe five or six yards from the boulder. With its flat top, it looked like a small version of one of those expensive granite food-prep islands you see in trendy kitchens. Shards of blue-and-white crockery were scattered on the boulder and on the ground next to it, as if a butterfingered cook had smashed a stack of plates. Heightening the sense of domesticity was the apparent presence of the klutz who'd dropped the china. Indeed, she seemed to have fainted at the sight of what she'd done. She lay on the ground on the far side of the boulder, her head visible to its right, her feet to its left. Even from a distance, the stench was strong and nauseating.

"There are a terrible number of skunks in Newton," Ceci remarked. "You wouldn't expect it, but there are. I'm afraid one of them . . ." She began to step forward.

"Don't!" I ordered. "Ceci, if she really has been

killed, we need to stay away. The worst thing we can do is get our footprints and everything all over the place."

To my amazement, instead of barging ahead or launching into a monologue about the broken china, Ceci held still and asked softly and pensively, "Holly, how did Douglas know it's Sylvia?"

"Is there something that makes you think it isn't?"

"No, no, it's Sylvia. That's her coat, Lord and Taylor, but she got it at Filene's Basement, and the shoes are Joan and David, from Frugal Fannie's, the scarf, too, she was wearing that outfit, and I said, how pretty, but Holly, she's face down."

"Yes?"

With a hint of panic in her voice, Ceci said, "You can't see her face!"

Calmly, I said, "No, you can't." *Thank heaven!*

"So how did *Douglas* know? Holly, I recognize her hair and her coat and her shoes and her scarf, but there's nothing special about her hair, it could be anyone's, and men don't notice clothes, do they? So how did Douglas know?"

"Maybe he moved her. To see who it was."

"He touched her?"

Sirens sounded in the distance and approached with what felt like impossible speed.

"The Newton police are—" Ceci started to say.

With unintended disrespect for the dead, Rowdy drowned her out by taking up the call of emergency vehicles. Planting himself in a solid sit, he raised his handsome head and emitted prolonged, responsive howls.

The dog has a great voice, tremendous tone, extraordinary range, basso profundo to high falsetto, and in most circumstances, his singing hits me as a magical incantation so powerful that I expect to see the aurora borealis light up the Massachusetts sky. If he'd actually been howling a dirge for Sylvia, I'd have let him go on. In fact, he'd barely known Sylvia. He wasn't mourning her; he was just howling in reply to the malamute-like sirens. Wrapping my hands around his muzzle, I said, "Not now! Rowdy, quiet!" And then, "Good boy!"

Heralded by the sound of voices and footsteps, uniformed police officers and EMTs arrived in astonishingly large numbers. The initial influx consisted of six police officers and four EMTs. In a lot of big cities, you'd be lucky to get that much help for a bank heist where the robbers had shot ten people dead and were threatening to kill ten more. Now, far from bothering my political conscience, the unfair privilege of wealthy suburbs made me sigh aloud in relief. I'd pressured Douglas to run and call the police, and I'd prevented Ceci from contaminating the scene with footprints, paw prints, Quest's hair, and who knew what else. Otherwise, I'd done nothing. Still, it felt wonderful to be free of the responsibility I hadn't assumed. Two of the officers were the handsome men who'd removed Sylvia from the park once before. The other four, three men and a woman, were also incredibly attractive. The unnatural good looks of all six cops created a sense of playacting. For a moment, the shattered pottery seemed to be a prop arranged by a stagehand, and the lifeless body looked ready to rise, brush the dirt off her coat, and take a coffee break.

Douglas, who'd led the way for the police and the EMTs, was flushed with what I suspected was pride in his starring, although hardly heroic, role. Ulysses was still with him. Of the three dogs, Quest, Ulysses, and Rowdy, mine was the only one who displayed an active interest in the sudden arrival of ten keyed-up strangers who talked softly to one another and loudly into cell phones, trampled the ground I'd kept Ceci from contaminating, and shooed us back up the narrow track and away from the clearing. Quest, as usual, sank to the ground and took a nap, and Ulysses sniffed dead leaves, bushes, earth, and Douglas's shoes. Rowdy, in contrast, joined me in studying the EMTs, all four of whom hovered around the body, and the cops, who unintentionally irked me by continuing to look more like movie stars than like the agents of law enforcement. Rowdy, I felt certain, was intent on discovering whether any of these newcomers happened to be carrying food that might somehow be induced to make its way from human pocket to malamute mouth. Being a mere human being, I watched just to see what would happen.

As I understood matters, the first cop who arrived was supposed to have the honor of officially deciding whether a crime had occurred. Since the six cops had reached the clearing almost simultaneously, I frivolously wondered whether they might quarrel among themselves about who had gotten there first. Somewhat to my disappointment, not a single spat broke out. Four cops now stood at the edge of the clearing. Another had run back up the track, presumably to lead reinforcements to the scene. The sixth, a tall, unbelievably gorgeous guy, stood near us. Since the cause of the stench was clearly not a skunk, the EMTs quickly finished what must have been a mandatory procedure to assure themselves that the victim was beyond help. As they stepped back, yet more people showed up, a few in uniform, most in mufti. No one asked us any questions, presumably because Douglas had talked to the police while he'd led them here.

"Holly," Ceci demanded, obviously aiming her voice at our guard, "aren't they supposed to be questioning us? After all, we found Sylvia! That's supposed to make us the prime suspects, isn't it?"

We hadn't found Sylvia; Douglas had. Still, after Ceci's remark about suspicion falling on the person who finds a body, I didn't want to make myself obnoxious by announcing that she and I had been late arrivals. Instead, I said, "It was Ulysses who found her, really."

"Althea won't like that one bit, you know, not that my sister wishes ill to anyone, in reality, but when you think about it, it's a cliché, you know, Holly, and not even a Sherlock Holmes cliché, the dog in the night, although Althea would be happier, of course, if a dog had done nothing in the night, Silver Blaze, even I know that one. But finding a body? Althea will be very disappointed. What am I saying? Poor Sylvia! And here I am—"

The cop turned to her. "You recognize her, ma'am? You know who she is?"

"Sylvia Metzner, of course," Ceci replied.

After the publicity about Sylvia's altercation with Officer Pasquarelli, half the population of Greater Boston would've known the name. In Newton? Without question, the entire police force had heard Sylvia Metzner's name hundreds of times. The muscles in the cop's face twitched. "You got close enough to see her, ma'am?" he asked.

"No." Ceci was offended. "I recognized Sylvia's clothes. Those are Sylvia's shoes and scarf and coat." She made no mention of Douglas at all.

I spoke up. "Douglas told us who it was." I turned to look at him.

The cop looked at Douglas, too. "That you, sir?"

Douglas nodded.

"So, how'd you know?"

Douglas shrugged. "The, uh, overall appearance. I just recognized her."

"You move the body?"

Douglas rapidly jerked his head back and forth. As he spoke, his voice climbed at least an octave. "No. I didn't touch a thing. Nothing. Not one thing."

"Strange that you knew who it was, sir. When you didn't see her face."

"Strange?" Douglas asked. "Well, yes. But I wasn't sure who it was. I wasn't sure at all."

CHAPTER 14

The police at the murder scene may have shared my concern about Ceci's health. She again looked chilled. Or maybe she was just grating on their nerves. For whatever reason, I was encouraged to remove her from the park. As soon as I put Rowdy and Quest in the car and settled Ceci in the passenger seat, my worry diminished. She immediately launched into her usual frenzied chattering. Now, as I drove her home, her focus switched from Officer Pasquarelli to the entire Metzner family, especially Eric.

"That Eric!" Ceci spoke of Eric Metzner as if *Eric* were his middle name. "All three of Sylvia's children were a perfect disgrace. But that Eric!"

"*Were?* When was this?"

Ceci said nothing for all of five seconds. "Thursday," she admitted. "Now, Holly, I *told* you it wasn't right to abandon Sylvia, didn't I? And I was certainly not the only concerned citizen there."

With an inaudible groan, I said, "You obeyed Pythagoras."

"Holly, are you all right? No, you're not! It's shock. On top of your concussion. Holly, dear, Pythagoras has nothing to do with anything. What I was saying was that after Sylvia was so brutally dragged off by the police, you were just as eager as I was to show your support for her, but you had already taken hours out of your workday and were simply too nice to tell me that you didn't have time. So after you dropped me off, I naturally hurried down there to headquarters, and I assure you that except for the appalling behavior of Sylvia's children, it was a deeply moving experience. Quite a few people from the park were there, and they were as horrified as we were at what we'd witnessed. And if I haven't happened to mention that I showed my support for Sylvia, it's only because I didn't want you to feel in the least tiny bit guilty for being unable to help. I have never doubted for a moment that you are just as strongly committed as I am to human rights."

"Of course I'm committed to human rights."

Ceci seized on a one-second pause. "Also, I have to confess, in all honesty, Holly, truthfully, that when I got back home and told Althea, she came very close to accusing me of being a busybody, which is patent nonsense, but without intending to hurt my feelings, Althea did leave me a teeny bit sensitive on the subject, and so I thought matters over and decided that sometimes the best thing to say is nothing at all. Holly, are you all right? Shock has dangerous effects on some people, you know. I think you should pull the car over."

"I'm fine. So what happened at headquarters?"

"That Eric! Well, you saw for yourself! He has pierced ears, and he wears earrings, two in one ear, and his hair stands on end as if he'd moussed it and then been frightened by a bear." Eric, Ceci informed me, was the youngest of Sylvia's three children. Together with the middle child, Oona, as well as Pia and Wilson, Eric lived with Sylvia. Furthermore, since graduating from college a few years earlier, Eric had worked full time at the unpaid job of deciding what he wanted to do with his life. "Sponging off poor Sylvia," Ceci said. "And that Oona isn't a lot better, but at least Sylvia had the sense to complain about Oona, who is quite a pretty girl, ruining her skin by exposing it to the sun, such a shame, but as I was saying, all that she, Oona, does morning, noon, and night is cadge rides on boats. What kind of life is that?"

Although Pia and Wilson, in contrast to Eric and Oona, held paying jobs, Ceci disapproved of them, too, primarily because they had participated in what sounded like a nasty family fight at police headquarters. The argument, according to Ceci, had initially centered on the subject of finding a lawyer for Sylvia. Wilson, Pia, or both had apparently contended that despite Sylvia's parting instruction at the park, there was no need to call a lawyer, since Sylvia would already have summoned one herself. Oona had wanted to call a lawyer she knew, but the others had disagreed with her choice of attorney because his only qualification had been the ownership of a yacht that Oona admired. All the family members had agreed that when Ian Metzner, Sylvia's husband, died, Sylvia's lawyer had been a woman. No one, however, could remember her name. The unfriendly exchange of views turned into an outright squabble when Eric asked to use Wilson's cell phone. Wilson refused. Eric persisted. Wilson remained firm.

"And then," Ceci said, "that Eric called Wilson some names too horrid for me to repeat, and Wilson up and told that Eric that he was a ne'er-do-well bloodsucker who ought to be ashamed of himself for taking advantage of his mother's misfortune by using it as a pitiful and transparent excuse for his own insatiable greed. 'Insatiable greed!' Those were his very words." Ceci said gleefully. "Those were Wilson's exact words, Holly, right there in the middle of the police station, and it was deplorable, although I must admit that there is some substance to Wilson's accusation, except that it applies equally well to the whole pack of them, parasites all, shamelessly living off Sylvia. And quarrelsome parasites to boot! I can just see that Eric as a little boy, and Wilson, too, the pair of them, silly, selfish children fighting over their toy trucks instead of this foolish cell phone, neither one of them wanting to share his toys. Poor, poor Sylvia!"

Since Sylvia was Eric's mother, it seemed to me that it was Sylvia's fault if Eric grabbed other people's toys. But Ceci's love of dogs extended to underdogs. Now that Sylvia had been murdered, she'd become, in Ceci's view, the ultimate underdog.

CHAPTER 15

Subj: Re: Genetic Clearances
From: HollyWinter@amrone.org
To: Jazzland@pnwmals.org

Hi Cindy,

A million thanks for the photos! Emma is just beautiful. I have to tell you that I am crazy about her rear angulation.

Best,
Holly

CHAPTER 16

Kevin Dennehy, my next-door neighbor, showed up at my door at six o'clock on that same Tuesday evening and invited me out to eat. He lives with his mother, a strict vegetarian, so he leaves home in search of flesh. Not mine. Since Kevin had started seeing his girlfriend, Jennie, a few months earlier, he hadn't even been seeking my company. I hadn't even met Jennie.

"Hey, Holly, how ya doing?" he greeted me, as usual. He didn't wait for my answer, which would, of course, have been that I'd had a ghastly day. Immediately, he asked Rowdy and Kimi the same question. They're crazy about Kevin, mainly because he feeds them whatever he happens to be eating, and since he is a great big man with a gigantic appetite, he eats all the time and doles out a stream of treats.

Kevin lowered the upper half of his mammoth body to dog level and made stupid growling noises that the

dogs love. In response, they scoured his face with their
big red tongues. Although Kevin is part Italian, he is
the most Irish-looking person I've ever seen. In Greater
Boston, that's saying something. He has red hair, fair
skin, freckles, and blue eyes, and in a gruff way, he
has that famous Irish charm, too. As I watched him
fool around with the dogs, it occurred to me that Kevin
was one cop who, unlike the voluptuous terrier who'd
arrested Sylvia, would never need to announce himself
as such. Studying him, I tried and failed to identify any
specific attribute that proclaimed his profession. He's
a lieutenant in homicide, so he doesn't wear a uniform;
at the moment, he wasn't even dressed in blue, but in
khaki pants and a tan crewneck sweater. Funny-looking
shoes and big flat feet were supposed to be hallmarks.
Like the rest of Kevin, his feet were big, but they
didn't look flat, and his white athletic shoes were obviously designed for fitness running rather than for
chasing down criminals. Still, if a menacing stranger
had suddenly broken into my kitchen and Kevin had
pulled out a badge and said, "Police," the intruder
would've been entirely justified in replying, "Yes, I
know."

I tried, of course, to tell Kevin about Sylvia's murder. One price I pay for having beautiful, friendly dogs
is, however, that people ignore me in favor of Rowdy
and Kimi. Kevin was now on the tile floor of the
kitchen flirting with the forbidden game of wrestling
with malamutes. He is also prohibited from giving
them beer. I know that he violates that ban when I'm
not looking because I smell brew on the dogs' breath.

Instead of breaking the wrestling taboo behind my back, he waits for the dogs to roll onto their backs for tummy rubs, and then under the guise of vigorously scratching their chests and bellies, he tussles in a fashion just short of wrestling. "Hey there, tough guy," he rumbled at Rowdy, "who you been beating up lately?"

"As a matter of fact," I said, "he *was* in a dog fight not all that long ago, and would you please stop giving them both the wrong message? Kevin, I have told you a million times that the message to give to them is that you do not like—"

Kevin mimicked me. "Anything that even begins to remind them of aggression toward blah, blah, blah. Who won?"

"Rowdy did. Well, I broke up the fight, but he did." I again tried to divert Kevin's attention from the dogs. "Kevin, I need to—"

"Then that's all right. You won, did you big fellow? They scrape the other guy off the sidewalk?"

"The other guy was a girl. Rowdy didn't hurt her. But—"

Gently grabbing both sides of Rowdy's substantial head, Kevin delivered a little congratulatory shake and said, "Sexist! Should've beat the pants off her like Kimi would've done."

Before I could break in, Kevin announced that he was starving, explained that we'd better take separate cars because he was going somewhere after dinner, and gave me directions to the restaurant he'd selected. Kevin's restaurant preferences are based largely, no pun intended, on quantity. He doesn't care whether the food is overcooked or the meat is tough if the portions are mountainous. He still hadn't stopped talking about a Spanish restaurant he'd mistakenly patronized because he hadn't understood that *tapas* didn't just mean appetizers; it meant small servings. Tonight, instead of going to the kind of Italian restaurant where everything swims in the same red sauce, we went to the kind of Chinese restaurant where everything swims in soy sauce made thick, slimy, and shiny with cornstarch. Cambridge has scores of excellent Chinese restaurants. This storefront place near Inman Square in Cambridge wasn't one of them. The outsides of the windows were so heavily coated with dirt and the insides with grease that the artificial plants shoving their plastic leaves to the plate glass windows managed to look sickly and light deprived. I shouldn't complain. We did get a booth. The noise level was low. The service was prompt. As you've probably guessed, there were only a few other customers, mostly because of rumors about poor sanitation and food poisoning. Kevin wasn't put off by the restaurant's bad reputation. On the contrary, with perverse pride he referred to it as the Taiwan Ptomaine.

Squeezed into his side of the booth, Kevin expanded left and right to fill the space meant for two people. He looked healthy and hungry. I felt filled with affection for him and guilty about the needlessly long and preachy lecture I'd given him about not wrestling with my dogs. "I got carried away," I said. "I'm sorry. It started with this article I'm doing about fatal dog attacks. The studies all focus on what's happening when the dog actually bites someone or kills someone, and no one pays enough attention to what's gone on with the dog before that. Dogs shouldn't be given the message that aggression is all right. But just because you growl at Rowdy and Kimi, it doesn't mean that they're going to go out and inflict fatal bites." Having apologized, I again started to raise the topic of Sylvia's murder, but a waiter appeared at the table to take our orders.

Kevin again announced that he was starving and stunned the waiter by bursting into Gilbert and Sullivan. " 'A policeman's lot is not a happy one,' " he caroled. "Jennie sings. Did I tell you that? Voice like lan angel." Abruptly addressing the waiter, he said, "General what's his name chicken, beef with cashews, sweet and sour shrimp, pork fried rice, for starters. No pancakes in any of that, is there?"

"You want mu shu?" the waiter asked.

"No," I said. "That's what he doesn't want. I do." The term *waiter* is politically incorrect. We're supposed to say *server,* but I hate the word. Given the choice, I'd rather wait than serve. And servers are presumably servile, whereas waiters are . . . ? Anyway, when the restaurant employee had departed, I said, "So your lot isn't happy? Mine isn't—"

"Not mine. Jennie's. She got attacked."

"How horrible!"

"By a *dog* walker." Kevin's tone suggested that I was somehow responsible. "She wasn't on duty. Just out for a run. I tell you she runs?" Hefty appearance to the contrary, Kevin is a dedicated long-distance runner. "She's in great shape."

Bully for her, I thought and also refrained from saying, *so am I.*

Kevin expanded. "She does Tai Chi. Tae Kwon Do." He gave a sly smile. "Sashimi. One of those things. Jennie's big on Asian. Eats nothing but vegetables. No calories in this stuff. Hey, you hear about the German Chinese restaurants?"

"Yes, Kevin. And so has everyone else."

An hour later, you're hungry for power.

"Snappish tonight, aren't we?" he said.

"I've had a horrible day. I really want to—"

The waiter interrupted me to cover the table with dishes of beef, chicken, shrimp, pork, and vegetables, all awash in brown glue. Then Kevin elaborated on Jennie's encounter with the dog walker. "She goes out for her run, and the park's full of loose dogs, and she goes by one, and the dog snarls at her." The waiter returned with my mu shu pancakes and a small platter of what looked like thousand-year-old cabbage. Kevin loaded his plate with big helpings, picked up his fork, and dug in. He does not believe in chopsticks. Between bites, he went on. "So Jennie asks the woman—dog's with a woman, older woman—to leash the dog, and like you always say, the woman gets her hackles up and tells Jennie it's her dog, and mind her own business."

"That must've gone over big," I said, struggling to encase the cabbage neatly in a pancake while hoping I was wrong. "So, what did Jennie do?"

"Identified herself." Kevin meant as a police officer. In his view, a cop has no other identity. "Told the woman to leash the dog. Woman refused. Jennie asked to see the dog's rabies tag. And, uh, something to clean up after the dog with." He looked embarrassed, and not because he was discussing an unmentionable subject over dinner. Is there a cop on earth who takes pride in enforcing the pooper-scooper law? "They're big on that in Newton. Fine for not having a plastic bag with you."

"Newton? I thought Jennie was a Cambridge cop." Even so, I'd made the connection. I'd also realized that Kevin couldn't have heard about Sylvia's murder. The body had, after all, been found not that many hours ago.

"Newton," Kevin said. "So what happened next was that the woman starts screaming, goes nuts, and shoves Jennie and knocks her to the ground."

"What about Tae Kwon Do?" I poured myself some tea. Only then did I notice that Kevin hadn't ordered beer. If he was enduring that sacrifice to decrease his girth, the relationship with Jennie was serious.

Ignoring my remark, Kevin said, "Assault on a police officer. Jennie told her she was under arrest, and she still didn't get it. Resisted. Had hysterics. When they took her in, she finally got the message. Kicked up a stink. This was all in the Sunday papers. Jennie's been suspended. There's a lot of political garbage going on. The woman's threatening to sue Jennie. Everyone knows the woman's lying"—Kevin meant everyone in blue—

"but they've still got to investigate, and that's hard on Jennie."

Instead of breaking the bad news, I said, "Kevin, I have to confess. I was there. At Cold Creek Park, when it happened. And I read about it in the papers. I just didn't connect Jennifer Pasquarelli with your Jennie. I thought you met Jennie here. In Cambridge."

"I did. At a ten-K road race."

"I assumed it was at work. Look, there's something you don't know." I started by telling Kevin all about Ceci and Quest and then outlined what I knew about Sylvia's arrest. With remarkable tact, I avoided pointing out the differences between the account he'd given me and what I'd seen, heard, and read. For instance, according to Kevin's report, which was presumably Jennie's, the officer had identified herself as such *before* she'd landed on the ground. In contrast, I'd seen her pull out her badge and identify herself as a cop *after* the shoving incident. She could have done it twice, of course. Maybe she had.

Kevin ate silently.

"The background," I said, "was that there really has been crime committed at the park. An exhibitionist. And there was the sense that the police weren't doing anything about him. And then this altercation about the *leash law.*"

"It's not about the leash law."

"It started that way," I insisted, feeling only a little guilty. Technically, I hadn't seen the beginning of the episode. "Admittedly, it escalated." That part, I had witnessed.

"And whose fault was that?" Kevin demanded.

"Don't yell at me! It wasn't mine!"

"I'm not yelling!" he yelled.

"Kevin, listen to me. Something else happened. The woman Jennie arrested, Sylvia Metzner . . ." I paused.

"The liar," Kevin said.

"Kevin, this is very serious. Rowdy and I were with Ceci today at Clear Creek Park. We were on one of the trails with a guy and his dog. The dog disappeared. The owner went after the dog. The two of them found Sylvia Metzner's body. She'd been shot. There was no weapon there. The wounds were not self-inflicted. The Newton police told me that."

Kevin put down his fork, wiped his mouth with his napkin, and tossed some cash on the table. Kevin and I were old friends: He didn't have to explain his departure, and neither of us had to say outright that his Jennie was the prime suspect. Still, as if establishing Jennie's innocence, Kevin said in parting, "That Metzner woman was a damned liar."

I said nothing. Sylvia Metzner was not lying about being dead.

CHAPTER 17

Before I tell you what happened next, I need to fill you in on a session I had with Dr. Foote in which I somehow drifted into talking at incredible length about a trivial, meaningless incident that wasn't worth two expensive seconds of a fifty-minute meeting. Instead of making maximal use of my therapy so-called hour, I wasted Dr. Foote's time and mine, as well as my insurance company's money, by telling her about a little episode that had occurred recently at a fast-food restaurant. Therapy is for big stuff. Conflict, torment, agony, panic. And mothers! Mothers! So what did I light on? Hamburger.

Anyway, what happened was that Kimi and I . . . "Have I mentioned Kimi?" I asked Dr. Foote. "My malamute bitch? Have I? Well, I'm pretty sure I have."

Little mental mementos of my head injury still lingered; my mind was apparently afraid that I might forget amnesia. Hah! Amnesia, let me tell you, was a bitch, and not a bitch of the Kimi variety. The tight-laced spell checker on my word processor purses its prissy lips when I write *bitch.* Instead of having the guts to come right out and order me to quit talking dirty, it expresses its prudish disdain by suggesting a ludicrous euphemism, namely, *arrogant woman.* In dog circles, *bitch* is clean. In feminist circles, *arrogant woman* is dirty. Ain't life strange.

Where was I? Oh, yes, as I told Dr. Foote, my malamute arrogant woman and I were on our way home from a freestyle obedience workshop when we stopped at S & I's Burgerhaven, a hamburger joint in one of Boston's western suburbs. Freestyle, as I explained to Dr. Foote, is dancing with dogs. It's fun. To return to the incident, the lawn next to the parking lot had picnic tables, and since it was a warm day, a few lone people and one big family were sitting at the tables enjoying the late afternoon sun. Arrogant women don't use ladies' rooms. Consequently, I was walking Kimi toward the designated pet exercise area when our route took us close to the table occupied by the family, whose large order of paper-wrapped burgers, french fries, and cold drinks was still piled on a tray. Worse, instead of sensibly occupying the center of the table, the tray rested at one end and not just any old end, either, but the end within easy leaping distance of Kimi, who took one whiff and squeezed her own trigger, as it were, thus shooting a large and wolflike gray bullet at the target, which she hit dead center. Bull's-eye! Not to brag or anything, but Kimi's aim is incredible, and is she fast! Rowdy is a perfectly decent food thief, but

Kimi is extraordinary. When this sport makes it to the Olympics, the U.S. Food Filching Team is going to consist mainly of Alaskan malamutes and Labrador retrievers, and even against that class of competition, Kimi will be a shoo-in for the gold. When she shows off like this around malamute people, I try to be modest, but it's difficult because they exclaim at her prowess and speed, as did the family at the picnic table, but not in quite the same tone of gasp. In brief, they were irate.

The family consisted of five people: a bedraggled mother, an oleaginous father, two neglected-looking little girls, and a vigorous old man with keen blue eyes. Individually and collectively, they exuded a heartrending air of poverty. With the exception of the old man, they looked as if they might have started out bright and vivid, but had repeatedly been run through the wash until their fabric was faded and threadbare. The mother's hair was in brush rollers, and her face was pitifully thin. Her husband was all grease, inside and out, big gut, sausage-shaped arms and fingers, lank hair, and oily skin. The little girls were maybe four and five. They still had baby teeth, the front ones brown with decay. Their identical outfits, dresses and coats, must once have been party wear. The cloth had originally been shiny, I thought, and, at a guess, baby blue. The old man was attired entirely in gray, but his expression was alert, and although the entire family was in an uproar, he seemed to be the only one with enough extra blood in his veins to redden his face. Especially since my switch from golden retrievers to malamutes, my dogs had stolen food from me and from a lot of other people on dozens of occasions. Never before, however, had one of my dogs stolen food from people who really needed it.

I was mortified. "I'm so terribly sorry," I said. "It was all my fault. I'll replace everything. This is horrible. She should never have done such a thing. Just tell me what you had, and I'll go order it."

Unappeased, the father continued bellowing. "Damn it! Damn it all! Damn it, damn it, damn it!" Meanwhile, the old man was swearing, and the malnourished girls were wailing. Tears and mucous ran down their pinched faces. Glaring at me, then exchanging glances with the men, the mother exclaimed, "Everything always goes wrong!"

"I'll fix it," I insisted, referring to this incident, of course, not to everything. "Just tell me what to order. Please! Double portions. With dessert. Anything!" So far, no one had responded to my offer. The restaurant's menu was limited to hamburgers, cheeseburgers, fried clams, french fries, and the like, so the original order couldn't have been complicated. In an effort to pry the information out of someone, I addressed the children. "I'm really sorry that my dog ate your food. Maybe she scared you, too."

The girls just stared at me.

"Did my dog scare you?"

Still no response.

"Well if she did, I'm sorry, and she is, too. Her name is Kimi, and she didn't mean to scare you. Now, let's get you some more food. What did you have? Or what

would you like?" These kids just had to speak English!
The adults did! "French fries?" I prompted. "Hamburgers? Ice cream?"

As the smaller girl seemed about to speak, the father
cut in. "They don't take presents from strangers." As
if I were luring them into a car with the promise of
candy!

"Of course," I told him. "But, look, please let me
make this right. I'll get whatever you want, or I can
just pay whatever the food cost."

To my surprise, the woman intervened. Addressing
the younger man, she said, "Tim, let her. It was a stupid idea to begin with. So just let her. The kids are
hungry."

"I can feed my kids, Brianna!" he hollered. "Give
me credit for that."

"That's not what I meant!" she protested. "And you
know it! This is all your fault! You and your bright
ideas!"

The older man spoke. "Tim, shut up. It wasn't what
she meant." To me, he said, "Look, it was an accident.
Forget it. We've got a dog, too. Dogs'll be dogs."

I smiled at him. "Yes, they will. Thank you." I renewed the offer to make good, and the family finally
accepted. To my relief, I didn't have to hang around
ordering food. The older man told me the amount of
the bill, and I persuaded him to take a few extra dollars
for dessert. The second I handed over the money, I
bolted. Kimi never even got to the pet exercise area.
Not that she deserved punishment. I'd been inattentive.

She'd been a dog. And it wasn't her fault that the family was poor.

"It was unsettling," I told Dr. Foote. "Oddly unsettling. It really got to me. The little girls, I could understand. A big dog jumped up and startled them and ate their dinner, although I must say that they didn't act afraid of Kimi. I can always tell when someone's scared of dogs. The body language gives it away, and there's an anti-life aura about those people. Not that I believe in auras, exactly, but there's a kind of global emotional constriction. Just take my word for it. The girls weren't phobic. And the grandfather, I guess that's what he was, said they had a dog. Even aside from that, the kids' reaction was understandable. The kids looked malnourished *and* undernourished. Both. And they were about to eat. Then the food was gone. So they started crying. That makes sense. But the adults were weird. They were angry and upset all out of proportion to what happened, even after I offered to get more food, pay, do anything. Maybe it was just what the woman said, that everything always goes wrong for them. I felt so sorry for them. They just looked so down and out. There was no resilience. A little incident was more than they could handle. Most of the time, I manage not to think that people live like that. And then I met them. It was very unsettling."

"What's been stolen from you recently?" Dr. Foote asked.

"Nothing. Nothing, really. Nothing of any value."

"Nothing of value?" She gave me one of those therapist looks. They're familiar to me. Rita is always casting them hither and yon.

"You mean Steve Delaney. Anita jumped in and . . . well, I guess you could say that Anita . . . Anita didn't exactly *steal* him, you know." Silence hung. "I get it. Anita staged a raid. She stole . . . resources. Nourishment. And no one paid. And now . . ."

"Poverty," she said. "And now you are reordering. Reordering your life, that is."

"Except," I said, "that fast food is replaceable. Steve isn't." I thought about Rita's probable response to my objection. "This is what therapists call resistance, isn't it?"

Dr. Foote smiled. "Is it?"

"Yes," I said, "it is."

CHAPTER 18

Winter, Holly

Perseveration a consequence of the head trauma? This wretched countertransference! Pt. goes on and on, anxiety rises, she picks up on it, it escalates! Tried commonsense approach: asked her to focus on *people* in her life. She replied, "Dogs *are* people!" Re her loneliness, she vigorously resists my suggestion of square dancing in favor of (imaginary?) organized dances for dogs!

Saw dear old Dr. S. for a consult. Suggests systematic desensitization, but it's not as if I have to confront the object themselves. What *are* objects, after all? Not introjects, that's what!

And then there's the unexamined matter of this miserable kitchen. Taking forever, costing hideously in excess of estimate. Did not mention to Dr. S. Should have! But with his encouragement, am concentrating on controlling my breathing as panic rises, avoiding hyperventilation when subject arises, as it inevitably does! And remains erect, so to speak! What would Freud have said?! Him and his damned chow chows, of which Dr. S. persisted in reminding me. "Love without ambivalence." Hah!

CHAPTER 19

As often happens in my local newspaper,
Wednesday's sports section was divided into two sub-
sections, the first of which concerned the NBA, the
NFL, pro hockey, tennis, golf, American and National
league baseball, and so on. The second part was devoted to deaths. It's a bit odd to see mortality cate-
gorized as a form of competitive recreation. *Tennis,
anyone? Fatality? Will that be singles or doubles?*
Still, there's nothing new about exploiting the possibilities of demise as a spectator event. Anyway, the
typical death notice here, as elsewhere, is written by
someone who flunked ESL because of a failure to
grasp English word order. It starts something like this:

HARBINGER—Of Melrose, Thalia (Conroy),
age 75, beloved wife of William L., devoted
daughter of the late James C. and Fiona W.
Conroy, dear sister of Penelope Conroy, loving

mother of Jane (Harbinger) Sheffield of Nahant and Harry C. Harbinger of Brookline, cherished grandmother of Mary Ellen Sheffield. Survived also by many adoring cousins, nieces, and nephews.

The notice goes on to give details about the funeral home, its location, visiting hours, the funeral itself, the interment, and the charity to which memorial donations should be made in lieu of flowers and in honor of the beloved, devoted, cherished, adored deceased.

Here's Sylvia's death notice, which appeared in Wednesday's paper:

METZNER—Of Newton, Sylvia (MacFarlane), age 54, wife of the late Ian Metzner, mother of Eric L. Metzner, Oona S. Metzner, and Pia (Metzner) Goodenough, all of Newton.

That's it. In its entirety. Not so much as a single *beloved* or *devoted,* not even the slightest hint about visits, services, flowers, charitable contributions, or anything else at all. Not so much as *Bye, Mom! Nice knowing you!*

On Thursday the paper ran a short article about the discovery of Sylvia's body. After popping a batch of liver brownies in the oven, I poured myself a third cup of morning coffee and read:

THE WICKED FLEA

Dog Finds Pooch Wrangle Adversary, Slain Sunday

NEWTON. The body of Sylvia M. Metzner, 54, was discovered on Tuesday afternoon by a dog walker in search of his wandering pet. According to a Newton police spokesperson, Metzner had been shot in the head and chest at close range. The victim is believed to have been killed on Sunday. The body was found in a secluded area of Clear Creek Park, scene of a recent and controversial altercation between Metzner and Newton Police Officer Jennifer Pasquarelli that resulted in Metzner's arrest on charges of assaulting a police officer and resisting arrest. Metzner, in turn, charged Pasquarelli with brutality and violations of civil rights. A dispute about Metzner's dog sparked the controversy. Conflict between dog owners and opponents has led to the widespread use in Clear Creek Park of noise-making devices to drive off unleashed dogs. It is thought that an aerosol alarm or similar device may have been used to mask the sounds of the gunshots. Authorities are pursuing their investigation of Metzner's death.

You could hardly expect the death notice to include a discussion of why there'd been a mess of broken pottery at the murder scene, but it would have been perfectly appropriate for the article to mention the oddity and maybe even explain it. Unless the police were

141

keeping the detail to themselves? When I'd given my name, address, and blessedly little other information to the Newton police, however, no one had ordered me to keep quiet about the blue and white china. No one had asked Ceci, either, and when she'd asked one of the handsome officers what the stuff was doing there, he'd said that he didn't know.

As I was pondering the problem, my eyes wandered over the newsprint and suddenly locked on a photo of a group of people and a golden retriever. Yes, take a wild guess what caught my eye first. But at second glance, I realized that the people looked familiar. A suety man and a scrawny woman with messy hair stood on either side of a rabbit-faced fellow in a suit. In front of this trio, two little girls flanked the dog. The children registered on me: the sad, undernourished kids whose food Kimi had stolen at the burger joint. Then the couple to the left and right of the human rabbit: the faded, threadbare mother and the oily father who'd violently overreacted to Kimi's naughtiness. The caption identified the couple as Timothy and Brianna Trask. The little girls were named, pitifully, Diana and Fergie. The rabbit, who wore a bellicose expression, was the family's attorney, James J. McSweeney. The paper didn't give the dog's name, presumably because the family pet was there only to suggest what nice people the Trasks were. They had their picture in the paper because they were suing S & I's Burgerhaven on the grounds that one of the children, Fergie, had been served a fried rat tail in what was supposed to have been an order of french-fried potatoes. McSweeney was representing the Trasks.

When the truth hit me, my coffee mug dropped from my hand. Fortunately, it fell only a few inches to the kitchen table, where it toppled over and spilled the dregs onto the newspaper. Ever alert, the dogs nonetheless came running. I could barely bring myself to look Kimi in the eye. "Those monsters," I told her. "No wonder they were so upset. You ruined their rotten little scheme. And when I offered to order everything all over again? To replace everything you ate? They didn't know what to say because they knew damn good and well that I wasn't about to be able to replace . . . oh, yuck! Well, let me tell you, never in a million years did I dream that you'd eaten . . . poor Kimi! This is disgusting."

If Kimi had known what she'd consumed, she wouldn't have been bothered at all. Even so! Yiiiiicck! When I'd put her back in the car before leaving the place, she hadn't licked my face, had she? I couldn't remember. She *might* have. Kimi is very affectionate. She loves me.

I contemplated revenge. Not on Kimi, of course, but on the Trasks, who, foiled once by Kimi, had armed themselves anew, returned to Burgerhaven at a later date, planted the disgusting object in a fresh order of fries, and thus successfully carried out their foul scheme. Had they committed a crime? Fraud, maybe? Conspiracy? If the innocent Burgerhaven lost all its customers, the failure of the business would be the Trasks' fault. I felt as if I should report my knowledge to someone. To whom? Kevin Dennehy would know whether vermin-planting for the purpose of launching a phony lawsuit constituted a crime in Massachusetts and, if so, what sort of crime. Extortion? Or maybe the whole thing was a civil matter. But what did I have to offer either the police or poor Burgerhaven? I felt absolutely certain that the Trasks had connived to insinuate the you-know-what into the fries. Burgerhaven presumably felt the same way I did. Feelings weren't evidence.

"Kevin," I said that evening as we sat at my kitchen table, "suppose I go to a restaurant and order french fries and plant a rat tail in them and then pretend to find it. And then I scream bloody murder and sue the restaurant. What's that called?"

"A stupid idea." Kevin sipped his Bud and swallowed. "Tired of dog writing? Exploring new career options?"

I recounted the story of Kimi's thievery at S & I's Burgerhaven and told Kevin about the photo and article in today's paper. "So when I saw it, I realized why the father, this Timothy Trask, came unglued, although the more I think about it, the more I think it was the grandfather, I guess he was, the older man, who planned it all. He was more intelligent-looking than the rest of the family. The others were kind of stupefied. Anyway, when it happened, I apologized over and over, I offered to replace all the food, I did everything humanly possibly, but the father, Timothy, totally overreacted. Now I know why."

"Hey, Holly, it's not like you bumped into this guy and knocked over a tray of food, you know. You gotta remember that these are ordinary citizens we're talking about."

"As opposed to what?"

"Dog nuts! Here's this family getting ready to eat, and all of a sudden, a great big dog that looks like a wolf comes flying out of nowhere. She must've scared the beejezus out of these people. For you, hey, it's all in a day's work, but you can't expect them to take it like *you* would, Holly. They're *normal.* That's the difference."

"I'm not *abnormal.* And these people, the Trasks, were not afraid of Kimi. They have a dog themselves. Their own dog is with them in the picture in the paper. A golden. These are not people who are afraid of dogs, and Kevin, I swear to you that their response was all out of proportion to what happened. And don't forget that they supposedly *found* the rat tail at the *same* place. S & I's Burgerhaven."

Kevin smiled. "They're regular customers." He shrugged "Let it go."

"Maybe they need the money," I said, trying to talk myself into taking Kevin's advice. "Maybe they were desperate, and that's why they concocted this business. Kevin, the little girls were so sad. They were dressed in these threadbare old party clothes. Their teeth were all brown. Baby teeth, rotting away. And they were very sweet kids. Shy, but nice. Still, you'd think there'd be some better way for the parents to take care of them than coming up with this idea of suing Burgerhaven."

"That'd be a funny target, anyway. Where's the payoff? A guy goes to the trouble of planting evidence so's he can sue McDonald's, Burger King, whatever.

Yeah, you can understand that. Deep pockets. But Burgerhaven?"

"I see what you mean. Maybe you're right," I conceded. "Maybe they're loyal customers who honestly were served filth. It does happen. Like that pasta factory? Remember? It was in Waltham or Medford or someplace like that. It got closed down because there were mouse droppings in the dough, and the owners resisted the order to throw out all the pasta they had on hand, five thousand pounds. Maybe they thought they'd invented a new flavor."

Let's step back a second. Here we have Lieutenant Kevin Dennehy of the Cambridge Police, who is involved in what is, to the best of my knowledge, the first serious romance of his adult life. The object of Kevin's affection, Officer Jennifer Pasquarelli of the Newton Police, is not on active duty at the moment because she engaged in a physical altercation with a woman who is charging her with brutality, violation of civil rights, and so forth. Now, of course, the woman, Sylvia Metzner, has been murdered in the very same park where the dispute took place. And the best Kevin and I can find to talk about is revoltingly contaminated food? Come on! I'd thought about pursuing the subject of the murder. But how? The possibilities felt impossible. *Did your girlfriend shoot Sylvia?* No wonder I write about dogs. They're easy. If you want to direct a dog's attention to a target, you put a delectable tidbit of cheese or meat on it, and what you get is rapt canine attention. Simple! Beautiful! You know all those books that promise to reveal the mystical secrets of communicating with your dog? Go into a trance, merge minds, read body language, tune into ESP, or pay hundreds of dollars for the services of the joker who wrote the book? Hah! I, Holly Winter, will now, free of charge, reveal the true secrets of communicating with dogs. There are two secrets. One is meat. The other is cheese. Ah, but the secrets of communicating with people? If I knew them, I'd tell.

"Another beer, Kevin?" I asked.

He accepted. After sipping it, he suddenly blurted out, "In case you wondered, Holly, Jennie had nothing to do with shooting Sylvia Metzner." Before I could reply, he said, "It was a small-caliber weapon."

Not a cop's gun. That was what Kevin meant. I nodded.

"Jennie can be hot tempered," Kevin informed me, "but she's a professional." As if I might have misunderstood, he added, "Law enforcement. That's what she does. *Law* enforcement," he repeated.

"Kevin, I never said otherwise."

"Handguns are all over. You might not expect it in Newton, but half the people at that park've got registered handguns."

"Half? Kevin, I really doubt—"

"Including the victim's deceased husband."

"Kevin, I know you're obsessed with family violence, but you can hardly suspect Sylvia's dead husband of shooting her. Do you think he came back from the grave?"

Kevin shook his big head. "Cremated. Ian Metzner was cremated."

"You checked? This is ridiculous! Sylvia was *not* murdered by a ghost! Kevin, this is totally unlike you."

Kevin had a sly expression. "The guy was there. In the park."

"Stop it!"

"Gotcha!" he exclaimed. His eyes crinkled in delight.

"Gotcha? I don't think so! I have no idea what you're talking about."

"His remains. Scattered near the body, human remains evidently belonging to the late Mr. Metzner. Who was cremated. Who owned a .22. And did not take it with him."

"Where is it?"

"The kids don't know. All innocence!" Kevin mimicked: " 'Did Daddy really own a gun? How terrible! How awful! *Where is it?* We don't know! We didn't even know he had one!' "

Kevin must've heard the story thirdhand. A Cambridge homicide lieutenant wouldn't have been working in Newton. And even if Jennifer hadn't been relieved of her duties, she'd have been the last person the Newton police would've assigned to interview Sylvia's family. Still, Kevin is an experienced cop. I felt certain that he accurately conveyed the family's attitude, if not their precise words.

"You ever met these people?" he asked.

I nodded. "All but the younger daughter. Oona, her name is. I've just heard about her. She sails. I've met the others, but I don't really know them. Wilson's the only one I've talked to much. He has a corgi he shows. Pembroke."

Kevin rolled his eyes.

I laughed. "I can hear what you're thinking. Wilson's a dog nut, so he's capable of anything. Actually, he's just getting started in dogs, so from your point of view, maybe that lets him off the hook. And he and Pia, his wife—Sylvia's daughter, the older one—are probably the two most normal people in that family. They both have regular jobs. They live—lived—with Sylvia, but for all I know, they paid rent. The other two probably couldn't have. Oona apparently does odd jobs for friends of hers who own boats. Sailboats. Yachts, maybe I should say. She crews. That can't pay, can it? And if she scrapes off barnacles and swabs decks, she probably gets something, but not much. The one Ceci really frowns on is Eric. He's the youngest. He graduated from college a few years ago, and I guess he hasn't done anything since, except hang around home. But Ceci's prejudiced about him. She isn't used to pierced ears on men."

"What's your take on him?" Kevin asked.

"Pierced ears don't bother me. Ceci, I guess, could be responding to a difference in style or a generational difference or something like that. But I met him myself. This was actually *after* his mother was killed, except that no one knew that. Well, someone did. But I didn't. Anyway, Sylvia's dog, Zsa Zsa, was running around in the park, and I got a leash on her and took her home. The one who answered the door was Eric. This was in the middle of the afternoon, and he looked as if he'd just gotten out of bed. Ceci makes him sound kind of punk, but he isn't, really."

"Known drug user," Kevin interjected. "Keep talking."

I shrugged. "He's more preppie than punk. Dissipated preppie. Mainly, he's a spoiled brat. Here I was, a stranger returning the family dog, and what he did was complain about how there was no food in the house. He wanted me to tell his mother if I saw her. As if he couldn't go to the store himself! Or cook. Or go out and look for his mother. But the point about Sylvia's family, Kevin, isn't any one person. It's everyone. I mean, Sylvia was killed on Sunday, and her body wasn't found until Tuesday afternoon, and so far as I know, no one in that family was worried about her. All three of her children and her son-in-law live with her, four adults, at least in terms of age, and not one of them even notices she's missing? Unless you count Eric and the food, I guess. You have to wonder how long it would've taken these people to start wondering where she was. A week? More?"

"They didn't all gang up and do it," Kevin said. "This's Newton. It's not Agatha Christie."

"That's not exactly her formula, is it? Except in the one on the train where all those people stab someone. But the formula is the least likely suspect, isn't it? It is in the movies, anyway, like that stabbing one. The least likely suspect is everyone. Anyway, the murderer is the one who couldn't have done it or the last one you'd suspect. Some twist on that."

"The police got a lot to learn," Kevin pronounced

with mock solemnity. "Take me for example." He tapped the side of his presumably thick head with one of his big fingers. "Geez, Holly, the correctional institutions of the Commonwealth of Massachusetts are packed with innocent guys I been locking up 'cause I'm so dumb. You see, I get taken in by *appearances.*"

I waited.

"Typical scenario," Kevin continued. "Junkie slithers into a convenience store and grabs the cash, scares the daylights out of two little old ladies and a mother with a babe in arms, and the clerk ends up with bullet holes where his brains used to be. And who takes the rap? Hey, next time it happens, I'm gonna know better. Instead of arresting the poor innocent junkie who just *looks* guilty because he happens to be holding the weapon, I'm gonna chase after the *real* perp, who's lo and behold, the last one the dumb cops'd ever suspect. The old ladies? Not them. They could've done it. The mother? No. She could've. And there are lots of rotten mothers around. Obvious suspects." He paused before his triumphal finish. "Yes, the baby! From now on, all the jails are going be filled with puking little babies, last people you'd ever suspect, right? See, Holly? The little suckers aren't called babes in *arms* for nothing."

CHAPTER 20

"Ceci," I said when she called the next morning, "what makes you think that the Metzners are sitting shivah? There was nothing in the paper about visiting the family. There wasn't even anything about a funeral. And it was her husband who was Jewish, wasn't it? Not Sylvia."

"In Newton," Ceci insisted, "everyone is more or less Jewish."

Or Catholic, I wanted to add. *Or Protestant. Not to mention Russian Orthodox, new age Buddhist, agnostic, atheist, and a lot of other things.* Instead, I kept quiet.

Ceci defended her claim. "Everyone in Newton eats bagels."

"Everyone in America eats bagels!"

"Taking food to the bereaved is not a strictly Jewish custom," Ceci lectured. "It's a lovely gesture for anyone to make to any family, and when you took Zsa

Zsa home, Eric told you that there was no food in the house, didn't he? Holly, I can simply *feel* that this is the right thing to do," by which she meant that she was itching to hear the latest news of Sylvia's murder and was determined to use any excuse to barge in.

If Ceci had been under the age of seventy-five, or if she hadn't taken care of me and my dogs after my head injury, I'd probably have informed her that if she wanted to turn up uninvited on someone's doorstep, she could do it by herself. If she'd pestered less vociferously, I'd have held out. As it was, I succeeded only in extracting a promise from Ceci that she'd call the Metzners before we stopped in and that we'd stay only long enough for her to leave her food offering.

Hah! Kind people over seventy-five are no more trustworthy than anyone else. As Ceci and I stood at the front door of the late Sylvia Metzner's brick Tudor waiting for someone to answer the bell, I suddenly experienced a flash of ESP. Maybe I just knew Ceci. Anyway, all of a sudden, I'd have bet anything that she had not, in fact, warned the family to expect us. Before I had time to question her, the door opened. One glance at the person who stood there confirmed my suspicion. A muscular young woman with a deep tan and sun-streaked brown hair, she wore jeans and a wrinkled chambray shirt. Instead of greeting Ceci, she eyed us with clear expectation of a pesky pitch for some religious movement, charity, or political cause. Or maybe she thought we were selling something, for example, the lemon cake swathed in plastic wrap that Ceci had made me carry.

"Oona, dear," Ceci said, "this is Holly Winter, who knew your mother. We've come to express our condolences. And I've brought you a cake. It's terribly difficult to think about food at times like this, isn't it? But it's terribly important to keep up your strength!"

As I was about to seize the mention of the cake as an opportunity to shove it into Oona's hands and make a rapid departure, a male voice sounded from inside the house. "Oona, is that UPS?"

Delicately brushing Oona aside, Ceci stepped through the foyer and into the hall. "We've just come to express our sympathy!" she called out. Too late, I understood that she'd refused to carry the damn cake because she'd wanted to be unencumbered, the better to avail herself of exactly this kind of opportunity. "Eric, dear, I'm so terribly sorry about your poor mother!" she gushed.

After rolling her eyes, Oona glared at me and said, "You might as well come in, too."

Toting the cake, which I now felt like tossing into Ceci's face, I followed Oona inside. The front hall was the size of my living room. There ended the resemblance. My living room has bare floors. Also, it's clean and neat. Underfoot here was an oriental rug that probably had one of those fancy names I never understand—*Kashan*, *Kerman*, *Sarab*, or some other foreign word meaning that a poor dog writer can't afford more than bare floors, so why bother mastering carpet terminology in Persian? It was a red rug with a pretty pattern obscured by dog hair, crumbs, and other, less readily identifiable, debris, some of which looked as if it could have been pulverized potato chips. An empty chip bag lay at the bottom of a carpeted staircase. Cuddled up to it to keep it from getting lonely were a couple of empty wine bottles and two stemmed glasses with red dregs. Jackets, newspapers, magazines, junk mail, an umbrella, running shoes, and a set of yellow oilskins also littered the floor. Leaning against a wall were a pair of cross-country skis and bamboo poles. The stale air bore a hint of what my educated nose identified as dog urine.

"I'm sorry about your mother," I told Oona.

"The place is bedlam. The kitchen is worse than this. It's disgusting." Oona sounded as if I'd offered condolences because her maid had quit. "You want some coffee? We're down to instant. There's no sugar. And the milk smells funny."

"No thanks," I said. "We can't stay long. Ceci just wanted to drop off this cake." Oona didn't reach out for it or show me a place to put it. The only table in the hallway held a phone, phone books, and a stack of papers, so I just stood there like a dope, still holding the cake.

"Come on in the living room," Oona offered, leading the way into a long room with wood trim and a high ceiling. Two big red couches on either side of a massive stone fireplace faced each other across a low table buried under pizza cartons and newspapers. Although quite a few standing lamps and table lamps were placed here and there, not one was on. The room seemed somehow filled with a dank and palpable darkness. Lying face down on one couch, apparently asleep, was a petite woman in a purple terrycloth bathrobe. Her short, dark hair identified her as Pia. Seated on the other couch were her husband, Wilson, and her brother, Eric, both of whom were dressed in rumpled khaki pants and polo shirts. Wilson looked, as usual, as if he hadn't bathed for a week. His hair was greasy, and his skin had a shiny look, as if he'd applied cold cream to it. Eric looked more awake than he had when I'd returned Zsa Zsa, and when I entered the room, he made an apparently token effort to rise to his feet. He did not, however, offer me a seat, and seemed content to leave the elderly Ceci standing. He'd have done better to remain seated altogether, because his gesture toward courtesy revealed that his fly was open. Neither Zsa Zsa nor Llio, Wilson's corgi, was in sight.

Ceci was talking nonstop about everything and nothing. "How nice that you have taken time off from work, Wilson, and Pia, too, prostrate with grief, how could she possibly have gone in and tried to concentrate? Neither of you would have gotten a thing done, and have the police been able to cast any light?" When no one responded, she barreled on. "Have you set a date for the memorial service?"

"Sylvia hated funerals," Oona said.

The whole scene was so depressing that I felt immobilized. No wonder Pia had fallen asleep. My own eyes were heavy. The cake plate might as well have been glued to my hands. I felt like a character in a surrealist drama, an absurd woman inexplicably trapped in a dark, smelly room, doomed forever to clutch a lemon cake that no one wants.

Wilson startled me out of my daze by addressing me in my native language. "You entered tomorrow?"

I shook myself. "No. But I'm going."

Like everyone else who shows regularly, I keep my own little heavily annotated book in which I rate judges. Sam Usher, who was judging malamutes at tomorrow's Micmac Kennel Club show, had earned his prominent place in my Absolutely Never Enter Under This Jerk class on the shameful—for him—occasion when he'd dumped both Rowdy and Kimi in favor of the most cow-hocked, swaybacked, snipey-muzzled, light-eyed, and otherwise pitifully unsound, incorrect, and just plain plug-ugly collection of supposed malamutes I'd ever seen in the ring. Not that I'm a poor sport! Ask anyone! I'm well known for my excellent sportsmanship. It's just that I don't believe in wasting my money asking for the opinion of an ignoramus who isn't qualified to judge stuffed animals.

But as I've remarked, I'm a good sport. Instead of explaining about Sam Usher, I politely asked Wilson about Llio, who, he replied, was entered. I said I'd look forward to seeing both of them. Since Wilson and I were now on chummy terms, I went on to point out the obvious, namely, that the cake I was holding was a gift from Ceci. What would he like me to do with it? In yet another display of what a good sport I am, I want to take full responsibility for what happened next. I have spent my entire life with dogs. By profession, I am a dog writer. I own, train, and show my dogs, who are, I should add, the most determined and voracious food thieves I have ever even heard of. And I knew that the Metzner household included two dogs. So, when Wilson belatedly thanked Ceci for the cake, moved a couple of pizza cartons to the floor, and told me to put the cake on the coffee table, I should have ignored him. Instead, I complied.

Where had Zsa Zsa been? I have no idea. Maybe she'd been sleeping. If so, the sound of the cake plate making contact with the table perhaps awakened her. In any case, a few seconds after I finally got rid of the cake, a golden-furred blob zoomed out of nowhere, crashed into Ceci, knocked her to the floor, made a dive at the cake, sent plate and cake flying off the table, hurled herself at her booty, and began gobbling it up.

"Bad dog!" Wilson yelled. "Bad, bad dog!"

Ceci had pulled herself to a sitting position. I lowered myself to her level. "Are you hurt?" I asked. "Is anything broken?" Within a few seconds, it became clear that she was more angry than injured. Luckily, she'd cushioned her fall by lurching against one of the couches. As I helped Ceci to her feet, Pia, jolted awake, began swearing about how no one ever gave her any consideration, and Eric made the mistake of trying to get the plate and the remains of the cake away from Zsa Zsa, whose response to his effort was a snarl.

I'd be curious to know how quickly I got us out of there. I have a clear memory of gripping Ceci's arm and almost dragging her to the door as I simultaneously and unnecessarily told anyone who might be listening— no one was—that we were going. It may have been as little as fifty seconds from the moment Ceci hit the floor to the moment she and I stood on the front walk catching our breath and recovering our sanity. The tidiness of the weed-free front lawn, the neatness of the heavily mulched rhododendron beds, the solidity of the big brick house on this infinitely suburban street were in such contrast to the chaos within that I felt momentarily disoriented.

"That," said Ceci, "was a mistake. Holly, those people are barbarians." To my relief, far from showing any ill effects, she had apparently been revitalized by her tumble to the floor. Her face was pink with excitement, and her eyes sparkled.

"You're sure you're okay?"

She gave her dainty hands a shake, as if to brush off my worry. "Zsa Zsa isn't even half the size I'm used to." Stepping briskly forward, she commented, "Won't it be perfectly lovely to see our dogs! Quest and Rowdy are such a contrast to people like *that.* Ugh! And to dogs like that one, too. Although I must admit, I can't help thinking that pain is contributing to that horrible behavior, and money is no excuse, there's obviously plenty, and if you ask me, Sylvia would've done well to push those children of hers out of the nest and take the money she'd've saved and get Zsa Zsa to a good veterinary surgeon for a full hip replacement, except that she's probably too fat, isn't she?"

By then, we'd reached my car, where Ceci was diverted from the topic of Zsa Zsa's appropriateness as a candidate for hip surgery. Having tapped on the rear window and waved to Quest, she got into the passenger seat and chatted to Rowdy about how nice it would be to get to the park and away from those horrid people.

Meanwhile, I got into the driver's seat, shut the door, and had just started the engine when a small, flashy silver sports car pulled up right in front of my Bronco. Out of it stepped a tall, thin, extraordinarily beautiful woman with long blond hair and a sour expression. She wore a very feminine version of the classic navy pin-striped suit. Tucked under her arm was a slim leather briefcase. My Bronco, I should mention, is distinctive, especially in fancy neighborhoods. Sylvia's neighborhood wasn't quite so dazzling as Ceci's. Still, Sylvia's street had a lot of brick pseudo-Tudors like hers, manicured lawns, and other features more compatible with new Volvo station wagons, shiny Mercedes sedans, and trendy sport-utility vehicles than with my rattletrap, which was readily identifiable not only by its dents, but by the bumper sticker I got for subscribing to *The Bark*, a fundamentalist religious publication ("The Modern Dog Culture Magazine") out of Berkeley, California, the West Coast Cambridge. Great reading! Check it out! (www.thebark.com) Anyway, as you've probably guessed, the bumper sticker reads DOG IS MY CO-PILOT, and it's identical to the one that used to be on Steve Delaney's van until that doGawful woman removed it. Okay, men! Let that be a warning to you! Today, she just tears off your bumper sticker. But tomorrow?

Where was I? Oh, yes, the beautiful woman with the briefcase must have recognized my distinctive car, but made no acknowledgment. Rather, she strode gracefully up the front walk of the late Sylvia Metzner's house.

"Real estate agents do that, you know," Ceci remarked censoriously. "It's disgraceful."

I didn't feel up to conversation. Still, I said, "What?"

"They ask owners if they're interested in selling. I get letters from them, and every once in a while, one of them turns up at my door and asks if I want to sell my house, and I don't like it one bit. This one must have heard about Sylvia. I think that must be it. At least she looks like a real estate agent, doesn't she?"

"She's a lawyer," I said. "And what she wants to look like is a movie star."

"You know her?"

"Her name is Anita Fairley. Fairley-Delaney. She's a lawyer, or maybe a disbarred lawyer, and she's Steve Delaney's wife."

"*Your* Steve Delaney?"

"Yes. But not anymore." I paused. "She's beautiful, isn't she?"

Ignoring the question, Ceci asked another one. "What on earth is she doing *here*?"

CHAPTER 21

"Damn Sylvia! She's an even worse problem dead than she was alive!" Noah's thick fuzzy brown fleece jacket enhanced his natural resemblance to a teddy bear, but he sounded like an enraged grizzly. "Why the hell did she have to go and get herself murdered!"

Even the mild swearing surprised me, coming as did from someone who'd named his dogs for the apostles. Ceci, a devout Episcopalian, seemed unoffended by the names and the curses; she liked Noah. At the moment, I was feeling especially fond of him myself. Five minutes after leaving the Metzners' house, we'd arrived at Clear Creek Park, where Ceci had undoubtedly wanted to hang around the playing field. Noah, however, had persuaded her that she and I should accompany him on an actual walk. By unspoken agreement, we'd avoided the trail that ran near the murder scene. Soon after we'd started down another one, a damp path that followed a polluted-looking stream—the Clear

Creek?—through murky woods, Douglas and Ulysses had joined us.

"Sylvia didn't set out to get herself murdered," Douglas pointed out.

Once again, I reminded myself that he wasn't bad looking. On the contrary, he had the mannequin looks of the models you see in ads for men's suits. Among other things, his hair was exactly the correct length. Steve Delaney's, I might mention irrelevantly, was usually too long or too short, because instead of getting it professionally cut every month or so, he prevailed on one of his vet techs to run clippers over his head a few times a year. Or that's what he'd done before. By now, Anita had probably bullied him into patronizing some trendy Newbury Street salon. At least she'd dug her talons into only one of my two males. If she'd been put in charge of Rowdy's grooming, she'd have subjected him to an English Saddle clip meant for a show poodle, half shaved to the skin with puffs here and there and a pompom bouncing around on the end of his poor malamute tail. But back to Douglas, whose most endearing quality was the possession of a charming dog. At the moment, the ungainly, mottled Ulysses was sniffing his way along the edge of the filthy water. For all I knew, the hound was hoping to discover another corpse. I liked the improbability of the big, awkward, nose-driven dog and tried to see Douglas as a whimsical, imaginative man who'd gone to a shelter and fallen for the funny-looking hound. When animal shelters fill up, the big, hairy dogs like Ulysses (and Rowdy, too) are the first to die. Douglas had probably saved the hound's life.

"Not that Sylvia went out and decided to get murdered," Noah conceded. "But you have to admit that Sylvia did cause trouble. Her and that damned Zsa Zsa. And the police! Honest to God! First, there was the exhibitionist. That's crime! A sick crime. Repeated. Cops ignored it. What'd they do instead? Who'd they go after? Us! Dogs. All of us. *Our* dogs. For what? For the crime of having fun! And then Pasquarelli waltzes in, and she's a whole new problem, her and her fascist tactics. And who gets blamed? Dogs! So, now the new problem's murder, and who would you think was to blame? Dogs! Us again."

On the contrary, Ceci had shown me a letter that had just appeared in the *Newton Pulse*:

> *More Dogs!*
> "Faithful and True Even to Death." The noble phrase from Senator Vest's famous Eulogy on the Dog sums up the compelling reasons why our City and our Parks need to shape up regarding Man's Best Friend by making our City and our Parks welcoming places for dogs and owners. The horrible Murder in one of our Parks and preceding terrorization of women by a PERVERT in that same Park happened only because there were not MORE dogs around. Dogs and dog walkers try and keep our Parks safe for everyone! Let's stop harassing the good guys!
>
> —ALVIN WILLETTE
> NEWTON UPPER FALLS

"Who's blaming dogs for the murder?" I asked. "I haven't heard anyone do that. Rowdy, leave it! Stop! That is disgusting!"

To my horror, he was scarfing down poisonous-looking mud. While I'm eating marked-down Brand X noodles, Rowdy and Kimi are dining on premium dog chow. Lately, the dogs had been feasting on homemade treats. So what delicacy did the big boy take it into his head to gobble up? Mud. I ask you!

Returning to the previous topic, I said, "If anything, dogs are the heroes. Or one dog." I smiled at Douglas. "Ulysses found her body. Well, you did, too, Douglas, but I'm sure you won't mind giving Ulysses all the credit."

"He's welcome to it," Douglas replied, "unless it means that suspicion automatically falls on him. Isn't that what's supposed to happen? The one who finds the body is the obvious suspect?"

"Not with Officer Pasquarelli around," I said, "although I can't imagine that the police are going to focus on one of their own."

Unconvinced, Noah said, "If someone comes along with an assault rifle and shoots everyone in the park, you know what the police are going to do? Hey, they're going to keep doing the same thing they've been doing—get tough about the leash law and really enforce the pooper-scooper law. Newton's the Garden City, you know, meaning that crime doesn't happen here."

Here, at that moment, bore no resemblance to a garden. Leafless branches of trashy-looking trees overhung the trail. The sludge oozing its way between the muddy banks of the stream gave off a vaguely petrochemical reek.

"It does seem as though no one's done much about the exhibitionist," I said.

"Maybe now that attention is turning in the direction it's turning," Ceci said incomprehensibly, "there'll finally be some long overdue progress, assuming that the police have the sense to put two and two together, and realize that it's a dirty sort of person who's driven to do dirty, dirty things!"

Noah, Douglas, and I exchanged glances. In unison, we shrugged our shoulders.

With no prompting, Ceci went on to clarify her point. In hushed tones, she said, "I could not help noticing, among other things, that he was not fully zipped!"

Taking pity on Noah and Douglas, I explained. "Ceci made a cake for Sylvia's children. We just delivered it. They really weren't prepared for visitors." At the risk of shocking Ceci, I added, "Eric's fly was open."

"*That* Eric," Ceci sputtered, "could charitably be described as a slob. Pia was asleep on the living room couch, of all places, and Oona was ... well, times change, but in my day, girls made an effort of some sort, even my sister Althea, not that Althea was an unattractive girl, but she's very tall and broad shouldered, and have you ever noticed her feet? It was dreadfully hard to find anything in size eleven except clodhoppers, we used to call them, not to mention gloves. And it's sadly clear that poor Sylvia was nothing more than a housemaid to the whole lazy pack of them because they're living like little piggies without her, and not the slightest indication of grief. But mark my words! That Eric is the one to keep your eye on." Evidently listening in on her own prattle, she blushed. "What am I saying! Or the one to keep your eye off, if he can't manage to do up his buttons and zippers, and I can't help wondering whether it was entirely accidental, if you understand me, or whether he had succumbed to a sick compulsion." Perhaps I should remark on the unmistakably titillated quality of Ceci's interest in the exhibitionist. Lingering beneath every sentence she spoke about him was an unvoiced and breathless question, namely, *Is he going to expose himself to ME?* Had she been his victim, she'd have hated the reality. But she adored the fantasy.

Douglas responded to what struck me as Ceci's ludicrous implication that the exhibitionist was Sylvia's son. "Eric as the exhibitionist. That's a new thought."

Noah promptly dismissed it. "Pia was the last victim. He wouldn't go around exposing himself to his own sister."

Woman of the world, Ceci chimed back in. "You never know, do you? After all, it's a sick individual we're talking about. What if Sylvia caught him at it? There that Eric is, lurking in the woods up to you know what, and along comes his mother, and he shoots her!"

Douglas cleared his throat. "He's carrying a gun in case his mother strolls along and catches him, because if she does, he intends to kill her. That's a bit far-fetched."

"Sylvia threatened him," Ceci hypothesized. "She threatened to turn him over to the police. And for all we know, Douglas, he carried a gun all the time. Maybe he still does!"

"Hey, this is Newton," Noah said. "A Newton mother who catches her son exposing himself packs him off to a psychiatrist. She doesn't call the police."

The word *psychiatrist* made me jump. I covered my embarrassment by looking in every direction except Douglas's. The stream was narrow and almost stagnant, its water brown with a greenish cast. Ulysses' feet were coated in filth. Noah's four dogs ran in a congenial little pack ahead of us. Their short coats would be easier to clean than Rowdy's thick double coat. Although Quest was on leash and hadn't left the path, his legs and feet were dirty, and Ceci would have a hard time removing the mud from his underbelly before she allowed him in the house. If you'll forgive an interjection, let me comment that free association is a weird phenomenon. *Psychiatrist* leads to *Douglas* leads to *dirt*. No wonder I was having my head examined.

And Douglas? What was his excuse?

"Still," I said, "I suppose it's possible that the exhibitionist is the one who killed Sylvia. She could have recognized him, whoever he is. For all we know, he's some fine, upstanding citizen with a lot to lose if Sylvia—"

"Exposed him!" Noah exclaimed.

I laughed obligingly. "Suppose he's a doctor, or he's in some other profession where that kind of scandal would do him in. Anyone would be humiliated, I guess, but not everyone's livelihood would be threatened. Maybe that's why he wears a ski mask. Exhibitionists don't necessarily do that kind of thing, do they?"

"The one they caught in the library didn't," Ceci said. "That one used to lurk on the third floor, and everyone knew what he looked like because there were those what-do-you-call-them drawings of him on posters all over the library, and then finally someone spotted him and had him arrested, but you have to wonder whether he didn't get some sick sort of enjoyment from seeing his face plastered all over the library, because after all, when you think about it, it's what these men want, isn't it? To be looked at?"

"On exhibition," I agreed.

"Like pictures," said Ceci. " 'Pictures at an Exhibition,' but I don't suppose that what's his name, Mussorgsky, was—"

Douglas smiled at her. "You never know."

"Yeah, but it's a whole different category," Noah said. "It's sick, but it's not violent. It's not in the same class as murder."

"That day when Pia ran into this guy?" I reminded everyone. "When she came running out of the woods? She looked like a crime victim to me. She was very frightened. The violence was emotional, or psycholog-ical maybe, but it was still violence. And this is a crime against women, meaning that it tends not to be taken seriously."

As if to prove my contention, Douglas said jocularly, "We'll have to start a campaign, persuade the guy, hey, he's being politically incorrect."

My hackles rose. "You see! It's a crime against women, so it gets joked about and dismissed. Pia didn't exactly have a hilarious experience. There was nothing funny about how she felt. It's possible that this guy exposed himself to Sylvia, too, and that he's the one who shot her. I don't tend to think of exhibitionists as physically violent types, either, but what do we really know about them? And we don't know anything about this particular man. He could be an exhibitionist and a murderer, too. The two things aren't mutually exclu-sive."

Rowdy had turned his attention to my face. His beautiful almond-shaped eyes glowed with approval. He approves of Kimi even more than he does of me. Anatomy has made her the feminist extremist in our family: she is blessed with malamute jaws, whereas I make do with a sharp tongue. Douglas looked abashed. Well, to be accurate, he looked like a men's suit ad model trying to look abashed.

From behind us, the sound of pounding feet and strained breathing presaged the appearance of Wilson and Llio. Llio was trotting along happily, maybe be-cause it was the first time in her life that she'd ever been taken for a run. Wilson was sucking in air. He'd

changed into gray sweatpants and a faded maroon
sweatshirt. To fortify himself for exercise, he'd apparently eaten a doughnut; his sweatshirt was dusted with
powdered sugar. As he approached us, he said, "Getting in a little conditioning before the show tomorrow!"

The sensible time to begin conditioning a dog for a
show is about six months before the dog is going to
enter the ring. Llio, however, was muscular and fit
from walking or playing; no judge was going to fault
her for flabbiness. I suspected that Wilson had suddenly taken up jogging in response to his own preshow
nerves. In any case, he slowed down and joined our
little group. "Sorry about the fiasco back there," he told
Ceci.

"No apologies are necessary," she said graciously.

"Without Sylvia, we're in chaos," he explained. "But
that's all too obvious. We don't know what to do.
We're barbarians. Here I am showing Llio tomorrow
when Sylvia—but what else am I going to do?"

Stay home, I thought. In my own show-fanatic family, the opposite would've been true. We'd expect a
family member to go right ahead and get into the ring
and win even if the entire rest of family had just per-
ished in a catastrophe. But that's because we're exceptionally religious. If an Orthodox Jew dies, the family
doesn't stay home from temple; on the contrary, everyone attends services. My family's just like that: Orthodox. But Wilson was a new convert, and the other
members of the family weren't show types at all. Still,
I had the feeling that none of them would give a damn
whether Wilson went to a dog show or to hell. They

probably wouldn't even notice he was gone.

"Sylvia wouldn't have cared," Wilson added.

"The police have any news?" Noah asked. "Have they got any idea what happened?"

"They're asking questions," Wilson replied, "not answering them. The one thing that hasn't been in the papers is what Sylvia was doing in the park, which was scattering Ian's ashes. That was her husband. Not that she shouldn't have been doing it. It's morbid to keep human remains in a vase in the house. You can call it an urn, but you could've put a bunch of flowers in this one, and no one would've known the difference."

I confessed. "Sylvia got the idea from me. Not the idea of the urn, but about scattering the ashes. Or a story I told her must've made her think about it. My stepmother inveigled me into helping her scatter her first husband's ashes in Harvard Yard. Only we got caught by the University Police. I remember that after I told the story, Sylvia said something about her husband's ashes."

"Ian was a bird-watcher," Wilson said. "Used to wander around here with binoculars. That's why she picked the park. Or that's what we think, although it's not my idea of a dignified resting place. And what happened was just awful, not that it was Sylvia's fault, but she must've been holding the urn when she was shot. It fell and hit a rock, and the urn, this vase thing, broke. The police did tell us that. That's all we know. Douglas, you found her. You probably know more than we do."

"Not really," Douglas answered. "All I did was go looking for Ulysses. But you're right about the, uh, urn. There was a lot of broken pottery. I wondered what it was doing there. I didn't know what it was. It could've been anything. Dishes. Cups. So it was the urn, huh?"

Wilson nodded.

Douglas said, "Pia told me something about that. Before all this. She said Eric'd found an unconventional use for it."

Considering Eric's police record and his drug-wasted look, the use wasn't hard to imagine. His father's ashes? His own stash. Maybe. If so, had his mother known? Not unless she'd been in the habit of sifting through the late Ian's dust. A scenario occurred to me: Sylvia takes the urn and goes to the park to scatter the ashes. Eric discovers what his mother is doing. He follows her. Confronts her? And stops her. Dead.

Sudden violence interrupted my speculation. One moment, the nasty little trail ahead of us was empty. Noah's four dogs were rambling in the nearby woods, Ulysses was a bit behind us on the trail of a fascinating scent, Quest was moseying along on leash at Ceci's side, and Rowdy was peacefully ambling at mine. Then all of a sudden, from around a bend in the trail, with no warning whatever, a snarling Yorkshire terrier in full attack mode came charging toward us at ninety miles an hour. What did the little dog weigh? Four pounds? Five? Nonetheless, growling his tiny head off, the Yorkie was hellbent on attack. His chosen victim? Rowdy! The peewee's entire body was smaller than a malamute forepaw. Still, with insane ferocity, he'd set himself on a direct course for Rowdy, who is a good dog, the best of dogs, and no bully. Even so, to Rowdy, a dog is a dog. Attacked, he retaliates. The Yorkie's surprise assault caught me completely off guard. Before I even thought of pulling the aerosol alarm from my pocket, the Yorkie was within a yard of Rowdy, ready to hurl himself, kamikaze fashion, into the big boy's jaws. If the Yorkie hit his target? With one shake of Rowdy's massive head, he'd break the toy dog's neck.

My rage was almost uncontrollable. What kind of stupid owner allowed this mindless, defenseless animal to run around challenging Alaskan malamutes? The owner should be in jail!

"Stop!" I screamed at the little dog. "No! Bad dog! Go home!" Desperate, I told Rowdy, "Watch me! Eyes on me! Leave it! Good boy! That's my boy, Rowdy! Keep watching!"

With three men there, Douglas, Noah, and Wilson, dogs owners all, all under the age of forty, who rescued us? For all her silliness, Ceci was a paragon of common sense when it came to dogs. Among other things, she'd been teaching Quest basic obedience from the moment he'd entered her house. "Down!" she told the Newfie, who was, I'm sure, happy to sink to the ground. "Stay!" Swiftly removing Quest's leash, she took brisk steps that positioned her behind the Yorkie, and with tremendous presence of mind, she neatly looped the leash around the toy's neck and hauled him firmly away. I thought I'd faint with relief.

The Yorkie's owner appeared. She was worse than I'd imagined. Sweetiekins, she informed us, hadn't been on leash because he never, ever left her side. She couldn't begin to imagine what he'd been thinking! As to her Yorkie's attempt at suicide by malamute? It had been no such thing. Sweetiekins, she was sure, had just wanted to play.

I got myself and my dog and Ceci and Quest the hell out of that park as fast as possible. After I dropped off Ceci and Quest, I found the old Dylan tune about how one should never be where one does not belong running through my head. Damned pet people! If that Yorkie had ended up dead, who'd have taken the blame? My Rowdy! Damn the murky woods, the polluted stream, the exhibitionist, Zsa Zsa, Sylvia Metzner's dissipated family, and Sylvia's murder! One *should* never be where one does not belong. I'd taken my dog and was going home. And tomorrow? Tomorrow, I was taking Dylan's advice. I was going to a show! A dog show. The ultimate place where I *did* belong.

CHAPTER 22

Winter, Holly
Yet more perseveration on the topic of these horrific symbols of phallic aggression! Pt. strongly resists interpretation as such—exhibits NO capacity for insight! Proposed bringing the brutes w/ her to my office to prove how "gentle" they are. I put a quick stop to that bid at acting out!

CHAPTER 23

Subj: Re: Your Rowdy
From: HollyWinter@amrone.org
To: Jazzland@pnwmals.org

Hi Cindy,

I'm relieved to report that Janet approves. (Janet
does not co-own Rowdy, but she's very possessive
about him—and about every other dog she's ever
bred.) I sent her Emma's pedigree and photos. As I
think I told you, Rowdy was bred twice to her Vanessa, but Vanessa resorbed* both litters. After

----

*The mother was pregnant, but absorbed the fetuses. Resorbtion oc-
curs in people, too. It's an explanation for the "vanishing twin syndrome," in which one ultrasound shows twins and the next shows a
singleton.—H. W.

that, Vanessa got pyo** and had to be spayed. Anyway, I can never predict how Janet is going to react to anything, but she is actually enthusiastic. We had only one slight misunderstanding. I told Janet that you were looking for a perfect tail set, and she initially decided that you were casting aspersions on her lines, but when I managed to get a word in, I straightened her out by saying that Rowdy's perfect tail set was one of the reasons you WANTED to use him.

Janet saw your Howie when he took a four-point major*** under C. J. Pastern. Janet says that he was stark naked—Howie, not Pastern! Maybe I'd better start that one again. Janet says that Howie was totally out of coat and none the worse for it, and that C. J. commented on Howie's excellent structure and movement.

I cannot begin to tell you how much I'd love a Rowdy-Emma puppy, but it's impossible for me to have a third dog here. I guess I'd better just take the stud fee. I'll send you a copy of my contract.

Holly

**Pyometra is a uterine disease of dogs (and cats, too).—H. W.
***Horrors! If you don't show your dogs, you may imagine all sorts of hideous scenarios. Let me explain that no military officers were involved and that Howie is a malamute, Emma's brother, CH Jazzland's How High the Moon, whom I've mentioned before, but briefly. When Howie took a four-point major, he won four championship points. In other words, he had lots of competition.—H. W.

CHAPTER 24

As you may have forgotten, but as Wilson certainly had not, the estimable Mrs. Nigel Waggenhoffer was a friend of my late mother's. At the risk of engaging in the ceaseless, shameless, repetitive bragging to which dog people are prone, let me simply report that my mother was well known and highly regarded in the dog fancy by virtue of her achievements as a breeder and exhibitor of numerous golden retrievers still remembered for their many successes in the conformation and obedience rings, as well as for their outstanding temperaments. Dedicated show person that she was, my mother, Marissa, belonged to various all-breed kennel clubs, golden retriever clubs, and obedience clubs, as well as to the Dog Writers Association of America and other dog organizations. In brief, Marissa was a power in purebred pooches, as is her friend Mrs. Waggenhoffer, a fellow breeder of goldens and the president of the club giving the show I was attending this Saturday, which, I remind you, was the show at which Wilson had entered his Pembroke Welsh corgi bitch, Llio. Although the Micmac Kennel Club was quite prestigious—you may recall that I belonged and Wilson didn't—the club's late autumn show was always held in what I deemed a somewhat unpleasant trade center in an industrially blighted community about an hour's drive from Cambridge. The trade center, which happened to be owned by a nephew of Mrs. Waggenhoffer's, was too old and shabby to attract important computer conferences, software job fairs, and executive training seminars featuring the kinds of motivational speakers who'd overcome challenges such as the loss of all four limbs and had gone on to win gold medals in Olympic events and, as if the medals weren't enough, had then gotten stinking rich making inspirational speeches and selling motivation-rousing tapes and CDs: *How I Did the Impossible and You Can, Too!* I buy these tapes. I need them. If you showed Alaskan malamutes in advanced obedience, you'd be in the same pitiable position I am, willing to spend any amount for the motivation instilled by anyone who promises you that optimism is everything and reality counts for nought.

Anyway, the Micmac show was strictly conformation, breed only, no obedience, and as I've already mentioned, the malamute judge was Sam Usher, who, I might add, had obviously lost the contents of his cranium, including the optic nerve and the power of rational thought, and had nonetheless gone on to get himself licensed to evaluate dogs when he should have pursued a career making motivational speeches. As I pulled the Bronco into the parking lot of the trade center at ten o'clock on Saturday morning and cruised around in search of an empty spot, I saw only one malamute-familiar vehicle, a beige van owned by a couple who also have Shiba Inus and were probably showing their Shibas today and not their malamutes. Like a lot of the other vans, minivans, cars, and motor homes in the lot, this one was plastered with breed-proud bumper stickers and warnings against tailgating. Paintings of purebred dogs adorned the sides of vehicles and the covers of rear-mounted spare tires, and here and there, exhibitors walked the real thing—show dogs of every size, color, and coat, giant, toy, red, white, black, brindle, smooth-coated, rough-coated, and even almost-no-coated hairless breeds like the Chinese crested, dogs all, great and small, bright and beautiful.

Oh my. With one exception. The oversized male golden retriever caught my eye, not only because goldens always catch my eye, but because every once in a while, a misinformed owner turns up in the show ring with an embarrassingly pet-quality dog. This poor dog sure was one. Finding an empty slot, I turned in, killed the engine, and studied the unfortunate animal, who had the same combination of a grotesquely over-developed front and a pitifully weak rear I'd noticed the second I'd seen Zsa Zsa. This dog, however, was tall and rangy, and in contrast to Zsa Zsa, he'd been kept lean. Still, he was horribly unsound and, in terms of the AKC standard, horribly incorrect, with a narrow skull, long ears, and a few dozen other serious faults. But his height was a disqualifying fault, that is, a mortal as opposed to merely venial fault, one that renders a dog ineligible for competition. A male golden is supposed to measure twenty-three to twenty-four inches at the withers. (Remember the withers? On the back, above the front legs.) The standard for the breed gives a bit of leeway, one inch in either direction, but this dog was at least twenty-seven inches. In terms of breed competition, he might as well have had no tail or three heads. If his owners tried to show him, they'd experience anything from mild humiliation to profound mortification.

As my thoughts turned to the owners, I finally took a good look at the people who accompanied the dog, and was astonished to realize that although I hadn't actually seen the dog before, I'd seen his picture in the newspaper. The article about the Trask family? The people suing S & I's for supposedly serving them filth in an order of fries? Yes, the very same rotten schemers who'd practically gone out of their way to feed the dirty, disgusting caudal appendage of a loathsome rodent to *my* beautiful Kimi! What on earth were they doing at a dog show?

The weather, I might mention, was, for once, seasonably cold. The temperature must have been in the high twenties, and the gray sky seemed to reflect the dull blackness of the asphalt. The little Trask girls, Diana and Fergie, wore matching pink polyester coats, probably bought for Easter Sunday. Neither child wore a hat or mittens. I got out of the car and headed toward the family, who, by unhappy coincidence, stood next to two open dumpsters overflowing with trash. Crows or roving animals had torn open the big green plastic bags that were piled next to the dumpsters. Litter blew around the Trasks and their dog, as if twisting their name in order to make a cruel judgment. In unintended protest, the dog was lifting his leg on one of the trash bags. As he lowered the leg, I approached the family. The older man, the one I guessed to be the grandfather, had been missing from the newspaper photo, but he was here today, and his face had the same alert expression I'd noticed before. The parents, Timothy and Brianna, had the washed-out, worn-out look I remembered. When the little girls smiled at me, there was no indication that they'd finally visited a dentist. I felt terrible. Rowdy and Kimi had strong white teeth, in part because our grooming sessions included dental care; I routinely scaled their teeth. If the dogs hadn't cooperated, I'd have had their teeth professionally cleaned. And here were these little children with their teeth— their baby teeth!—rotting out of their heads! The sight melted my rage. Besides sparing the children my anger, there was almost nothing I could do to make life easier for them. Almost. There was one small thing. If the Trasks intended to show this awful-looking dog today, I could try to save the little girls the pain of listening to strangers disparage their pet.

"I'm Holly Winter," I said, directing my words mainly at the grandfather. "My dog stole your lunch. I'm really sorry. I should've been paying attention."

The three adults were much more forgiving now

than they'd been at S & I's. Probably because I hadn't just foiled a plan to establish the grounds for a lawsuit, they were, in fact, friendly and pleasant. They even went so far as to introduce themselves.

"Tim Trask," said the father. "Brianna, my wife. And my father, George. Fergie and Diana." He pointed at the girls. Fergie was the taller of the two.

"And Charlie," little Diana piped up. "Charlie's our dog!" She wrapped her arms around his neck.

"*And* Charlie!" I replied. "I'll bet Charlie is a really good dog."

Fergie responded. "Charlie is the best dog in the whole world!"

The three adults exchanged sad-faced glances.

Addressing the children, I asked, "And how come Charlie is at the dog show today?"

The children's exclamations had aroused my hopes. American Kennel Club shows sometimes include Canine Good Citizen testing, for which Charlie would be eligible. The CGC program is open to all dogs, including mixed-breed dogs and purebreds with disqualifying faults.

Fergie answered my question. "I told you! Because Charlie is the best dog in the world!"

"Have you entered him?" I asked Tim Trask. "You're showing him today?"

The response was immediate and vehement. "Put him in a dog show? He can hardly walk! You ever heard of what they call hip dysplasia?" Tim demanded.

In a sympathetic tone, I said, "All too often."

"You know what it costs to fix?"

"I know what a full hip replacement costs."

For the price of having both hips replaced, you could buy a new car instead of new hip joints for your dog. The car would be used, and it wouldn't be a two-year-old Mercedes. But this family couldn't've come up with the money for a new bicycle.

I asked, "It's severe dysplasia? Is Charlie in pain?"

Brianna answered. "If you touch Charlie on the rear, he yelps. The kids are good about it. They're real gentle with him. We give him aspirin, but it doesn't do much, and there's this other medicine we tried, but it didn't do too much, either, and you could feed your family on what it cost. The vet did an X-ray, and he said the medicine was a waste of money. He said to get the operation or—"

Her husband interrupted her. "Brianna, shut up! We're not doing that, and for Christ's sake, not in front of the kids!"

Euthanasia.

"There's another kind of surgery," I said. "Your vet probably mentioned—"

Sensibly, Tim Trask glared at me. As I should've kept in mind, this wasn't the first time these people had discussed the dog's ailment. Tim's expression said that the dozens of questions that came to me had already been asked and answered.

The elder Mr. Trask, George, spoke up. "For all practical purposes, the dog's got no hip sockets. The hip joints are deformed, both sides."

"Any chance of talking to Charlie's breeder about

it?" I asked, half expecting to hear they'd bought the dog at a pet shop.

But in a sweet, high-pitched voice, little Diana said, "The lady died."

"Every once in a while, people get what they deserve," Brianna said.

George Trask told me what I already knew. "Breeders are supposed to take X-rays of their dogs before they breed them so's this doesn't happen."

"That's not foolproof," I said.

"I know it's not!" George hollered. "Hey, I could pass a vet school test on hip dysplasia! I read up at the library, including on the Internet. And you wanna know what's not there? What's not there is why the hell they let people get away with not doing a damn thing. This dog's got papers. There's all kinds of clubs about dogs, you know, fanciers of everything, official this and that, Golden Retriever You Name It, Everything Kennel Club, and did any of them give a shit how people were gonna feel when this happened?" His eyes were wild, and he was beating the cold air with his bare fist.

Sorriness goes only so far. The violence in George Trask's voice and gestures made me want out. Immediately. "It should never have happened," I said, careful to agree with him. Not that I disagreed. "I'm really sorry." Turning to the children, I said, "And I can see what a good dog Charlie is." Pointedly looking at my watch, I said, "I have to run. I'm late for something." With an awkward wave of my gloved hand, I headed for the entrance to the trade center.

The lawsuit? The aim wasn't money for the children. Or not exactly. The little girls loved the dog. The dog was in pain. The choices? Let him live in pain that would inevitably grow worse and worse. Or end his misery by ending his life. Or come up with enough cash to pay for surgery. How? By planting vermin in an order of french fries. I no longer felt angry about Kimi. I understand the love of dogs.

CHAPTER 25

What about the blameless owners of the restaurant? Why should *they* pay? I really did feel sorry
for them. But I felt worse for the little girls with the
bad teeth and for the dog they loved. After the sad,
vaguely frightening encounter with the Trask family, I
needed an antidote, and my assignment for *Dog's Life*
provided the perfect one. As I may already have said,
I write a column for that respected publication, but I
also get assignments and do a lot of freelance work,
too. Today, for example, I was interviewing a niece of
Mrs. Waggenhoffer's who was in charge of a demon-
stration of freestyle at the Micmac show. Freestyle, I
remind you, is dancing with dogs and was the subject
Kimi and I had been studying on the infamous Day of
the Tail. Freestyle was a fairly new canine performance
event, and the niece, Erna L. Sporter, was forever trying to recruit support for it by organizing demos at
fairs, parades, and other public festivities as well as at

dog shows. Like every other organized dog activity, freestyle involves competition and titles, but it distinguishes itself from conformation, obedience, tracking, agility, and such by emphasizing the aesthetic element in the performance of dog and handler. And the humorous one. I mean, just how seriously can you take dancing with dogs? Well, in Erna L. Sporter's case, pretty seriously, but to other people, freestyle is the canine equivalent of pairs figure skating crossed with a wacky form of Vaudeville. It has rules and regulations, of course. For instance, the dog and handler are supposed to move in time to the music. But it has only one real point: it's supposed to slap a grin on your face that you can't wipe off. And it does!

So there I was, standing outside the freestyle ring beaming my face off at the sight of a tiny Yorkie and a great big woman in matching gold costumes boogieing to "The Chattanooga Choo Choo," when Wilson lurched into me, apologized, and tried to drag me off to Llio's crate to give him my opinion of her nails. Dog toenails!

"They're too long." I spoke from memory. Keeping my eyes on the Yorkie, I added, "You could take a tiny bit off, but be careful you don't hit the quick, or she'll go lame on you."

Mistake!

"I hate to ask you," Wilson said, "but could you do it? I'm new at all this. And my handler doesn't do any grooming."

"Maybe Llio's aren't too long after all," I lied. "They're probably all right. And if Llio doesn't like having her nails clipped, it might put her in a bad mood, and then she won't show very well."

"They're too long," he persisted.

"When are you due in the ring?" As may not be obvious, I posed the question in my native dialect, which succinctly encodes the assumption that you and your dog are one. In standard English, Llio would be in the ring with her handler and without Wilson, but in the heartfelt English of the dog fancy, where the dog is, there the owner is, too.

"Not for a long time. It's for the group," he said modestly and, I must add, deviantly. The guy obviously hadn't mastered the social conventions yet. When your dog goes Best of Breed, you aren't required to make yourself obnoxious, but you damned well are supposed to brag. Not that you even need to say anything! A smug expression is fine. But you are supposed to display pride! Why? Because you owe it to your dog, that's why! Anyway, in English, Llio had already been in the Pembroke Welsh corgi ring, where she'd won. Consequently, she'd represent her breed in the judging of the Herding Group, which, like the judging of the Sporting Group, the Working Group, and so on, and eventually the judging of Best in Show, would take place much later in the day.

"Congratulations! That's well deserved," I said. "Were there a lot of specials?" Specials: dogs and bitches, technical term, who've already finished their championships. Going Best of Breed is good. Going B.O.B. over specials is worth a big, big brag.

"No. And it wasn't a major." (That's a major win,

one worth three or more points.) "A lot of people don't like the judge." In other words, there'd been a small entry, that is, a small number of Pembrokes in competition. The size of the entry determines the number of points awarded. The greater the competition, the more points given for winning. Sensible! Indeed, like many other aspects of dog shows, a model for the rest of the world. I could go on. And often have.

Before long Wilson had me where he wanted me, which was next to his brand-new grooming table with a pair of clippers in my right hand and Llio standing on the table casting beautiful but unhappy eyes at me. As I was informing Wilson that Llio's nails weren't too bad and that I was not going to trim them for fear of leaving her with a tender toe or a sour attitude, my eyes were taking an inventory of the incredible collection of equipment he'd brought to a smallish show for one smallish bitch.

The grooming table was new but fairly ordinary. The heavy-duty crate dolly was also new. The tack box from which he'd produced the clippers was the kind of large metal affair that professional handlers and big-time breeder-handlers use, and to my amazement, Llio's crate was one of those luxurious, expensive wooden ones, a brand-new version of an old-fashioned model, fitted with brass hardware and probably weighing in the vicinity of a zillion pounds. Well, not quite. And I do admire those crates. I even own a few, antiques, really, that I inherited from my mother. But for shows, I use Vari-Kennels, which weigh almost nothing, or my Central Metal folding crates, not some

weighty collection of flashy, unnecessary, and imprac-
tical gear that has to be loaded into the car, unloaded
onto a dolly, hauled to the grooming area, set up, and
eventually, broken down, reloaded onto the dolly,
hauled back to the car, and loaded into the car, only
to be unloaded at home, and so forth. For a cluster of
three or four shows where Rowdy and Kimi are both
entered, my cousin Leah and I take a fair amount of
paraphernalia: crates, crate dolly, grooming table, tack
box, chairs for ourselves, a cooler, maybe, and other
odds and ends. But heavy, cumbersome wooden crates,
no matter how impressive? They're for people who pay
other people to do the lifting and moving. I wondered
how many trips it had taken Wilson to get this stuff in
here. And how much he'd paid for all of it.

Then I turned my attention to Llio. Like malamutes,
corgis are extremely intelligent and curious, but unlike
malamutes, they don't go out of their way to ingratiate
themselves with every fool who comes along. For a
corgi, Llio was almost cuddly. As I was stroking her
throat, advising Wilson to think about putting herding
and tracking titles on her, chatting with him about what
he fed her and what I fed my dogs, and so forth, Mrs.
Waggenhoffer's melodious but penetrating voice suddenly rang out. "Holly! I had no idea you had a Pembroke! Nice bitch!"

Mrs. Waggenhoffer occupied lots of space, vertically
and horizontally. In defiance of the stereotype, she
didn't have a pretty face. Her nose was tiny and
pointed, and her jowls large and prominent. Her wavy
white hair had always reminded me of the wigs worn

by barristers and judges in English courtroom dramas. Today, she had on a robelike black dress.

I waved and said, "Hi, Mrs. Waggenhoffer! The bitch isn't mine. Too bad for me! She took the breed today."

The grande dame—she really was one—came striding down the aisle of crates, and when she reached me, looked Llio over carefully and pronounced, "Very typey head! Really, overall, very nice!" *Typey* means "correct for the breed." If Lassie looks like what she is, a rough collie, then she's typey, but if a malamute's head reminds you of Lassie's, it's called a "collie head" and—horrors!—isn't typey.

"I heard your father got married," Mrs. Waggenhoffer said in a tone of odd triumph. "Is that true?"

After saying that it was, I immediately presented Gabrielle's credentials. "She has a bichon. They met at a show."

"Well, then, that's all right." Mrs. Waggenhoffer nodded her big head in such hearty approval that her jowls bounced. Pointing at Llio, she asked, "Who's handling this bitch? You?"

"I should hope not. Actually, I don't know who's handling her. Wilson?"

The next few moments threatened to become awkward. The day I'd first met Wilson, he'd given me the impression that he knew Mrs. Waggenhoffer. Now, it was clear that he merely knew who she was. I quickly introduced the two. Wilson looked painfully intimidated, as if he were being presented at the Court of Saint James's and not to the president of the Micmac

Kennel Club. Instead of just saying that he was happy to meet Mrs. Waggenhoffer and then immediately making some socially appropriate remark, in other words, almost anything about dogs, he stammered a shy, formal, "How do you do?"

The silence lasted only a few seconds. I was about to break it, but didn't have to, because the elder Mr. Trask did it for me. Navigating his way between the rows of crates that formed the aisle and around grooming tables, gear bags, jugs of water, coils of electric cord, and other dog-show accoutrements, he was trailed by Tim, Brianna, and the little girls. Pointing an accusatory finger as Mrs. Waggenhoffer, he abruptly demanded, "You! Are you Winifred?"

As I knew perfectly well, Winifred was Mrs. Waggenhoffer's first name. I was probably old enough to call her by it. I never did. She wouldn't have liked it.

Sounding more arrogant than she intended, I think, Mrs. Waggenhoffer responded with a question. "And who might you be?" Mrs. Waggenhoffer, as I hope I've suggested, is not the sort of ruffian who growls, *Yeah, and who wants to know?* But that was what she meant.

Instead of making sure that she was who she was, and instead of answering her question, George Trask pulled a sheet of paper from one of the pockets of his shabby jacket and began to shake it in the air and pelt her with questions. "Do you know what this is? And do you know how much my son paid for this dog? Is this your idea of fair? Is this—"

Mrs. Waggenhoffer blinked. Then she smiled in a way that people who didn't know her must have seen as condescending. I saw it as an effort to make light of an unpleasantness. But, of course, I'd known her all my life. "How could I possibly tell what that is when you're waving it around like that?" she said. "What in heaven's name is all this about?" By now, to my annoyance, she'd taken a step forward and was blocking my view. Still, her tone of voice suggested that rather than speaking directly to George Trask, she was addressing some distant personage far superior to the man right in front of her.

George Trask finally quit shaking the piece of paper. Peering around the bulk of Mrs. Waggenhoffer, I got a quick look at the paper and easily identified it as a pedigree. I also got a glimpse of the rest of the Trask family. Tim, now standing next to George, wore a sullen, bullish expression. Brianna's face was pale and pinched. The girls were peering through the wire mesh door of a Vari-Kennel. I hoped they knew better than to stick their fingers into the crate of an unfamiliar dog.

Feeling sorry for the Trasks, although far less sorry for George than for the others, I intervened. "These people, the Trasks," I said, "have a dysplastic golden. Naturally, they're very—"

"Pissed!" Tim Trask finished my sentence, although not quite as I'd intended. "Damn straight we are! Rightly so! And we're not stupid, you know! My father went to the library and looked it all up in books and on the computer, the Internet, and this isn't supposed to happen."

Mrs. Waggenhoffer was all sympathy. "Hip dysplasia is a real heartbreaker," she agreed. "But the good news is that in many, many cases, there's lots to be done about it. I can give you the name of an absolutely marvelous orthopedic surgeon, not that I've ever needed his services. Not with *my* lines." She paused. "Where did you get the dog?"

George Trask still had the pedigree in his hand. He thrust it at her. Unfortunately, she held it where I couldn't see it. In a few seconds, she said, "Now, I find this really quite odd. Timothy Trask?"

"That's me," the father said.

"But that's your dog's name!" Mrs. Waggenhoffer crowed.

Tim Trask was red faced. He looked even oilier than ever, but the shininess of his face seemed now to result from perspiration. "That was a mistake," he muttered. "The dog's name is Charlie."

His father sprang to his defense. "All that's beside the point. The point is that you people let these goddamn breeders get away with this, that's what the point is. You're head of this outfit, right?"

Mrs. Waggenhoffer couldn't let go of the error Tim had made in filling out the registration form. "You put *your* name where the dog's name was supposed to go? Well, I must admit that that's a new one to me!" Without intending to be mean, I think, she laughed merrily. "But the point, if you really do want to get to the point, is that all this pedigree shows is that your dog came from a backyard breeder. And that's that." She shrugged her broad shoulders. "This is exactly the sort of thing that happens when people don't do their homework. If you'd read up and surfed the web and so forth before you bought a puppy, you'd have ended up with a reputable breeder, and the chances are excellent that you'd have a lovely, sound, healthy dog." She tapped the pedigree with one finger. "Careful breeders, you know, screen for hip dysplasia. Sometimes the roll of the genetic dice tricks us, but we really do our best." Shaking her head back and forth, she added, "I'm terribly sorry to hear about the trouble you're having, but you should have gone to a careful breeder to begin with and not to this"—she consulted the pedigree—"to this Sylvia Metzner, whoever *she* is."

Standing just in back of me, Wilson caught his breath.

"The lying bitch isn't anyone anymore," George Trask said. "Sylvia Metzner is dead."

CHAPTER 26

"I owe you one for that." Wilson did indeed look pitifully grateful. He was referring, I felt certain, to my discretion in not telling Mrs. Waggenhoffer that the late Sylvia Metzner had been his mother-in-law. If I'd spoken up, the Trasks would probably have given him a hard time, but I'd have bet anything that Mrs. Waggenhoffer was the one he cared about. As it was, he'd been presented to that formidable lady as the owner of the admirable Pembroke Welsh corgi bitch who'd just gone Best of Breed, and I hadn't spoiled Mrs. Waggenhoffer's glowing first impression of Wilson by announcing that he was also the son-in-law of a backyard breeder of dysplastic golden retrievers, in other words, the kin by marriage of scum.

Wilson and I were once again outside the freestyle ring. This time, Llio was with us, mainly because her owner had used her as an excuse to escape the scene with Mrs. Waggenhoffer and the Trasks. A dog, of course, is a great social convenience when it comes to gracefully fleeing any awkward, nasty, or boring situation that occurs indoors. All you do is glance at the dog, slap an expression of urgency on your face, and cry, *Sorry to rush off, but my dog needs to go out—now!* Who's going to argue with that? Off you go!

Displaying the opportunism drummed into me by Alaskan malamutes, I'd seized on Wilson's departure as the chance to make my own retreat. Offering no explanation, I'd simply told Mrs. Waggenhoffer that I'd see her later. Then I'd tried to disappear. Unfortunately, I'd made my move so fast that when Wilson had happened to look back, he'd spotted me and waited, and I'd been unable to shake him. Here he still was, outside the freestyle ring. Inside, a thin woman in black and white and her black-and-white Border collie moved fluidly and rhythmically to the music of "Embraceable You." The very name of Rowdy's intended! Well, the name of my intended for him, Emma, CH Jazzland's Embraceable You, and at the risk of digressing, let me note that we dog devotees appreciate such apparent serendipity for what it really is, namely, a welcome reminder of the divine purpose and celestial harmony everywhere evident here in our happy constellation of Canis Major.

Where was I? In truth, scanning for Steve Delaney, who turned up at shows now and then, sometimes in obedience with his shepherd, India, sometimes alone. He liked to wander around and watch the competition. I ran my eyes over the crowd, but didn't see him. In marrying Anita, he'd probably ended his dog-show

THE WICKED FLEA

days. Goddamn! So, he married someone else. But did
he have to marry someone who hated dogs? With my
own eyes, I'd seen Anita kick Steve's gentle, timid
pointer, Lady. On another occasion, Anita had stepped
on Lady's foot. Sneak that Anita was, she'd made sure
Steve wasn't watching. By now, he must have seen or
at least sensed her viciousness.

"You don't owe me anything," I told Wilson. Irra-
tionally, I blurted out, "No one owes me anything!"

Ignoring the outburst, he said, "Yes, I do!"

"You didn't decide to breed Zsa Zsa."

"Neither did Mrs. Waggenhoffer," Wilson pointed
out. "But you can see why those people decided to go
after her. She's *very* eminent in goldens. And in the
entire fancy. They probably imagine that people like
her can get rid of irresponsible people like Sylvia."

I must have looked startled. Someone *had* gotten rid
of Sylvia.

Having evidently absorbed what he'd just said, Wilson looked embarrassed and added, "You know, stop
them from breeding."

"If only," I said.

"Those people called Sylvia, you know," Wilson
confided. "And Sylvia treated them like dirt. Her attitude was that it was their dog, so it was their problem.
She thought the whole thing was a big fuss over nothing. Sylvia *would* think that. You touch Zsa Zsa's rear,
and she hollers, and Sylvia never even took her to a
vet—no shots, no heartworm test, nothing. And there
she is, running around loose. She probably *has* heartworm, for God's sake."

With Sylvia dead, whose dog was Zsa Zsa? The sad, nasty golden was an inheritance no one would want. But who was inheriting the house? And anything else Sylvia might've owned? At a guess, Pia, Oona, and Eric, her three children, would inherit equally. But maybe not. If I'd been in the heirs' situation, I'd've felt a moral responsibility to make things right with the Trasks; the cost of Charlie's surgery would've felt like a debt that had to be paid. When it comes to dogs, though, and especially when it comes to responsibility for puppies, I get carried away. I struggled not to impose my exacting standards on Sylvia's children. If they'd felt like helping the Trasks, I'd have admired them. But if Wilson, the only dog person in the family, sensed no obligation, it seemed highly unlikely that any of the others would assume responsibility.

"What's going to happen to her now?" I asked. "To Zsa Zsa?"

"Eric wants to keep her. I told him he had to take her to the vet. Her hips are bad. You can tell by looking at her. Her elbows are probably bad, too. She's obese. Her teeth are a mess. God knows what else. But I'm not having her around Llio unless Eric gets her shots and gets her wormed. At a minimum."

The weird thing about Wilson's take on Zsa Zsa was its strong resemblance to my take on him. Not that his hips or elbows were bad, but his teeth did need cleaning, and whenever I'd seen him, he'd looked as if he could use a good bath. At a guess, he wasn't up to date on his tetanus shots, either.

"You know," he went on, "you can't blame those people, those Trasks."

"I don't. I feel sorry for them. How do they tell those little girls that their dog has to die because there's no money for surgery? Or are they supposed to keep the dog the way he is? That dog is in pain. You can tell. And the pain is only going to get worse. It's a degenerative disease. What are they supposed to do?"

"Sylvia bought our house twenty-five years ago," Wilson said in a near whisper. "She bred that litter before I even met Pia, but Sylvia was living there when those puppies were whelped. So the people who bought the puppies must've come to the house."

"And?"

"And so these Trasks knew where to find Sylvia."

"Are you suggesting. . . ?"

"They *could've*. And it's not just that Sylvia sold them that puppy. It's how she treated them when they called."

"Did you actually hear the conversation?"

"Sylvia's end of it. And what she said about it after. She thought it was a joke. She was nasty. Condescending. The truth is that Sylvia was a condescending person. She had no sympathy for people who were less fortunate than she was. You couldn't blame these Trasks if they wanted to get back at her. Well, if they just *hated* her, you couldn't blame them. But you know, they could've hung around the house and watched until they saw her go out. Alone. They *could've*."

"Not all of them," I said lightly.

"That old man looks like the brightest of them."

With some misgivings, I said, "George, that's his name. George Trask. I know what you mean. He has some spark."

The matching black-and-white Border collie team bowed and drew loud applause. Wishing I'd been free to give their performance my full attention, I joined in. Picking up on the break as a cue to move along, Llio trained her intelligent eyes on Wilson's face and shifted on her short Corgi legs. I wished that Wilson had her social savvy. For one thing, if I couldn't really watch the freestyle demo, how was I going to write about it? For another, greatly though I admired Llio, I just didn't like Wilson. For one thing, his dirtiness repelled me. I shower all the time, and my dogs are so clean that you could eat off them, at least if you didn't mind picking a few hairs off your tongue. For another, I didn't like his bootlicking attitude toward Mrs. Waggenhoffer and, to some extent, toward me, too.

Idly reflecting on my preference for clean, proud men, I felt a wave of longing for Steve Delaney and was busily pining for his subtle odor of veterinary disinfectant and his total incapacity for sucking up to anyone when Wilson interrupted my romantic musing. "The more I think about it," he said, "the more I think . . . look, you know what?"

Slovenly, bootlicking, and vacuous, too. Q.E.D., as certain residents of Cambridge say. Aloud! Which reminds me, Wilson was pretentious, too. The million-dollar crate? To my annoyance, he persisted in building a case against the Trasks, especially the elder Mr.

Trask, as the culprits in Sylvia's murder. Until then, I'd assumed that Wilson's powers of imagination extended maybe as far as envisioning Llio's taking a Group I—first place—later this same afternoon. To my surprise, he elaborated on his murder-by-Trask theory with lurid relish. "That George plans it, and they lurk around, the two of them, George and the son, what's his name—"

"Tim," I supplied.

"Whatever. And they follow Sylvia into the park, and the plan is, see, that they're going to *threaten* her with the gun. So there she is, saying a few last words over Ian's ashes, you see, that's why she's off the beaten path, so to speak, so she can have a few, uh, reverent moments alone and not just dump him in the dirt, and these guys sneak up on her. And it's the young one who's holding the gun, but the sneaky old man does the talking. 'Fork over the dough, or you're dead meat, Sylvia!' "

Dead meat? Everything about the proposed scenario struck me as ludicrous. Among other things, I couldn't see George Trask turning over control of anything, including a gun, to someone else. Besides, as I knew and Wilson didn't, the Trasks had already concocted a scheme to get the money for Charlie's surgery, namely, the plot into which Kimi had unintentionally leaped.

"Only," Wilson continued, his little eyes bright with enthusiasm, "the son, Tim, he's not the cool customer the old man is, and he panics, and his finger jerks, and BANG! The gun goes off! And Sylvia drops the urn and smashes it, and she goes, uh, tumbling after." He blinked as the Jack-and-Jill phrase registered on him.

"Wasn't Sylvia shot twice?" I asked.

"Well," said Wilson, "once they shot her by accident, they had to finish the job, didn't they? When they saw what they'd done . . ."

Just like Lizzie Borden, I thought. *And when she saw what she had done . . .*

"She gave her father forty-one," I blurted out.

"What?"

"Nothing," I muttered.

"Someone's got to go to the police about this," Wilson said.

I brought a finger to my lips. Only a few yards away, Brianna Trask and the children, Di and Fergie, were easing their way to ringside. Once again, I cursed Wilson for interfering with my freedom to watch the performances. In the ring now were a tiny Asian woman and her P.B.G.V—Petit Basset Griffon Vendeen, low to the ground like the familiar basset hound, but with a wiry coat and other more subtle differences. Same sense of humor, though! The music was country, a song I didn't recognize with themes I did: loss, cheating, and revenge. The dog was fantastic. He heeled on the handler's right, switched to the left, spun around, raised his right forepaw, then his left, and took a flashy bow. Fantastic, yes, but probably no better than my dogs could be . . . with a little work. Rowdy and Kimi were bright and agile, and not to brag or anything, but their heeling was already close to dancing, and as to showmanship, Rowdy, in particular, glittered with charisma. The tiniest bit of work, and my dogs . . .

The faces of the little girls interrupted my dreams of glory, probably because their expressions were identical to mine. With enchantment in their eyes, they followed the P.B.G.V.'s exit from the ring. Little Di's high voice rose above the applause. "Charlie can do that!" she announced. "Charlie can do that, only better!" Her pride in her dog was as strong as my pride in Rowdy and Kimi. The difference was this: my dogs were sound and healthy, whereas Charlie couldn't walk without pain, never mind dance.

Turning to Wilson, I said quietly, "This family had every reason to hold a grudge against Sylvia, and since they're here today and going after Mrs. Waggenhoffer, it's obvious that they want moral satisfaction, justice, something like that. And they must've had it in for Sylvia, too. But they did not kill her for money, Wilson. They've already got a plan for that. I know because I stumbled into it. Well, I didn't. My Kimi did." As objectively as possible, I summarized the incident at S & I's Burgerhaven and described the article in the paper about the lawsuit. "What they're up to," I said urgently, "isn't exactly ethical or admirable. But they're desperate. Those children love that dog! And these are children who have almost nothing. I know it's not right. There's no reason why the restaurant should suffer. And even if the Trasks had *found* something revolting in the food, I'm not sure that suing S & I's would be the best thing. But I'm in no position to judge. And I obviously can't go to the police or the courts or whatever, because I *know* what the Trasks are up to, but I don't have any proof at all. But when you see those little girls with the dog, and when you listen to them and hear how much they love him, you can see why the grownups would stoop to this phony lawsuit. Wilson, it's obvious that after they called Sylvia and didn't get anywhere with her, they gave up on her, and they decided to go after the breed clubs and the kennel clubs, for the moral satisfaction. They hatched this scheme—"

I broke off. Wilson was staring at me. "S & I's," he said.

"Yes. It's a burger joint, really. Fried clams. That kind of thing. This was the one on Route 20. It's a local chain. But—"

"I know what S & I's is," he said, looking stunned. "And you don't?"

"Yes I do. I just told you."

"S & I's," he informed me, "is the family business. Pia's father started it. Then Sylvia took over. Get it? S and I. Sylvia and Ian. It was *Sylvia's* restaurant."

CHAPTER 27

Subj: Re: Genetic Clearances
From: HollyWinter@amrone.org
To: Jazzland@pnwmals.org

Hi Cindy,

Many thanks for sending Emma's OFA* information
and all the rest. My scanner is acting up, so I have
Xeroxed and snail-mailed you the information about
Rowdy. You've probably checked the OFA database
online, but I've sent the certificates, anyway. His
hips are OFA Excellent, and his elbows are normal.
Obviously, chondrodysplasia** isn't an issue in our

---

*OFA, the Orthopedic Foundation for Animals, maintains databases
that allow breeders to assess inherited problems, including hip dysplasia. Search online! http://www.offa.org.—H. W.
**CHD, chondrodysplasia ("dwarfism"), is a genetic disease that af-

lines, but he's CHD clear. As you can see on the CERF*** web site, Rowdy's last eye exam was in August, and his eyes are clear. I have mailed you a copy of Dr. Fabian's full report. Everything was normal. I had a full thyroid panel**** done in June. The Michigan State report is in the packet I sent, all normal. By the way, Rowdy has full dentition and a PERFECT scissors bite. If dogs could model for toothpaste commercials, I'd be rich.

Holly

---

fects the bones and joints. In Alaskan malamutes, it causes a particular kind of anemia. The trait is recessive. Rowdy has a very low probability of being a carrier.—H. W.

***CERF, the Canine Eye Research Foundation, is more or less the OFA for eye disease. See for yourself at http:///www.umdb.org/cerf.html.—H. W.

****Hypothyroidism is quite common in dogs. Here, I am presenting evidence that Rowdy is not hypothyroid. Careful breeders place their greatest trust in the results of thyroid testing done by the Animal Health Diagnostic Laboratory at Michigan State University's College of Veterinary Medicine, Interested? http://www.ahdl.msu.edu/ahdl/ctr.htm.—H. W.

CHAPTER 28

Subj: Re: Genetic Clearances
From: HollyWinter@amrone.org
To: Jazzland@pnwmals.org

Hi Cindy,

It isn't exactly a genetic clearance, but I forgot to mention that Rowdy has absolutely outstanding pigment. His eyes are so dark that they're almost black. Even his gums are black.

I'll get a new brucellosis* test. At the moment, I'm without a regular vet. It's complicated. I'll tell you

---

*Canine brucellosis is a contagious disease that causes sterility and miscarriage. A sexually transmitted disease, it can also spread via infected tissue and bodily fluids.—H. W.

about it when you and Emma are here. My animals aren't the issue. I am. I can always use Angell Memorial. Come to think of it, I could do with an angel myself.

Holly

CHAPTER 29

S & I's. Sylvia and Ian's. The Trasks' rodent ruse
no longer seemed quite so foolish, and Wilson's sus-
picions about the Trasks didn't seem quite so ridiculous. As I interviewed Erna L. Sporter, my mind's eye
kept seeing the faces of the little Trask girls, and my
ears rang with little Di's proud claim about her dog:
Charlie can do that! Charlie can do that, only better!
In dog heaven. In this life, what lay ahead for Charlie
was a shaved foreleg and then a green needle. Unless
the Trasks won their lawsuit. Now that I knew who
owned—or had owned—S & I's, I half hoped they did.

Although freestyle is a super upbeat sport and although Erna and her Dalmatian were two of its most
upbeat enthusiasts, the interview depressed me, mainly
because I'd already written the same kind of article a
few hundred times, as had a few hundred other dog
writers. The topic could've been worse, meaning that
I could've been writing about what to feed (or not to

feed) your dog, how to keep your dog cool in the summer heat, or how to prevent and cure flea infestations, an itchy subject I'd scratched so many times that merely thinking about it gave me human hot spots. Anyway, Erna's Dalmatian, Eddie, had three legs. Not credits-toward-a-title legs, earned by qualifying the required number of times, but four Dalmatian legs minus the one he'd had removed.

Dogs with three legs do so well that it seems apparent that every dog is born with a spare one, and Eddie was perfectly used to having only three legs and performed nimbly on them, so he was not the cause of my bad mood. Or maybe I should say that Eddie wasn't the direct cause. What got to me was that Erna, who was tiny and wiry, kept chirping about how much Eddie loved the music he'd chosen for his routine and how excited he got about performing and on and on until I couldn't help asking myself, If this dog can *love* and *dance* and have *fun* for God's sake on three legs, why can't I manage to shuffle along a little more happily without Steve Delaney? To make matters worse, as if comparing Steve to an amputated Dalmatian leg weren't bad enough, I immediately realized that he was the only man on earth who wouldn't feel even mildly insulted by the analogy. So then I started thinking about that feminist slogan. You know the one? *A woman without a man is like a fish without a bicycle.* And what I started thinking was—need I remind you that I train dogs?—that a clever animal trainer would have no difficulty in teaching a fish to ride a specially constructed underwater bicycle. Fin-propelled pedals.

Bubble steering. And after the fish had gotten really good at riding the bicycle? And you went and took the bicycle away? Well, you'd end up with a fish who missed the bicycle, which is to say, one very sad fish.

"Holly, are you all right?" Erna asked gently. "I heard about your accident. Is there anything I can do?"

With that, she began rummaging in a capacious tote bag and was soon offering me antidotes for anything that might ail me. Beware of accepting medical help from dog people, including me. Half the time, we'll dose you with ordinary over-the-human-pharmacy-counter medications that are good for both dogs and people, but we're equally likely to offer the veterinary salve that worked wonders on Fido's sore ear or the painkillers Lady didn't use up after she was spayed. In this case, Erna produced a vial of dried vegetation that looked like marijuana, but was, she insisted, a potent herbal remedy that cured Eddie of his periodic bouts of stage fright. I was supposed to put the stuff under my tongue and hold it there for as long as I could without swallowing. I was on the verge of asking how she got Eddie to comply with those instructions when all of a sudden, I saw myself as if from afar, and everything hit me as simply too crazy, the tiny woman who danced with the three-legged dog, the prospect of doping myself with dog medicine, the training possibilities of fish and bicycles, and I rapidly excused myself and fled. According to the Bible, it's the wicked who flee—when no man pursueth.

When I got home, Kimi and Rowdy were so thrilled to see me that they dashed around, bounced in the air, and sang loud peals of *woo-woo-woo*. As Kimi had so forcefully demonstrated at S & I's, malamutes exhibit what is known as "genetic hunger," meaning that they enjoy a genetically programmed conviction that they are in ever-present danger of starving to death. In the breed's Arctic homeland, the danger was real. In my well-stocked Cambridge kitchen, Rowdy and Kimi eat as if it still were. For that reason, I cannot just feed my dogs in a normal sort of way by dumping kibble into dishes and putting them on the floor, and I wouldn't dream of just leaving food out. Even with peaceable breeds, free feeding is usually a bad idea. Dogs with constant access to a full bowl often get fat. Some, in contrast, turn into picky eaters. Worse, free-fed dogs have a tendency to become aggressive, in part because they are spared frequent reminders of their dependence on human beings for life's essentials. Well, enough preaching. My dogs eat twice a day, the second meal being dinner, served at approximately five o'clock, and since the time was now five-fifteen, Rowdy and Kimi were performing their own version of freestyle to their own music. To prevent them from getting into a snarling, bloody fight, I have to separate them. I'd just finished hitching Kimi to the hall door at one end of the kitchen and Rowdy to the living room door at the other end when the phone rang.

I grabbed it. "Hello?" Or that's what I presume I said. The dogs' shrieking made it impossible to hear anything. I should've let the machine pick up, but I'm active in malamute rescue, and I'm always afraid of missing a life-or-death call. Most people will leave a message, call back, or visit our web site (www.malamuterescue.org), but every once in a while, the call is from a malamute owner or a shelter worker who tells me that a sweet, friendly malamute is going to be put down immediately unless someone helps. Since I couldn't hear this caller at all, I shouted a plea to call me back in a few minutes. Then I hung up and fed the dogs. In the twenty seconds it took them to clean their bowls, I checked the caller-ID box. Its display read Private Call Number Blocked. He'd been ringing me quite often, probably to invite me to dinner at a trendy restaurant. My most ardent suitor, however, was Out of Area, who was always trying to reach me in the hope, no doubt, of seducing me into spending a romantic weekend with him in some charming out-of-area country inn. Data Error called occasionally, but I didn't like the sound of him one single bit (Date Error?) and was happy to miss his calls.

Not that I needed to feel like Miss Popularity. After all, even though it was Saturday evening, I had plenty of things to occupy me and was a few years beyond the absolute need for a date. Reminding myself of my age didn't help a lot. To boost my spirits, I decided to walk the dogs. They, at least, wanted to go out with me, even if no one else did. And when they're with me, I draw a whole lot of admiring glances. The dogs and I had barely descended my back stairs when we ran into Rita. By now, night had fallen, and the temperature with it, and Rita was hurrying to get indoors to warm up and get ready to go out with Artie Spicer, who was her birding mentor and the man in her life.

Approximately two seconds after the back door had shut itself behind Rita, the dogs and I reached the sidewalk, and Kevin Dennehy's great bulk loomed out of a shadow and startled me. He was leaving to pick up Jennifer Pasquarelli and didn't have time to talk.

I should mention that my neighborhood is interesting and diverse. It has single-family and multifamily dwellings, the Hi-Rise bakery, the Fishmonger, gourmet take-out shops, a branch of the Cambridge Public Library, a fabulous restaurant—Aspasia, on Walden Street—and an extraordinary number of renovated three-deckers cut up into psychotherapy offices. So why had Rita sent me all the way out to Newton? If I was too crazy for Cambridge, I was in terrible trouble. Anyway, my heterogeneous neighborhood borders the homogeneous magnificence of the area around Brattle Street, and the dogs and I often take advantage of our proximity to the grand colonials and Victorians and the splendid gardens of Off Brattle. I gawk and fantasize. Rowdy and Kimi snuffle with special enthusiasm, as if the privileged dogs who inhabit the twenty-room houses anoint their shrubs and trees with posh-smelling urine that simply begs for overmarking by tough-guy malamutes.

Tonight, instead of choosing the opulent route, I made the mistake of heading up Concord Avenue in the direction of the Square, turning right onto Huron, and following it, thus passing shops where couples had bought wine, cheese, and other delicacies that they were now sharing, a pizzeria where couples were placing orders and nibbling slices, and, worst of all, couples themselves. Cambridge being Cambridge, the couples were old, young, academic, townie, heterosexual, gay, lesbian, and ethnically everything. It should, but perhaps does not, go without saying that all these people had one thing in common: each member of every couple was paired off. Kevin Dennehy was with Jennifer Pasquarelli. Rita was going out with Artie Spicer. Grubby Wilson was married to athletic Pia. My father was married to Gabrielle. Tim and Brianna Trask had each another. Sylvia and Ian Metzner had been united as S & I. In front of a toy store on Huron Avenue, an expectant mother pointed out something in the window to a man whose arm rested on her shoulders. Rowdy would, I hoped, be bred to Emma. Still, he and Kimi were a pair. Ahead of me, they made a handsome brace.

Steve Delaney would have married me. He'd asked. Often. I'd refused. Often. It had never crossed my mind that he'd marry someone else.

Cutting our walk short, I headed home. When I reached the back door, the phone was ringing, but by the time I answered it, Private Call Number Blocked had hung up. The answering machine showed no messages.

Sitting on the kitchen counter near the machine was a terrific book that Gabrielle had given me, *Urban Foxes* by Stephen Harris. I tried to read it, but it depressed me. Foxes live in family groups. My third-floor tenants, a couple, naturally, were away for the weekend, and since Rita was also going out, I decided that I was free to stink up the place by working on my own book. A friend had E-mailed me a new recipe for liver brownies. Like brownies for people, liver brownies (no chocolate, which is toxic to dogs) are an old standby, so I didn't want to embarrass myself by including a recipe that didn't work. To forestall another kind of embarrassment, let me mention that testing the recipes didn't require my tasting the products. Ugh. Rather, the testing consisted simply of making sure that the goodies solidified in proper dog-treat fashion and held together after they'd cooled. As taste-testers, Rowdy and Kimi were useless, since they gave dewclaws up to absolutely anything. Their own recipes are simple and effortless, but a bit too disgusting and, in some cases, graphic to appear in my book. The dogs have, however, persuaded me to share a few here.

Master Recipe for Garbage
Toss on floor. Turn dog loose.

Smorgasbord
Open refrigerator door. Forget to close.

Lapin Tartare
Turn loose in confined area:
1 live rabbit

Turn loose in same confined area:
1 live malamute

Yield: 1 live malamute

Revolting! You can see why I'd never publish so-called recipes like those. Having subjected you to dog recipes, I feel compelled to compensate by offering a real one. My basic recipe for the liver used to bait show dogs came from Charlene LaBelle, a comrade in malamutes and the author of the classic book about backpacking with dogs.

Charlene's Famous Liver Bait

Put liver in a big pot, cover with water, and add one clove of garlic for every pound of liver. Boil for twenty minutes. Drain. Remove accumulated gunk by rinsing liver under running lukewarm water. Towel it dry. Bake it at 250 degrees for two to three hours, depending on its thickness. It's done when it's dry.

A few hints. Unless you have truly nauseating food preferences, discard the garlic as soon as possible. You can freeze liver and probably should, because liver contains lots of vitamin A and therefore should be doled out in small amounts to prevent an overdose. Oh, and if you can't stand the stink of liver, substitute beef heart, not that it smells fabulous. If it did, would dogs like it? And the very idea of eating *heart*!

As in eating your heart out?

Anyway, I was preparing to test the brownie recipe. The oven was preheating, and a mess of chicken liver was defrosting in the microwave when the phone rang again. The second I answered, Private Call Number Blocked hung up, but called again ten minutes later and then ten minutes after that, each time cutting the connection as soon as I'd said hello. By that time, the brownies were baking, and the house reeked, so I opened a lot of windows and took refuge in my study, which is the home of my computer and my cat, Tracker, and is off limits to the dogs. A short-haired black cat, Tracker was attractive if you couldn't see her face, which was disfigured by a white splotch, a squiggly birthmark, and the remains of a torn ear. She was as ill tempered as she was homely. Steve Delaney was the only person she'd ever liked. She purred for him. So far, my efforts to befriend her hadn't been reciprocated, and the behavior-modification program I was following to train the dogs to accept her was moving much more slowly than I had hoped. I still had to be careful to keep the study door closed, with Tracker on one side and the dogs on the other. Life in the confines of one room was less than ideal for Tracker, but she got food, water, shelter, clean litter, and offers of human companionship, and I continued to feel hopeful about convincing the dogs that she was a member of our pack.

After slipping dogless into my study, I closed the door, dislodged Tracker from the mouse pad, checked my E-mail, and worked on organizing the recipes into chapters. I'd just finished inserting Liver Baba au Rhum in the dessert chapter when, to my surprise, the doorbell rang—and the bell for the front door at that. My friends use the back door. The front bell means a delivery from UPS or FedEx, or a visit from a stranger. On Saturday night?

Taking care to shut Tracker in my study, I headed for the front door. The dogs were more interested in our unexpected visitor than they were in the cat, anyway. Malamute interest in visitors is usually inaudible. Rowdy and Kimi ran ahead of me, tails happily wagging, and waited silently at the door. I had to push past them to ease it open.

Standing there all by herself on *my* porch at *my* door on Saturday night was Anita Fairley, also known as Anita Fairley-Delaney, the wife of Steve Delaney, and not a person who was in the habit of paying me visits. The porch light shone on her coat, which I told myself must be raccoon, even though its thick, dark gray fur was conspicuously reminiscent of the glorious coats of my own dogs. On Anita's otherwise beautiful face was an expression of distaste. If I hadn't known her, I'd have assumed she was responding to the stench of liver that emanated from the oven. But I knew Anita and recognized her characteristic expression.

Before I had time to think of something unwelcoming to say to Anita, she barged in. Turning her perfectly coiffed head left and right to make her long blond hair sway, she demanded with her usual arrogance, "Where is he?"

Kimi and Tracker are female. Anita obviously didn't mean Rowdy. For one thing, his presence at my left side was impossible to miss. For another, Anita hated dogs. I didn't answer the question.

"Has something died here?"

Once again, I didn't answer. Why bother? Literary endeavor such as mine was far beyond the comprehension of philistines like Anita.

Striding ahead of me, Anita entered my living room.

Finding no one there, she surveyed the kitchen, where she peered at the open windows. The brownies were obviously beginning to scorch, but I left them in the hot oven. The burning liver provided the perfect olfactory equivalent to a sound track. The thought crossed my mind that this stinking situation was beyond the understanding of the dogs and that it was a shame to subject them to all the bad feeling without being able to explain its cause. Stupid thought. As if dogs didn't understand territory, possession, rivalry, loyalty, and rage.

Tossing her head and picking a door at random, Anita abruptly threw open the one to my bedroom. Kimi followed her in. Then out. It was clear to me by now that Rowdy had placed himself in charge of me and my safety and that Kimi had assigned herself the task of monitoring Anita. Under Kimi's gaze, Anita checked out the bathroom. Then the guest room. Each time she entered a room, I nodded lightly to the dogs, who understood perfectly that I was tolerating this search of the premises, but could bring it to a halt whenever I chose.

When Anita reached toward the door of my study, I made that choice. "No," I said in my dog-training voice. "My cat's in there. She can't be loose with the dogs."

Anita made eye contact with me. She said nothing.

"Steve isn't the kind of man who'd cheat on his wife," I told her. "Any wife. He just wouldn't. No matter what."

With a nasty smile, Anita exclaimed, "Ever the little moralist!"

I didn't know whether she meant Steve or me, and I didn't ask.

"I saw you at the house," Anita said. "Spying on me."

Spying? By getting there first? Still, I didn't challenge the interpretation. I just said, "At the Metzners'."

Anita corrected me. "The Delaneys'." Then she laughed. "The Metzners! Horrible little people! Mommy couldn't get the kiddies to move, so she decided to sell the house out from under them! Pitiful!"

"Sylvia Metzner is dead," I pointed out. "She was murdered."

"Yes, wasn't she." With that, Anita darted her hand to the study door and threw it open. Her purpose? By now, she must've realized that Steve wasn't hiding in a closet in the manner of a cuckold in some French farce. Among other things, if I'd been harboring a secret lover, would I have chosen the time of the tryst to char liver? Anita's purpose, then, could only have been senseless malice: she was deliberately trying to expose my poor Tracker to my predatory dogs.

"Rowdy! Kimi!" I reached into a pocket and grabbed what were by now the ubiquitous liver treats. "This way!" I bounded toward my bedroom. The dogs followed. I shoved the goodies into their mouths and shut them in. Then I returned to Anita. "You fooled Steve," I told her, "and you've fooled a lot of other people, but you don't fool me. You just tried to kill my cat, and what's worse, you tried to use my dogs to do it. I don't know where Steve is, but if he's avoiding you, I don't blame him one bit. Get out of my house, and get out now!"

With a sneer, Anita put her nose in the air, wrapped herself tightly in her simulated malamute coat, and marched out my front door.

Good riddance! But when Anita left, the house felt empty. Steve wasn't, of course, hiding in a closet or under the bed. Still, I couldn't help wishing she'd been right.

CHAPTER 30

I was a fan of Sherlock Holmes even before I met Althea Battlefield, but my friendship with her renewed my interest and pleasure in the adventures of the Great Detective. Not that I'm exactly eligible for membership in the Baker Street Irregulars or the Adventuresses of Sherlock Holmes. But my admiration and enthusiasm pleased Althea, in part because my attitude contrasted sharply with Ceci's refusal to share the absorbing passion of Althea's life. Ceci's late husband was also an ardent Sherlockian, as were Althea's closest friends, Hugh and Robert, and Ceci maintained that she had endured all that one person could be expected to tolerate of Holmes, Watson, Greek interpreters, and the like. Although Althea never said so outright, in her heart she believed that Ceci was too stupid to appreciate the brilliance of Holmes. On that point, I disagreed with Althea; Ceci was silly, I thought, but not stupid. Still, I valued Althea's good

opinion of me and took pains not to be lumped with
the Sherlock-ignorant likes of Ceci. As Rita once remarked, "Althea is one of your good mothers." I
pointed out that the original, my own mother, had been
a good one, but Rita said that all of us could use all
the good mothers we could get. Consequently, my feelings about Althea were nothing to be ashamed of. Wise
Rita! Had Dr. Foote ever said anything half so insight-
ful? Not in my hearing.

On Sunday morning, with the presumed blessing of
at least one of my good mothers—Althea—I phoned
Steve's clinic and played Sherlock Holmes by cleverly
disguising my voice. On Sunday? Steve kept the clinic
open on Sundays, albeit only from nine to one and with
a small staff. Even so, that's a committed vet for you.
But I digress. Anita had probably stopped Steve from
working on Sundays himself except in emergencies,
but I felt confident that someone other than Steve's
answering service would pick up the phone. I didn't
intend to talk to Steve, anyway. I just wanted to find
out where he was. Indeed, where *was* he? His wife
might not know, but his staff would.

I recognized the voice of the person who answered,
an assistant named Mary Kelly. Whenever Holmes
went undercover, so complete was his success in assuming his new identity that even Watson was taken
in. Feeling wonderfully self-confident, I spoke in the
low, gravelly, and sophisticated tones I'd practiced.
Hurling myself into the role, I said, "Hello! I wonder
whether you could tell me which veterinarians you
have there today?" I regretted the phrase as soon as it

left my lips. *Which veterinarians you have . . . ?* It sounded as if they were for sale! *Which brands of dog food do you carry?* But my verbal clumsiness turned out not to matter.

With no hesitation, Mary said, to my disappointment, "Holly, you sound terrible! Do you have the flu or something? Oh, no! It's one of your animals! You're crying. I'm so sorry. Which one is it? Steve isn't here. He's at a conference in Cleveland. But Dr. Greenberg can see you right away. It's not Rowdy, is it?"

Ignoring the slight to Kimi and Tracker, I assured Mary that my animals were fine. Stammering a little, I said, "I, uh, just had a question. It can wait. When did he leave for Cleveland? I, uh, happened to see Anita yesterday, so I assumed . . ."

"You won't catch her at a veterinary conference," Mary said sharply. "For God's sake, there just might be an animal there! I don't know if you've seen Steve lately, but he looks terrible. His skin is kind of gray, and you can hardly get a word out of him, not that he used to be exactly talkative, but we're all worried about him. That bitch is driving him crazy. She's totally paranoid! I mean, Holly, you know him, he doesn't even complain about her, for God's sake, and Friday she decided he wasn't really at the conference, and she must've called here ten times. He's in Cleveland! I talked to him yesterday. And *I* called him. I *placed* the call. He's *there*. But I think he must be avoiding her, so she's decided he's up to something. I hope he is! But he's not. I think he must just be avoiding her. Who could blame him? You know she's trying to make him move to Newton? Whoops. Someone's here. Gotta go. Bye."

If Mary was going to gossip like that, it was a good thing for her that Steve was, in fact, in Cleveland. If he'd overheard her talking like that about anyone, he'd have fired her instantly. But Mary had answered my question about where Steve was. So Steve looked terrible, did he? He might look ashen, but to my eyes, he'd still look pretty good. It cheered me to hear that he was probably just avoiding his horrible wife. What buoyed my spirits even more than that news was Mary's confirmation, more or less, of Anita's claim that she was buying Sylvia Metzner's house. Or had bought it? Just in case I haven't mentioned it recently, let me say that Anita was a crook. I'm not joking. Or exaggerating. She was under indictment, admittedly for the nonviolent crime of embezzlement. Still, Sylvia *had* been murdered. And Anita the criminal *had* been involved with Sylvia.

My spirits soaring, I made a fresh pot of coffee, all the while engaging in wishful thinking about Anita and Sylvia's murder. There was, I should emphasize, no question in my mind about whether Anita would have committed murder to get what she wanted; my only question—hope?—was whether she's actually done so. As I poured the coffee into a mug and added milk and sugar, I found myself thinking about the possible reinstatement of the death penalty in the Commonwealth of Massachusetts. I'd always opposed the death penalty. At the moment, I wavered. Settling at the kitchen table, I did what dog writers do when confronting the typical problems of the profession, such as dreaming up new and fresh ways to tell readers how to win the battle against fleas, except in this case, I was setting out to explain to myself how to win the battle against an evil rival by proving her guilty of homicide. My method was the familiar one. No matter what the nature of the task, it's a matter of pride with me to take a professional approach, meaning that I overdose on caffeine and talk to my dogs.

"Chronological order," I said to Rowdy. "Kimi, the dishwasher is securely latched, so don't bother even trying to open it. Besides, the dishes are clean, so you're wasting your time. Chronology. Ian Metzner dies. I don't know when. A few years ago. Sylvia has his body cremated. She puts his ashes in a blue-and-white ceramic urn. And leaves them there. Sylvia breeds Zsa Zsa. The Trasks buy one of the puppies. They name him Charlie. Wilson marries Pia, who is one of Sylvia's two daughters. Pia and Wilson live with Sylvia in her house in Newton, near the park. Sylvia's other daughter, Oona, is as crazy about sailing as I am about training and showing dogs, so instead of throwing away her money on rent, she also lives with Sylvia. The son, Eric, graduates from college and moves back home. He gets in minor trouble for drugs. He keeps his stash in the urn with his father's ashes. That's the background. Kimi, do not try to open the refrigerator! If you learn to do that, I am going to have to find some drastic and bizarre way to keep it shut, and I am quite eccentric enough already, thank you."

I poured myself more coffee and again took a seat at the table.

"Rowdy, you are a good boy to sit and listen to me. As I was saying, the Trasks really love Charlie, who has severe hip dysplasia. George Trask, the grandfather, reads up on it. He knows what hip replacements cost. The alternative is euthanasia. So the Trasks do what the books and the web say to do: they call the breeder, Sylvia Metzner. And Sylvia treats the Trasks like dirt. George Trask concocts a plan. Tim and Brianna follow it. They find out that Sylvia owns S & I's, they get hold of a rat tail, and they plant it in their food. Kimi intervenes. They try again. This time, they succeed. They get a lawyer. The aim: money for surgery and revenge on Sylvia. Rowdy, you are a much better Watson than Kimi is, do you know that? Kimi, there is no liver in the oven, as you can undoubtedly smell for yourself, young lady."

The better Watson, Rowdy, yawned, sank to the floor, and closed his eyes. Can you imagine Holmes being treated this way? But Kimi took on the role of Watson by leaping over the dozing Rowdy to plant herself next to me. "Strictly between us," I told her, "although both of you are brilliant, you are, in fact, the more intellectually gifted. Maybe you're Holmes and I'm Watson."

Kimi replied by tilting her head up and locking eyes with me.

"Assorted facts," I said to her. "An exhibitionist starts exposing himself in the park. To Pia, among others. Self-evidently, my dear Kimi, it's a crime that Anita Fairley couldn't have committed. Meanwhile, Wilson pours an insane amount of money even by my liberal standards into showing Llio. We all know what that costs, don't we? All the while Oona is earning little or nothing, and Eric is earning nothing and still spending on stuff that goes up his nose or in his veins. Sylvia wants to get this pack of bloodsuckers, A.K.A. her children, out of the house. In desperation, she sells it out from under them. To Anita. And Steve. I stupidly arm everyone in the park with air horns to drive off Zsa Zsa, who picks fights with the other dogs. Officer Jennifer Pasquarelli picks a fight with another woman, namely Sylvia, and arrests her. Not too long after that, Sylvia takes the urn with Ian's ashes to the park, presumably to scatter his remains. Someone shoots and kills her with a small-caliber handgun. She drops the urn on a rock. It breaks. That's on Sunday. On Tuesday her devoted family hasn't noticed her absence, except to observe that there's no food in the house. Douglas's admirable dog, but not half so admirable as you, Kimi, finds the body. And that's that. Always, Kimi, always start with what you know."

As if on their own, my eyes wandered in apparent search of knowledge I'd overlooked. My gaze moved from Kimi to Rowdy, then from spot to spot (no pun intended) in my kitchen. On the back door hung dozens of leashes. On top of the refrigerator were the results of my latest recipe research: dog treats. The refrigerator itself held the cheese and roast beef I use to train the dogs. On the floor next to the dogs' water bowls lay two fleece dog toys: a bear and a dinosaur. In the closet was dog food. Wisps of dog hair loitered near the baseboards. Stacked on the kitchen table were my notes about fatal dog attacks. And so forth. Dogs, dogs, dogs!

"Kimi," I said, "if it sometimes seems to you that I'm a little dense and slow, I can understand why you might form that opinion. So, let's start with what we *really* know, meaning malamutes, goldens, spaniels, mastiffs, Yorkies, Dalmatians, Labs, terriers . . . yes! Jennifer Pasquarelli, the voluptuous terrier. A lot of sparring and yapping. Strong character. Anita Fairley: a slinky, elegant hound, a spoiled house pet. Noah, the mayor of Clear Creek Park: a teddy bear of a dog. Nothing deadly so far. The Trasks? Kimi, you're the real dog expert here. After all, you're a dog yourself. What *are* the Trasks?"

I got up to pour myself another hit of caffeine. Regrettably, Kimi did not offer a verbal reply to my question. Instead, she tagged along as I added sugar to my coffee. Then she tried to poke her nose into the refrigerator when I got milk and had another go when I put the milk back. Since the book on urban foxes was lying in plain sight near the answering machine, I would dearly love to report that Kimi rose up, whacked the book with her paw, and sent it scuttling across the floor. Alas, *Urban Foxes* drew my attention with no help from Kimi.

Even so, I said, "Right you are, Kimi. The Trasks are doglike without actually being dogs. They live on the margin in a small family group. They cooperatively scrape by. They are scavengers. They are, in fact, urban foxes, especially that wily old George Trask. Do foxes kill people? They're too small. A rabid fox might bite someone. Otherwise, foxes don't even attack people. So, on to the Metzners."

Before I report what happened next, I must point out that fleas are the flies in the ointment of professional dog writing—not the insects themselves, but the need to write article after article, year after year, about flea control. I am an overpublished authority on the subject. My dogs do *not* have fleas. Nonetheless, Kimi suddenly dropped to the floor and began madly nibbling at her hindquarters exactly as if she had just been bitten.

"A dog with fleas," I said. "Thank you. *That's* what Sylvia Metzner was. Her house was infested with her own children. They lived off her. She chewed at them." When Llio had drenched Wilson's foot with urine, Sylvia had humiliated him. How had Sylvia responded to Pia's encounter with the exhibitionist? By ridiculing Pia, by nipping her own daughter.

Kimi was now peacefully sprawled out full length on her back. "And once again, you're right. I'm a dog expert, not a flea expert, and viewed as a dog, Oona is an open book, as you so graphically suggest. Oona is a sailor. Obsessed with water. A Chesapeake Bay retriever? No, a Portuguese water dog. No harm in that. And Pia? A poorly bred standard poodle. High strung, dependent, yes, but not nippy. We're down to two, kid. Eric and Wilson."

I remembered Ceci's account of the childish quarrel between Eric and Wilson at Newton Police Headquarters. Eric had wanted to use Wilson's cell phone. Wilson had refused. *I can just see that Eric as a little boy,* Ceci had commented, *and Wilson, too, the pair of them, silly, selfish children fighting over their toy trucks instead of this foolish cell phone, neither one of them wanting to share his toys.*

My view differed only slightly from Ceci's. Being who I emphatically am, I saw Eric and Wilson not as silly, selfish children, but as badly behaved dogs, the kinds of dogs who'll bite you if you try to take away their toys. I knew more than I wanted to know about dogs that inflicted fatal bites. According to my article-in-progress, the typical fatal-attacker was an intact male, improperly socialized, untrained or harshly trained, given inadequate nutrition and veterinary care, and—rather obviously—allowed loose or tied to a chain, not kept safely confined. Unsocialized dogs. Eric, untrained by his mother. Wilson, harshly treated by his ridiculing mother-in-law. Emotionally malnourished. Both, in effect, chained to Sylvia's money. Intact males. Dangerous? Fatally so.

CHAPTER 31

Subj: Update!
From: lizgreenberg@idwasegobe.com
To: Ritatheshrink@psychesrus.net

Rita, you were right, I do like E-mail! Tired as I am
of E-business, E-commerce, and E-everything E-
else, it is miraculous to be able to stay in touch
with Harvey while he is in the Netherlands without
waking him up by mistake. You'd think that they
wouldn't have given us our doctorates without making sure that we could remember which way the
time zones worked, wouldn't you? Boston is earlier
than here in the Bay Area, isn't it? Or is it later?
Well, hurrah for E-mail! Now I don't have to struggle to work out the planets spinning, the sun rising
in the east, and all the rest of that boring scientific
crap.

Sorry you couldn't make it to the Berkeley Countertransference Conference. The only person from your part of the country was Vee Foote, and I have to tell you, I was NOT impressed! Her presentation was banal and IMHO (aren't you impressed by my mastery of the jargon!:) In My Humble Opinion!!) probably unethical. How could any responsible therapist possibly try to justify using (abusing?) a patient to treat her own phobia? I was not really surprised. After all, Vee IS a psychiatrist! Honestly, psychologists are the only people who get any training at all in doing therapy. Thank God we didn't waste our time and creativity by going to medical school. Besides, I never have liked Vee.

Have to fly! Bowlby wants his walkies.

Liz

PS Don't show this to anyone!

CHAPTER 32

Subj: Re: Update!
From: Ritatheshrink@psychesrus.net
To: lizgreenberg@idwasegobe.com

Hi Liz,

Could I beg you for details about Vee's presentation? I referred a friend of mine to her—there are possible neurological issues—but I must confess that I'm now having second thoughts.

This may sound odd, but did Vee's case have anything to do with dogs?

Rita

CHAPTER 33

I see the world through dog-colored glasses. And just exactly what's *that* supposed to mean? If you have to ask, you're wearing the wrong spectacles.

Once I looked at Sylvia's murder from an unabashedly dog-centered perspective, everything fell into place. The profile of the fatal attacker pointed to the solution, and the solution felt right. Or the solutions, I should say. Plural. There obviously remained the trivial question of which of the men, Eric or Wilson, was actually guilty of the murder. Could they have acted together? Considered as dogs, Eric and Wilson did not constitute the kind of affiliated pair that would hunt as a pack.

The phone interrupted my thoughts. The caller was Althea. "Tea at four!" she reminded me. I had completely forgotten. "Ceci has splurged on raspberries," Althea continued. "And she wonders whether you would like to take the dogs to the park first. That's why I'm calling. She's run out to the store for cream." Althea paused. "I want you to know that you should feel entirely free to keep whatever previous engagement you may have made that will prevent you from accepting her suggestion."

I was tempted to seize on Althea's tactful offer of an easy way out, but the elderly sisters were my adopted aunts. I succumbed to a sense of family obligation. Also, Ceci knew how crazy I am about raspberries. I owed her one. I told Althea that I'd pick up Ceci and Quest at two o'clock.

And I did. To my surprise, when Ceci, Quest, Rowdy, and I arrived at the park, I felt happy to be there. The freakishly warm weather had returned. A few white clouds decorated the sky, and the grass remained unseasonably green. Better yet, the field had been claimed by a few dozen people who were engaged in an energetic game of baseball, and not a single member of the dog group was in sight, so I wouldn't be expected to accomplish the paradoxical task of walking Rowdy while both of us stood still.

"No one's here," remarked Ceci, meaning no one who counted, in other words, no one with a dog. People who show their dogs cling to the erroneous belief that pet owners can't be real dog people. Hah! Ceci was proof to the contrary.

I pointed out the self-evident: "We are."

To my relief, Ceci made no effort to linger around the parking area or the field, but eagerly strode toward the woods. Thriving under her care, Quest ambled at a pace that was slow for Rowdy and me, but decent for him. Taking the same trail we'd used the day Ulysses and Douglas had found Sylvia's body, we talked dog talk: Quest's positive response to his new drug regimen, the pros and cons of various brands of senior dog foods. We encountered remarkably few other people, with or without dogs: two or three runners, a grim-faced woman with a merry golden retriever, a young man who looked too exhausted to bear the weight of the yellow-haired baby in his backpack. The golden was on leash, and for once, no loose dogs were in sight. I heard not a single blast of an air horn; maybe the horrible fad I'd foolishly introduced had peaked and was declining. The footpath we'd followed to the scene of Sylvia's murder was now behind us, and we'd gone beyond the place where Douglas had turned back to search for Ulysses on the day the improbable hound had discovered her body.

Just ahead of us, the trail forked, and noticing the split, Ceci switched from the topic of dogs. "Like the Robert Frost poem! Except that they're paths, not roads, are they? And the woods are more brown than yellow, and those pines or spruces or whatever they are are still green, well, not *still*, since they're evergreens . . ."

Knowing Ceci, I expected her to add that the non-roads in the non-yellow wood hadn't actually diverged. She didn't. For once, she fell suddenly silent. Turning to her to see what was wrong, I found that she'd stopped to stare into the deep woods to our right. I felt no alarm, and neither of the dogs gave any indication of anything amiss. Quest was his usual bearlike, giant self. Rowdy's tail was sailing back and forth over his back, but malamutes carry their tails over their backs, and even for a malamute, Rowdy is an exceptionally happy boy. For a second, I panicked at the possibility that Ceci was having a heart attack. Quest had been setting the pace, which was a near creep for Rowdy and me, but perhaps a near sprint for Ceci. Her expression, however, didn't suggest pain, and she wasn't clutching her chest or showing any other alarming signs. She didn't look sick. What she looked was stunned. My eyes followed the direction of her gaze. A stranger watching my face would probably have worried that I was having a heart attack. Like Ceci, though, I was simply astounded.

In the woods, perhaps, forty feet from us, framed by a pair of six-foot hemlocks, stood a tall man wearing a long trench coat and a black ski mask. The knitted hood covered his head and face. It had small slits for his eyes and a smallish mouth opening to permit breathing. He needed it. For heavy breathing. The trench coat was buttoned from his neck down to his waist. Below, it was open. As was his fly.

Weirdly enough, it took a moment for the reality of the exhibitionism to register on me. I'd certainly heard about the exhibitionist in the park. Being an adult speaker of English, I knew the right words. Still, they did not immediately occur to me, probably because their connotations were so static, so entirely immobile. An art *exhibition.* Paintings. Oils on canvas. But this exhibition was no still life! Hey, in case you're as naive as I was, let me warn you: *Flashing* suggests speed: *in a flash.* Well, his right hand was moving fast enough, but he didn't just *expose* himself briefly and take off.

When the reality hit me, it crossed my mind that maybe I should feel scared. Pia had been horribly frightened by this same experience. But she'd been alone. I glanced at Ceci, whose initial amazement was turning to shocked bewilderment and what looked to me like fear. Suddenly, I was enraged. Reaching into my pocket, I grabbed my key ring, thrust it at Ceci, and said, "Car keys! Go back to the car! Can you do that?"

She nodded.

"Go!" I'm a dog trainer. I'm used to giving orders.

Ceci nodded again.

As she turned and began to lead Quest back down the trail, I whispered fiercely, "Rowdy, let's go!" And off we went, into the woods, after the man, who must've taken advantage of my delay to zip or at least button his pants. Damn it! He'd turned and was fleeing nimbly, not hampered by clothes falling off. But he was in sight. Enraptured with the primitive joy of the chase, Rowdy plunged through the low underbrush, taking the lead, pulling me after him, inspiring me to holler to our quarry, "You picked the wrong woman this time, you son of a bitch! I am no one's goddamned victim! And I'm going to get you!"

Ahead of me, Rowdy leaped over a log. High on adrenaline and hellbent on vengeance, I mimicked Rowdy, cleared the log, landed lightly, and pounded on, dashing around and under low-hanging branches,

and shrieking, "Go, Rowdy! Go! We're going to catch
this bastard! Run, Rowdy, run!"

Run he did! His ears flattened against his head, his
mighty legs eating up the ground, his tail flying boldly
like a banner of war, Rowdy charged ahead, and
through the leather leash that joined us and through the
intangible bond of love that united us, his wild strength
and his savage speed flowed into me until I was
stronger and faster than myself, half woman, half malamute, invincible!

Rowdy and I gained ground. Our prey was about
twenty feet ahead of us. "I'm going to get you!" I
snarled. "I'm stronger and faster than you, you sick
son of a bitch! Watch out, because you're going to trip
and fall, and I'm going to catch you and kick the shit
out of you and tear you into thin little strips of skin
and flesh, do you hear me? Watch out!"

Ah, the power of suggestion! The ski-masked head
bobbed briefly as the man checked to see exactly what
would trip him. Something did. His own feet? Suddenly, he faltered. And fell. Hard! His body gave a
loud *whomp.* Until then, I'd been all wrath and speed,
ferociously determined to catch the villain. What on
earth had I intended to do with him once I did? Deliver
a lecture on keeping his pants zipped? During the
chase, I'd been in aggressive pursuit. Rowdy had been
having fun. I'd growled, threatened, and snarled.
Rowdy'd been playing a happy game. Even now, when
the object of the chase lay ahead of us, when our en-
emy had been felled, Rowdy showed no intention of
transforming himself into the sort of dog who could be

commanded—*Guard him!*—to pounce on the evildoer
and wrap massive, toothy jaws around the scoundrel's
throat while I, ignobly if safely, scurried off to call the
police. If the situation had been reversed, if the man
had chased me, if he'd threatened me in any way at
all, commands to Rowdy would have been equally useless and entirely unnecessary. All on his own, Rowdy'd
have stopped him. The dog was eighty-eight pounds of
muscle and bone. He loved me. And he didn't need
my advice.

It occurred to me that I should take his. Contem-
plating the man, Rowdy saw no threat. Because there
was none? Enjoying the last of the adrenaline, I felt
more puzzled than brave. Above all, I felt determined
to see the damned man's face. Even if he got up and
bolted, I'd know the face, and I'd pick it out in a mug
book or a police lineup.

I trust Rowdy. Even so, swooping quickly down, I
grabbed a rock far bigger than I'd have chosen to fend
off an aggressive dog. The man stirred. Before he had
a chance to recover from the fall, I was standing over
him. The ski mask had twisted to become a blindfold.
With one hand signal, I dropped Rowdy. With a second
signal, I ordered him to stay. Holding the rock in my
strong right hand, directly above the man's head, I
reached out with my left, grabbed the ski mask, and
ripped it off.

For the second time, I was utterly stunned. Surprised, amazed, astonished, incredulous!

"Douglas?" I blurted out. *"You?"*

Ceci's eligible gentleman, the man she'd insisted I
just had to meet. Douglas, the lovely person.

CHAPTER 34

Imagine the letdown! The damned crash! I'll tell you, the sight of Douglas's ever so sickeningly *nice* face knocked the emotional wind out of me. Only seconds before, Rowdy and I had been soaring godlike through the woods in glorious pursuit of truth, justice, and the rights of women. And how had our noble and zealous chase ended? With the apprehension of this piddling nonentity.

"You!" I exclaimed. "You perverted nebbish!"

Douglas had fallen face down. When I'd pulled off that ridiculous ski helmet, he'd rolled onto his side. Now that I was yelling at him, he turned onto his back and looked directly at me. He made no effort even to sit up, never mind to rise to his feet and run.

"What's a nebbish?" he asked.

"This is Newton! How can you not know the word *nebbish*? It's Yiddish for a goddamned nobody. You, for example. Nice, wholesome, polite, inoffensive, clean-cut Douglas." As I've just said, he was now lying on his back. His trousers were buttoned, but his fly was still open. He knew it, too. His eyes were on me. "Zip your pants," I added vehemently. "And keep them zipped."

Still flat on his back, he complied. "I didn't have time before," he said. "I was in a hurry."

"And exactly why was that? I'll tell you why. Because you were too busy giving offense to an elderly woman who has been nothing but friendly and pleasant to you. You know, I am perfectly happy to give no thought at all to anything anyone wants to do in private. Or anything between consenting adults. But what you have been committing is a crime *with* victims. Pia was terrified. Ceci is undoubtedly still upset. And these are women who are supposed to be your friends." Out of the corner of my eye, I saw Rowdy stir. No wonder he hadn't sensed a threat. I caught his eye and mouthed a silent *Stay!*

Douglas let his body relax completely, as if he were sinking into the depths of a soft couch. An analyst's couch? "It's a compulsion," he said somberly. "A compulsion beyond my control."

"This is why you're seeing Dr. Foote," I said. "Is that what she told you? That this was beyond your control?"

He sighed. "She's a terrible therapist, isn't she? Useless. To me, that is. I hope she's been more helpful to you."

"Well, no, as a matter of fact, she hasn't been very helpful," I admitted. "But that's different, because my problems . . . Douglas, this entire time, Dr. Foote has known about you?"

"Of course she's known about me. What are shrinks for?"

"That you've been exposing yourself in the park? All this time, she's known, and she's done nothing to stop you from victimizing innocent women? How long have you been seeing her?"

"Six months."

"She's let this go on for *six goddamned months*?"

"Well, what do you expect her to do?"

"Cure you. That's what you're paying her for, isn't it?"

"Dr. Foote says it's a normal impulse."

"Your problem has nothing to do with *impulses*. It has to do with behavior." Thus spoke the dog trainer.

Sounding genuinely curious and gratified, he asked, "Do you really think so?"

Now, he'd switched to flashing his symptoms. Damn it! I was about to remind Douglas that his career as a victim of impulse had just undergone a radical change because he'd finally been caught. Before I spoke, I felt a twinge of fear. As a dog trainer, I trust fear. When a strange dog gets a certain glint in his eye, fear is the saving voice that warns you to move smoothly out of range of his teeth. Sometimes, you don't even see the glint. You just feel scared. You take a step back. The dog lunges. And misses your throat. So far, Douglas had remained flat on the ground. Fear, the dog trainer's salvation, reminded me that it had been Douglas's dog, Ulysses, who'd found Sylvia's body and that this belly-up creature at my feet had been the first person at the scene of her murder. Had Ulysses really *found* Sylvia? Or had Douglas seized on the dog's disappearance in these same woods to "find" his own victim? Maybe Sylvia's murder had nothing to do with her family and no correspondence with fatal dog attacks. The alternative scenario was simple: Carrying the urn containing her husband's ashes, Sylvia followed the footpath to the clearing with the small boulder. Douglas exposed himself to her. Somehow, she recognized him and threatened, in turn, to expose him. To the police, to the community, to ridicule and humiliation. And he shot her. Had he used an air horn to cover the sound of the gunshots? Douglas probably owned one of the wretched devices. They'd been handed out freely to the dog group, of which Douglas was a member. Why hadn't I thought of that? Because, as usual, I'd been obsessed with dogs and had seen human beings through my dog-colored glasses. Wilson presumably had an air horn, but so far as I knew, Eric didn't. Eric wasn't a dog walker and hadn't needed one. And Douglas was, all too conspicuously, an intact male. If he'd killed one woman who'd caught him, I had every reason to feel more than a twinge of fear.

I still hadn't answered his question. Belatedly, I said, "Yes, but I'm a dog trainer. I think in terms of behavior. What I'm sure of is that you need to see someone who can help you stop, uh, doing this."

"I need a new therapist," he agreed, adding thoughtfully, "So do you."

"I know someone good. She's a friend of mine, so

I can't go to her. But you could. I'm sure she's a lot better than Dr. Foote."

"Who isn't!" Douglas gave me a conspiratorial smile.

Throughout this Theater of the Absurd exchange, his expression remained mild. Except for the oversized trench coat, he could've passed for a picnicker who'd stretched out on the ground to relax after a good lunch.

"You know, Douglas," I said amiably, "you could get in terrible trouble. What if you get caught? By someone other than me, obviously." I remembered an ad I'd seen for a book that promised to teach the reader how to tell whether someone was lying. I hoped Douglas hadn't read it. I wished I'd ordered it. Did he believe me? Did he trust me to keep his secret? Or was he waiting for me to turn my back so he could pull out a gun and guarantee my silence? Should I take the risk of finding out? Douglas was prone, and I was on my feet. Rowdy and I had outrun him once. What's more, Sylvia had been killed with a small-caliber handgun. With that weapon, his chances of getting in an accurate, fatal shot at a distant, moving target were slight, weren't they? But what if I tripped and fell? And a bullet aimed at me could hit Rowdy.

Keeping my eyes locked on Douglas, I said, "Everyone always says what a wonderful person you are. It's terrible that you have to struggle with this problem."

"Worse than you know." His voice was grim.

Don't confess! I want to shriek. *Don't tell me! I'm safe not knowing! Don't confess!*

Pronouncing each word as if it were a stone he let drop from his mouth, he said, "I . . . was . . . there."

In desperation, I quickly spoke for him. "You were a witness." Hoping I wasn't pushing him too far, I added, "You were an innocent bystander."

"If I'd been entirely innocent," he said wryly, "I'd've gone to the police. But they'd've wanted to know what I was doing there. I'd've had no explanation! Ulysses wasn't with me. And I might've blurted it all out. It's a compulsion. It might've hit me all of a sudden, and I might've blurted it all out. Besides . . ."

I believed him. Maybe it was a good thing I hadn't wasted my money on that book. Maybe I didn't need it. "The man who killed Sylvia," I said gently. "Her murderer. You saw him. And he saw you." When Douglas found the body, how did he know it was Sylvia's? Ceci's question finally had an answer: because Douglas had seen Sylvia die.

Rowdy had been patiently resting his big head on his forelegs. As Douglas slowly sat up, Rowdy echoed the movement by lifting his head. For a second, I felt alarmed. But Douglas reached a sitting position only to bend his knees, slump his shoulders, and let his head sag. The trench coat formed a tent around him. Despite it, I could see his ribs heave as he moaned and sobbed. "I tried to tell Dr. Foote," he managed to say, "but she didn't want to hear it. She wouldn't listen. And I didn't know what to do."

I felt horribly sorry for him. It would have been kind of me to put a hand on his back and kinder to hold him. I couldn't bring myself to touch him. My repulsion made me even more sorry for him than I'd been before.

"You remember that song Sylvia used to sing?" Douglas asked suddenly. " 'There'll Be Some Changes Made.' "

"I did hear her hum that," I said.

"Sylvia wasn't really a very nice woman. She was hostile. She needled people. Mostly, her family. She used to sing snatches of that song or hum it when she'd been going after one of them. After he shot her, he sang that song. Not all of it. Just a little. Just the way Sylvia used to. It was creepy—hearing him sing off-key about what he'd done. I was sick to my stomach. I couldn't help it. Before that, he didn't know I was there. Then this nausea hit me, all of a sudden, and it was like food poisoning. No warning. I pulled off the, uh, ski mask. I had to. And he saw me."

"Who?" I finally asked.

CHAPTER 35

The answer had almost—but not quite—left Douglas's lips when out of the corner of my eye, I spied Zsa Zsa lumbering through the woods. Simultaneously, Rowdy broke his solid down-stay.

"Damn it!" I yelled, not at Rowdy but at the golden, who picked up speed, accidentally barreled into Douglas, and deliberately hurled herself at Rowdy. My big dog had seen her coming. And he owed her one. The last time Zsa Zsa had attacked Rowdy, I'd spoiled the fun by sounding my air horn and bringing the fight to a halt. This time, Rowdy intended to teach her a bone-crunching lesson about the inadvisability of tackling a malamute. Only seconds after Zsa Zsa's onslaught, the two big dogs were a writhing, yelping mass of fur, flesh, and teeth. Douglas rose to his feet and had the sense to rid himself of that encumbering trench coat as he prepared to help break up the fight. The second Zsa Zsa appeared, I should've nabbed her. But I'd been slow to respond, in part because the nasty reality of Zsa Zsa's viciousness toward other dogs was so atypical of her breed, so completely aberrant, that I found it hard to comprehend; despite my previous observations of Zsa Zsa, I found it almost impossible to convince myself that a female golden retriever would actually attack Rowdy.

The sight and sound of the battle persuaded me. It was far worse than their previous skirmish. That time, Rowdy'd been at my side, his leash securely in my grasp. This time, I'd been standing near Douglas, not right next to Rowdy. What's more, one end of Rowdy's leash remained fastened to his collar, but I'd left the six-foot length of leather on the ground at his side. God almighty, how I hate a dog fight! Already, my heart was pounding, my face felt flushed, and I was sweating profusely. I knew Rowdy'd win the fight. So what! Even if he'd simply been a beloved pet, I wouldn't have wanted him injured. But he was entered at four upcoming shows, and I had plans for his future. If that damned Zsa Zsa ripped him open, she could leave permanent scars that would end his career in the ring.

"Douglas!" I ordered. "The second I grab Rowdy's leash, grab Zsa Zsa's tail! Then pull hard and let go." Hollering to make myself heard over the roar, I warned, "Don't touch her collar. Or she'll nail you. Ready?" I reached into my pocket for the air horn. After weeks of being blasted with the horrific noise by countless dog walkers, Zsa Zsa probably wouldn't react at all. But if Rowdy's jaws were locked on her flesh, the sudden clamor just might startle him into loosening his grip.

With my feet spread apart, my knees bent, the horn in my left hand, my right hand free to snatch Rowdy's leash, I positioned myself just beyond the range of the dogs' jaws. The tangle of gray and golden coats took a sudden heave as Zsa Zsa lost strength. Seizing his chance, Rowdy pinned her. She shrieked. Rowdy's leash lay across his back. My hand darted for it, and I'd just seized the familiar leather loop when a third dog spoiled my spur-of-the-moment peace plan by dashing from the woods and plunging into the fray. Wilson's beautiful corgi bitch, Llio, arrived with blood flying from a badly torn ear. Don't get me wrong about Pembrokes! As a breed, Pembroke Welsh corgis are kindly, if spunky, creatures, and Llio in particular was a sweetheart. But dogs are dogs, and Llio had not only had to tolerate Zsa Zsa as a housemate, but had evidently just taken a trouncing from her.

Rapidly revising my plan, I opportunistically decided to use Llio's surprise arrival to remove Rowdy from the melee. "Douglas, stay out of it," I hollered. "You'll just get bitten." With that, I let the air horn fall to the ground, clenched Rowdy's leash in both hands, and applied all my strength to it. Just when I began to fear that Rowdy would slip his collar or that the leash would break before I could budge him, the pressure on the leash eased, and I called, "Rowdy, leave! This way! This way! That's my boy! That's my good boy!" Now that I'd succeeded in getting his attention, I made a fool of myself keeping him focused on me. Whistling, clucking my tongue, and babbling lunatic verities about what a great dog he was, I took the risk of bolting from what was now a two-dog fight.

Rowdy could have veered around and jumped back in, or Zsa Zsa could have gone for him again. But my gamble paid off. With Rowdy bounding at my heels, I dashed up a little slope to a spot where two waist-high boulders leaned into each other. Pulling and cajoling, I managed to get Rowdy behind the rocks. Exhausted, I rested my weight on one of them. At a guess, only two minutes had elapsed since Zsa Zsa had appeared through the trees and attacked Rowdy, perhaps thirty seconds since Llio had joined the brawl. I felt as if the fight had started hours ago. My arms and legs were trembling. Exertion and relief had me panting like a dog. Rowdy was breathing far more lightly than I was. If I'd had a tail, it wouldn't have been wagging, but his was zipping back and forth. His ears weren't torn or bleeding, and neither was his face, which, in fact, wore a smug, obnoxious smile.

A short distance downhill, the remaining combatants were alarmingly quiet. Zsa Zsa, back on her feet, was circling the blood-spattered Llio, who, I suspected, would've been content to call it quits. Douglas stood only a yard or two from the dogs, his body tense, his face contorted with what I felt sure was agonized indecision about how to rescue Llio. Without human intervention, the lull in the hostilities would've reached a natural end either in Llio's quick and probably successful flight or in Zsa Zsa's renewed attack. The young, strong corgi seemed to me to have an excellent chance of making a swift escape. Catching Douglas's eyes, I was trying to signal him to do nothing, when screams broke the silence.

"HELP! HELP! HELP ME!" The woman came flying out of the woods. "He's going to kill me!" she shrieked. Even in a state of obviously genuine terror, Anita Fairley-Delaney looked as if she were posing for the kind of fashion magazine in which the typical model is five feet ten and evidently suffers from self-induced colitis while also incubating the Ebola virus, but is gorgeous anyway. You know the type? The mannequin's eyes are dissipated and her combined pallor and rigor suggest that she recently died of fright. Who cares! She's got hollow cheeks, incredible bone structure, mile-long legs, and great hair, and she really can *wear* outfits so grotesque that no normal person would be caught dead in them even on Halloween. In fact, Anita wore a full-length black coat piped in red, slim black trousers, and shiny black high-heeled boots. Her entrance was stagy, but there was nothing fake about the panic in her voice. "Help me!" she screamed at Douglas. "He's trying to kill me!"

Yes, who?

Almost immediately, Wilson answered the unasked question by emerging from the woods in pursuit of Anita, who, in spite of the dress boots, had been too fast for him. At the sight of Wilson, Anita renewed her shrieking and tried to take shelter behind Douglas. Wilson, meanwhile, was hurling invectives at Anita and pleading with either Douglas or God—I honestly don't know which—to save Llio from Zsa Zsa.

"Never mind your fucking dog!" Anita bellowed. Her self-confidence restored by Douglas's presence, I suppose, she added, "I just want my money back! Just give me back my deposit and you'll never see me again!"

"Llio! Llio!" Wilson wailed. "Her ear! Look at her ear! Goddamn you, look what you did! This is all your fault!" I assumed for a second that he meant Zsa Zsa. The object of his rage was, however, Anita. Stamping his foot and pounding the air with his fist, he demanded, "What'd you have to kick Zsa Zsa for! Zsa Zsa wouldn't've done this if you hadn't kicked her, goddamn it! Llio's a show dog, for Christ's sake! And you've wrecked her! Look at her ear!"

"You moron!" Anita responded. Suddenly, she was her cool, snotty self again. "Forget the goddamn dogs! I didn't kick the dog, I just nudged it with my foot, and it turned vicious and flew at the other one. For that, you had to pull a gun on me? Are you crazy? Think about what just happened! I showed up because I don't want to buy the house after all. Happens all the time. No big deal. I just want my deposit back. And I end up getting chased by a lunatic with a gun! Jesus!" To emphasize her point, she stretched out one leg, rotated her ankle a bit, smiled admiringly at her shiny boot, and then delivered a light kick to one of Zsa Zsa's hind feet.

As if to demonstrate exactly how the original fight between Zsa Zsa and Llio had begun, Zsa Zsa reacted to the blow by lunging at Llio and digging her teeth into the corgi's uninjured ear. The corgi cried out in pain and struggled to shake off the larger dog, but Zsa Zsa held the ear in her jaws and, I believe, dug her teeth yet more deeply into Llio's flesh. In a desperate effort to free Llio, Douglas stooped to retrieve the rock I'd left lying on the ground. Holding it in both hands, he shouted uselessly and inarticulately at the dogs. If he'd brought the rock down on Zsa Zsa, he'd simply have incited her, as he evidently realized.

But Llio was Wilson's dog, not Douglas's, and her hideous yelps of pain drove him to action. Spotting the air horn I'd dropped, Wilson picked it up and sounded it in a prolonged, ear-shattering blast that drowned out Douglas's shouts. Far from breaking up the dog fight, the bawling of the air horn frightened the wounded corgi, who screeched more loudly than ever and began to twist her sturdy body in terror and agony. Aching with sorrow and empathy for Llio, I clutched Rowdy's leash in one sweating hand and dug the other into his great wolf-gray ruff.

Desperate to rescue Llio, Wilson suddenly tossed the air horn into the woods, reached into his pocket, pulled something out, and took a remarkably calm, deliberate step forward. From my perch behind the boulders, I watched attentively. I trust my impression, which was that Wilson, like Douglas, was searching for the chance to knock Zsa Zsa out of action without causing additional, unintended harm to Llio. The object in Wilson's right hand was an automatic so small that only an inch or so of the diminutive barrel projected beyond his fist. With his feet spread apart, his knees slightly bent, his right arm extended, he was almost leaning over the dogs when Llio suddenly fought back at Zsa Zsa. With a monumental thrust of her short, strong hind legs, Llio managed to throw the big dog off balance. Lowering his weapon an inch or two, Wilson took aim at Zsa Zsa's chest. As Wilson was about to pull the trigger, Zsa Zsa gave an unexpected lurch that sent her careening against Anita. As Wilson fired, Anita tumbled off her feet, hit the ground, and took the bullet that had been meant to save the corgi. Then, still hellbent on rescuing Llio, Wilson coolly moved his arm and again took aim. His target appeared to be Zsa Zsa's chest. I'm sure he meant to shoot her in the heart.

I'm equally sure that he never noticed Douglas at all. Still holding the big rock in both hands, Douglas, the lovely person, the exhibitionist, took long, smooth steps that placed him directly behind Wilson. Raising his arms high above Wilson, he paused for a second and then slammed the rock down on Wilson's skull. As Wilson collapsed, Douglas glanced at me and said, with no emotion in his voice, "He shot Sylvia. If I've killed him, he had it coming."

Turning back to the dogs, Douglas lunged at Zsa Zsa, who had finally loosened her hold on Llio's ear. Or what was left of it. And Douglas did precisely what I'd warned him not to do: He reached out, grabbed Zsa Zsa's collar, and dragged her away from the corgi. As I'd predicted, Zsa Zsa nailed him; she veered abruptly around and sank her teeth into his free arm. He didn't seem to notice the bite.

Did he notice the blood? It flowed from his forearm,

from the corgi's mauled ears, and from Anita Fairley's veins. Llio shook her head. Her blood flew everywhere. It showered Anita's body and mingled with Anita's human blood.

CHAPTER 36

The bullet had entered Anita's chest. She bled heavily. She survived. Rowdy had his brucellosis test done at Boston's famous Angell Memorial Animal Hospital, not at Steve's clinic. I heard that Steve and Anita were getting a divorce. I didn't write, call, or E-mail Steve. I knew he wasn't entirely alone. Steve had his dogs and his work.

I had my dogs, too, of course. And my work. Not that there's a sharp distinction between the two. During the month that followed the horror, as I thought of it, I did some final liver-recipe testing, put the finishing touches on my cookbook, and trained Rowdy and Kimi with homemade treats. Kimi picked up one championship point at the Boston shows in December, and Rowdy took two B.O.B.'s—Best of Breed wins—and on both days, he went on to place in the group—Working Group—one second place, one third place, not bad except that Rowdy is drop-dead gorgeous and . . . the expression is unfortunate.

Speaking of show dogs, Wilson wrote to me from prison to thank me for rushing Llio to Angell on that nightmare day. Llio's show career had ended, as Wilson knew it would the moment he saw Zsa Zsa rip into the corgi's uninjured ear. The surgeons at Angell did a wonderful job of restoring Llio to close-to-normal, but the show ring is about perfection, and from a judge's viewpoint, Llio is now imperfect. She does, however, seem perfectly happy, and that's what matters most, isn't it? I expected to get stuck with the whopping bill from Angell, but to my surprise, Pia not only paid it but took Llio home and now devotes herself to pampering her jailed husband's dog.

When, at Wilson's request, I made a visit to check on Llio, Pia talked on and on about Llio, and also had a few things to say about Wilson, all of them nasty. According to Pia, her husband should be charged with attempted homicide for shooting Anita. Pia hadn't even been there. I had. "A would-be double murderer," Pia insisted. "That's what he is." Without waiting for the results of ballistics tests, Wilson had confessed to using the same gun on Sylvia that he'd used on Anita. He was claiming, truthfully I might add, that he hadn't aimed at Anita and that in Sylvia's case, he was guilty only of manslaughter. Eric intends to testify against Wilson, Pia told me, and anyway, she added, it was apparent to everyone that her rotten husband was—and I quote—"a sneaky, mooching liar."

According to his wife, Wilson ferreted around in

Sylvia's desk and discovered that she intended to sell the house, move to a small condo, and leave her children and son-in-law to fend for themselves. But if Sylvia died? Wilson and Pia, as well as Oona and Eric, could continue to occupy the house or could sell it. Furthermore, the children would inherit the rest of Sylvia's estate.

Interestingly enough, Pia did not allude to Wilson's dog-show extravagances, which she perhaps does not view as such. Maybe she imagines that Wilson paid fifty dollars for Llio's palatial wooden crate. Maybe Wilson lied to her about its cost. Pia not only accused Wilson of being a liar, but cited what she considered to be irrefutable evidence. "Do you know what Wilson has the gall to say about Douglas?" she demanded. "Well, according to Wilson, Douglas is the exhibitionist. Is that the most outrageous thing you've ever heard? I mean, Douglas of all people! Let me tell you, Holly, Douglas is really a lovely person. As a matter of fact, we've started spending a little time together. Walking dogs. And we're having dinner on Saturday. I keep telling Douglas that he should sue Wilson for defamation. But naturally Douglas would never do that. He's much too nice. The exhibitionist, for Christ's sake, is Wilson. The creep! I should know, shouldn't I? To think that I ever shared the same bed with that pervert."

Oona Metzner, I might mention, bought a boat and sailed away, but Pia and Eric are still living at home in Sylvia's house. Someone told someone who told Ceci who told me that Sylvia's children are quite well off. Sylvia's life insurance policy was a big one, and the children sold S & I's for a ton of money, despite the fuss about contamination. The Trasks settled the case out of court. The settlement was generous, or so George Trask said. I ran into the whole family a few days ago outside my dentist's office in Newton. The Trask girls, Di and Fergie, had appointments with a children's dentist in the adjoining office. Charlie's hip surgery is scheduled for next month. I still can't decide whether I was right to keep my inside knowledge of the Trasks' wily-fox scheme to myself. On the one hand, the scam was none of my business. On the other hand, Charlie *is* a dog, and dogs *are* my business. Morally speaking, where does that leave me? On the side of the dog. Where else?

That reminds me. Zsa Zsa. All along, it had seemed to me that there was something terribly wrong with her. Her bad hips must have caused her terrible pain, she probably had an aggressive temperament to begin with, and Sylvia was an irresponsible owner. All true. But there was more. On the day of horrors, the cops had no sooner shown up, taken Wilson into custody, and set about taping off the area and taking down names, when Zsa Zsa collapsed and had a seizure that went on and on. I had the comfort of knowing that although she looked as if she were suffering, she was deeply unconscious. Even so, I threw hysterics until the police agreed to call a vet. But Zsa Zsa died. Although she'd instigated the dog fight, I felt sick at the idea that Rowdy had inflicted a mortal wound. To my relief, the police ordered a necropsy—a veterinary autopsy—just in case Zsa Zsa's death had some connection with Sylvia's. It didn't. And according to the vet who performed the necropsy, the stress of the dog fights may have triggered the seizure activity, but Rowdy hadn't killed Zsa Zsa. The main finding of the necropsy was a brain tumor. I felt stupid. I'd known all along that there was something aberrant about Zsa Zsa. I should've guessed what it was. All the members of Ceci's dog group felt the same way I did. In the peculiar fashion of people devoted to dogs, we mourned a dog we hadn't even liked.

The dog group is in partial hibernation for the winter, but Ceci has stayed in close touch with Noah, who is planning to regularize and upgrade his position as mayor of the dog group by running for mayor of Newton. Ceci is working hard on his one-issue campaign: Noah promises that if elected, he will lead Newton into a new era of fully fenced off-leash dog parks throughout the city. If I lived in Newton, he'd have my vote. On the subject of Newton's public servants, let me report that Officer Jennifer Pasquarelli has been reinstated after successfully completing a social skills training program. Kevin informs me that Jennie graduated at the top of her class. I notice, however, that Kevin has still not introduced Jennie to his mother.

Douglas has also entered a social-skills program of sorts. It's a self-help group for sexual addicts. He dropped out of treatment with Dr. Foote. So did I. Dr. Foote knew that Douglas was frightening women by exposing himself in the park, she knew that he had witnessed Sylvia's murder, and she did nothing to protect the women or to bring Sylvia's murderer to justice. Furthermore, she was of no help to Douglas or to me. But those aren't the reasons I quit seeing her. No, I dropped out because of an incident that occurred only a few days after Anita's near-slaying. The incident should have amounted to nothing. In the shrink-infested quarters of Cambridge and Newton, therapists and their patients run into one another all the time at restaurants, theaters, health clubs, parties, and everywhere else. Big deal. As it happened, I ran into Dr. Foote in Harvard Square. She was crossing the street from the Harvard Coop to the kiosk, and we were crossing in the opposite direction. By "we" I mean, as always, Rowdy and Kimi. Being the sort of friendly human being who does not need to be sent off for social skills training, I smiled, nodded, and said hello to Dr. Foote just as if she were a normal human being instead of a psychiatrist. The dogs, who are even more socially skilled than I am, were as quick as ever to pick up on my gregarious attitude and to add their own conviviality, which took the form of bouncing up and down in an unmistakably merry and entirely nonthreatening manner while issuing throaty peals of *woo-woo-woo*. And instead of returning our greetings and going on to admire the dogs, just what did Dr. Foote do? I'll tell you. She screamed and ran. Since I couldn't imagine what had upset her, I tried to go to her aid. The dogs, I'm proud to report, were just as solicitous as I was. In brief, Rowdy, Kimi, and I sprinted through the crowd by the Coop and had no difficulty catching up with Dr. Foote before she reached Brattle Square.

When we did, she keeled over. Abruptly. I'd never before seen anyone black out so rapidly. One second, she was on her feet, and the next, she lay on the brick pavement. She immediately drew a crowd that included my sympathetic dogs, who did their best to revive her by licking her alarmingly pale face. Someone who announced herself as a doctor gently nudged the dogs aside, kneeled, and hovered over the ailing Dr. Foote. As I watched, Dr. Foote whispered something to the doctor, who rose and spoke to me.

"This woman is having a severe panic attack," the doctor said. "If you'll take the dogs away, she'll be fine."

"What?" I said.

"She's phobic," the doctor said. "She's deathly afraid of dogs. Yours are beautiful, by the way. I have a malamute myself."

As it turned out, by what the non-dog world foolishly calls coincidence, she'd bought her dog from Kimi's breeder and was thus a long-lost cousin of my own. Naturally, we simply had to spend the briefest possible moment or two comparing notes about pedigrees, and then I simply had to tell her about breeding Rowdy, and after that we devoted practically no time at all to figuring out exactly how her dog was related to Emma. Anyway, although we devoted only a second to two to exchanging these snippets of family history, when we looked for Dr. Foote, she'd mysteriously vanished. If she'd risen to her feet, we'd have noticed. I assume that she crawled ignominiously away. Poor woman! I hate to think of the psychotherapy hours we wasted together. If only she'd been open and honest with me about her fears, I'm sure I'd have been able to help her.

Rita was entirely and uncharacteristically unsympathetic to Dr. Foote's plight. She apologized profusely for having referred me to Dr. Foote and explained that she'd done so only because of Dr. Foote's supposed knowledge of neurology. If I'd told Rita the truth about Douglas, she'd probably have filed an official complaint against Dr. Foote. As it was, Rita settled for making Dr. Foote hand over every note she'd written about me. Rita presented me with the lot in a sealed envelope. Also, she made Dr. Foote promise to go into treatment herself with a therapist of Rita's choosing. Never supposing that I'd recognize the name, Rita told me that she'd sent Dr. Foote to Dr. Harvey Bremmer, whom Rita described as a skilled clinician whose speciality was ethics. As I didn't tell Rita, I'd known Harvey for ages. He breeds and shows Gordon setters. Very nice dogs. Sound. Typey.

But to return to the matter of Sylvia Metzner's murder, it was Althea Battlefield, Adventuress of Sherlock Holmes, member of the Baker Street Irregulars, and Ceci's sister, of course, who pointed out the inadequacies of my dog-attack analysis and of Pia's explanation of her husband's motives. Instead of enumerating my stupidities and telling me that the truth was elementary-my-dear-Holly, Althea straightened me out in the kindest possible way. She invited me to tea. As Ceci dished out cream and fresh raspberries, Althea told me that it wasn't necessarily a mistake to view murder through dog-colored glasses. According to Althea, if I'd looked through my lenses at my own egregiously opportunistic dogs, I'd have seen that a concatenation of motives triggered the murder by constituting an opportunity that Wilson couldn't resist.

When Sherlock Holmes summed up a case, Watson was always staggered by the Great Detective's brilliance. From Watson's astonished admiration, it's clear he understood what Holmes was talking about.

Forgetting my manners, I said, "What?"

"The concatenation of *other people's* motives." Althea's eyes sparkled. "There being no such thing as a condogenation."

"Yet," I said.

Althea smiled. "Motives. The victim, Sylvia Metzner, had just had a dramatic public confrontation with Officer Jennifer Pasquarelli, who had every reason to be angry. The Trasks were justifiably furious at the victim because of the suffering of their beloved pet. My sister's dog-walker companions at the park, especially our mayoral candidate, Noah, had been repeatedly harassed by the victim's dog and, indeed, saw the victim's failure to control her dog as a threat to their own dogs' freedom to enjoy the park."

"Enjoy? Really, Althea—"

"Let me finish! And before I do, let's add as a little aside that in a misguided effort to assist in the control of the victim's dog, you offered the murderer a handy means of covering, or diverting attention from, the sound of gun shots, a means available to a great many people at the park. And used by a great many. Meanwhile, at this same park, the exhibitionist was engaging in criminal acts. Motive for murder: the victim could have been in a position to disclose the man's identity. At the same time, the victim's son, Eric, was making irreverent use of the urn containing his father's remains to hide his *stash.* Lovely word, isn't it? And at your inadvertent prompting, so Ceci tells me, the victim chose rather belatedly to scatter those remains, thus providing a motive for the son, who would presumably have tried to prevent his mother from throwing away his supply of whatever drug it was. Cocaine, dare I wonder? But there we have the fortuitous concatenation of motives. Wilson hated his mother-in-law. She needled him. He was greedy. He wanted her money. And Fate, the careless owner of us all, left unguarded before him this delectable smorgasbord of other people's motives. Those motives were Wilson's opportunity. He pounced. Like a big, hungry dog."

CHAPTER 37

Subj:AfriCam
From: SDelaney@hightailit.com
To:Ritatheshrink@psychesrus.net

Rita,

There's a web site you've probably visited that has cameras trained on waterholes in Africa. I spend a lot of time watching those murky waterholes, hoping to see lions or leopards. No luck so far.

That's my life lately—all mud, no big cats. The only thing worse than divorce was marriage.

Steve

CHAPTER 3 8

Subj: Re: AfriCam
From:Ritatheshrink@psychesrus.net
To: SDelaney@hightailit.com

Steve,

No big cats here, either—but you're not really a cat person, so what does it matter? I suspect you'd have better luck if you trained your sights on half-wild dogs.

Rita

CHAPTER 39

One evening in mid-January, my stepmother and I finally disposed of her first husband. The credit for our success belongs to Kimi, who created our excuse to linger in Harvard Yard when she marked the base of a certain famous statue in front of University Hall. Happily—*God* spelled you know how—Kimi thus chose a suitable and dignified resting place for Professor Beamon, who lies in perpetuity at John Harvard's feet. *Requiescat in pace.* Good riddance! After what happened to Sylvia Metzner when she belatedly scattered the ashes of *her* late husband, I'd developed a superstitious dread concerning the sprinkling of dead spouses and was actually surprised when we dispersed Professor Beamon without being murdered.

Despite my gratitude to Kimi, I sent her to Maine with Gabrielle. Cindy Neely had phoned with the welcome news that Emma's litter brother, Howie, had announced that the time was right to breed his sister. In Howie's view, the proper stud dog was undoubtedly himself rather than Rowdy. Even so, Cindy and Emma were flying from Washington to Boston the next day. If you don't breed dogs, perhaps I should mention a fixed rule of purebred canine etiquette, which is that the gentleman invites the lady home to see *his* etchings, and not the other way around. The custom is falsely believed to be based on the male's preference for his own turf, where he feels so self-confident that he doesn't keep interrupting the proceedings to gulp Viagra. Another myth I'd like to dispel is that stud dogs own large and expensive art collections and therefore have etchings worth seeing. Hah! The true explanation is that if *he* went to *her* house, she'd make him pick up his socks and empty the dishwasher instead of devoting himself exclusively to siring puppies, which is what breeding is all about, isn't it?

Speaking of siring puppies, the plan was that Cindy would drop off Emma with me for the breeding and then go on to visit her family in Pennsylvania and friends in Connecticut. I felt honored to have Cindy entrust Emma to me. Kimi would've spoiled our carefully made plans. The feminist extremism that impels Kimi to leave her mark on public icons of human paternalism somehow fails to translate into a friendly sense of sororal obligation to creatures of her own breed and sex, especially when they are in standing heat.

Emma was an outrageous flirt. Rowdy was smitten. When Ira Gershwin wrote the lyrics to "Embraceable

You," the procreation of show dogs probably wasn't foremost on his mind—was it?—but in Rowdy's opinion, CH Jazzland's Embraceable You lived up to her name.

Repeatedly.

Afterward, Rowdy's lady love flew back home to the Pacific Northwest. Practically before the plane had landed in Seattle, I began to check my E-mail every hour. When I wasn't logging on, I was hovering by the phone. Filled with nervous energy, I finished my cookbook and mailed the manuscript. My notes about fatal dog attacks ended up at curbside on trash day; my interest had shifted from death to birth. I had no intention of breeding Kimi. Knowing her as I did, I felt certain that she'd produce a litter of ten or twelve vigorous little female-rights fanatics. What would I do with them? There's barely room enough in the world for one Kimi, never mind a whole litter. As for me, there wasn't a suitable stud in sight. Besides, I'm ordinary. Rowdy is special. Kimi agrees. As I tell him, he's our boy. That's an understatement. Rowdy is *the* dog.

The gestation period of *Canis familiaris* is sixty-three days, give or take. In some cases, each of those days is a hundred years long. A few weeks after the breeding, Cindy sent E-mail to report that Emma was suffering from all-day-long morning sickness. According to Cindy, Emma was ravenously hungry. When Emma had stayed here, she'd tried to convince me that she was starving. Rowdy and Kimi always act famished. But at about four weeks, Emma showed a subtle raising of the hairline along the side, and soon after that, she lost hair around her nipples. Finally, Cindy called with the happy announcement that Emma looked as if she'd swallowed a Thanksgiving turkey whole. Afraid to get my hopes up, I reminded myself that although Thanksgiving was long past, Emma, like Rowdy or Kimi, would've happily dispatched a turkey, including a live one, feathers and all, and might have done just that. But when the vet counted six puppies, I was finally convinced.

Nine weeks after the breeding, at seven o'clock in the morning, which is, of course, four A.M. Pacific time, I happened to be sitting in the kitchen eating scrambled eggs, drinking coffee, and staring at the phone. When it rang, I grabbed it, not because I have ESP, but because I'd been leaping at it like Kimi after liver every time it had rung for the past five days. This time, the call was the one I'd been waiting for. Cindy spoke in that exhausted, blissful voice that's unique to devoted breeders who've been up in the night whelping puppies. Emma had had seven strong, healthy puppies so far, five males, two females, with at least one more on the way. According to Cindy, the puppies were beautiful. It's a universal truth that whereas newborn puppies of other people's breeding look exactly like drowned rats, those of one's own breeding are staggeringly gorgeous even before they're dry. Since these were Rowdy puppies, I had no doubt that they really were beautiful. In the background, I heard the puppies mewling. The little cries were plaintive and miraculous.

The bawling of the puppies stayed with me after I hung up. It rang in my head until my eyes filled with tears. My weeping began softly and gently, but the more I cried, the harder I cried. Just before Cindy had gone back to attend to Emma, she'd said, "You know, Holly, you can still have a puppy instead of a stud fee." I wailed for the puppy I couldn't introduce into my two-malamute pack and couldn't keep in my little house with its small yard. I hate crying and seldom do it. Once I started, monumental sadness poured out, never-ending grief at my mother's death, longing for my long-dead golden retrievers, and the overwhelming loneliness of life without Steve Delaney. Rowdy and Kimi stared at me with wide eyes. Rowdy leaned against me, and Kimi licked and licked my damp hands as if they were her own newborn pups. Eventually, I staggered to the bathroom, blew my nose, and washed my face in cold water. I simply had to pull myself together. Rowdy and Kimi trusted me. They deserved better than this blubbering mess. The puppies were *good* news. I was blessed with a family and friends who'd celebrate it—Rowdy's breeder, my father, Gabrielle, my cousin Leah, even my annoying cousin Janice, Rita, Kevin Dennehy, Ceci and Althea, friends from dog training, my editor at *Dog's Life* magazine, E-mail friends I'd made on Malamute-L, the AMHotline, caninebackpackers, Dogwriters-L . . . I was continuing this ineffectual internal pep talk and blotting my haggard face dry when the phone rang once more. Bolting for it, I snatched the receiver without even checking caller-ID. I pray as seldom as I cry. Now, I was pleading for the well-being of Emma and her Rowdy puppies.

"Holly," the familiar voice said. It was octaves lower than Cindy's.

"Steve."

"I heard that you bred Rowdy. I hope you don't mind . . ."

"I don't mind." The sobbing had left my voice thick.

Anyone else would've asked whether I was okay. Steve said, "Are your dogs all right?"

"Fine. Both of them."

"The breeding. Did something go wrong?"

"No. In fact, I just heard. There are seven puppies so far, five boys, two girls, and at least one more on the way."

"All spoken for?"

"Some. Not all."

"I'm interested."

Steve had always preferred civilized breeds. "You're joking. They're *malamutes*," I said. "Obviously."

"I'm a vet. Remember? They taught us that in school. Malamutes produce malamutes." After a second or two, he repeated, "I'm interested."

I can read him better than I can read myself. "The terms of the contract are pretty tough," I said. "What are you looking for? A pet? Or a show dog?"

"Show. And obedience, too."

"Steve, if you want *obedience*, mine is the wrong breed."

"Love or honor would do," Steve said. "Love would be more than enough."